As they finally reached the alley, they stopped for a moment to breathe in the night air.

"I'd forgotten what open space feels like," Rawlings said.

Before they could take another step, Wilson stood and blocked their way. "You boys going somewhere?" he said, then laughed as he pointed his gun at Dalton. "You first," he said, "since I figure you to try running. Your friend, he don't look capable of any quick moves, so he'll be next."

They heard the click of his pistol being cocked.

RALPH COMPTON

DALTON'S JUSTICE

A Ralph Compton Novel by

CARLTON STOWERS

BERKLEY
New York

BERKLEY
An imprint of Penguin Random House LLC
penguinrandomhouse.com

Copyright © 2021 by The Estate of Ralph Compton
Penguin Random House supports copyright. Copyright fuels creativity, encourages
diverse voices, promotes free speech, and creates a vibrant culture. Thank you for buying
an authorized edition of this book and for complying with copyright laws by not
reproducing, scanning, or distributing any part of it in any form without permission.
You are supporting writers and allowing Penguin Random House to continue to
publish books for every reader.

BERKLEY and the BERKLEY & B colophon are registered trademarks of
Penguin Random House LLC.

ISBN: 9780593102466

First Edition: March 2021

Printed in the United States of America
1   3   5   7   9   10   8   6   4   2

Cover art by Dennis Lyall
Cover design by Steve Meditz
Book design by George Towne

THE IMMORTAL COWBOY

This is respectfully dedicated to the "American Cowboy." His was the saga sparked by the turmoil that followed the Civil War, and the passing of more than a century has by no means diminished the flame.

———◆———

True, the old days and the old ways are but treasured memories, and the old trails have grown dim with the ravages of time, but the spirit of the cowboy lives on.

———◆———

In my travels—to Texas, Oklahoma, Kansas, Nebraska, Colorado, Wyoming, New Mexico, and Arizona—I always find something that reminds me of the Old West. While I am walking these plains and mountains for the first time, there is this feeling that a part of me is eternal, that I have known these old trails before. I believe it is the undying spirit of the frontier calling me, through the mind's eye, to step back into time. What is the appeal of the Old West of the American frontier?

———◆———

It has been epitomized by some as the dark and bloody period in American history. Its heroes—Crockett, Bowie, Hickok, Earp—have been reviled and criticized. Yet the Old West lives on, larger than life.

———◆———

It has become a symbol of freedom, when there was always another mountain to climb and another river to cross; when a dispute between two men was settled not with expensive lawyers, but with fists, knives, or guns. Barbaric? Maybe. But some things never change. When the cowboy rode into the pages of American history, he left behind a legacy that lives within the hearts of us all.

—*Ralph Compton*

PROLOGUE

FOR MARSHAL BEN Dalton, the dream is always the same.

It is a bright, warm day, cloudless, with the sweet scent of lantana and honeysuckle wafting in a gentle breeze. Wearing overalls and a floppy hat pulled low on his brow, he is in his father's wagon, delivering a load of cooking wood to the café. As his mule, LuLu, lazily pulls him through town, he passes the Aberdene churchyard where a noonday social is under way. There is energetic singing, laughter, and wooden tables laden with dishes of food and jars of sweet tea provided by the women of the church. Children play games of tag, giggling as they chase after one another. A happy old dog barks and joins in their fun.

But all he really sees is her. She stands out in the crowd, wearing a flowing white dress that seems to glow, her long blond hair, all waves and curls, falling over her shoulders, her eyes as blue as the sky. In the dream, she always smiles and waves as he passes.

And then he is wakened, sometimes by the gray dawn that peeks through a window, sometimes by a rooster's crow or the bellow of his milk cow, signaling to him it is time to fetch his bucket and head to the barn.

Or, occasionally, it comes in the dark of night with the urgent calling of his name.

M ARSHAL . . . MARSHAL DALTON . . . you up and got your pants on? We got us a problem . . . needs tending right away." It was the high-pitched voice of his young deputy, Rolly Blair, whom he had assigned late-night watch duty so he might sleep in his own bed for a change instead of on one of the jail cell cots.

Blair was already through the front door of the small farmhouse by the time his boss was stepping into his britches.

"You fix us some coffee while I get myself dressed," Dalton grumbled, pointing toward the glowing embers that remained in the fireplace. "This better be important."

He doubted it was. In the two years since Blair had begun working for him, the marshal had grown to expect that not all of his deputy's "emergencies" were as urgent as his tone of voice might suggest. Ben Dalton passed it off as youthful energy and enthusiasm that he couldn't help but admire. He had a vague recollection of once being that way himself.

Aberdene was a quiet little town where lawbreaking and threats to the well-being of the townspeople were rare. Such had been the case in the years since Dalton returned home from the North-South war and began wearing his badge. Oh, there were always drunken Saturday night fights at the Clear Water Saloon to break up; there was that Christmas Eve night when lightning struck the feedstore and set the roof afire, and the brief disappearance of a couple of young schoolboys who frightened the wits out of their parents by choosing to spend a day skinny-dipping at Loving Creek instead of sitting in class, reading and doing arithmetic. But Dalton could count on one hand the times a rancher's horse or farmer's cow had been stolen, a life had been threatened, or a business had been broken into. Aside from the time he had single-handedly aborted the robbery of the bank by three young and woefully inept Confederate deserters, his career enforcing law and order had been considerably short on excitement or high drama.

All of which suited him just fine. He had secretly resigned himself to the fact that he and a stagnant daily routine were for now and evermore on a first-name basis.

Truth be known, Ben Dalton really wasn't much of a town marshal. Still, he was generally liked by most. Folks always nodded and smiled when he took his slow walks along Aberdene's main street, making his presence known two or three times a day. He had never been the subject of scandal or whispered gossip, even when Maizy Benton named her first child after him.

What had happened was her labor pains had come during one of the worst winter storms in the county's history. Neither the doctor nor the midwife could get into town, so her husband had managed to trudge the half mile to the marshal's office, seeking help. Then, in his frostbitten and anxious state, the soon-to-be father fainted dead away. Dalton dragged him to a cot in one of the cells, covered him with blankets, then braved the ice storm and arrived to the painful screams of Mrs. Benton. It was left to the marshal to help deliver a healthy seven-pound boy. "He'll be called Ben," the exhausted and thankful mother had whispered to him as she clutched her newborn to her breast.

D ALTON WAS SIPPING at the coffee the deputy had handed him before he finally asked for details of the current emergency.

"Ol' lady Akins, she finally got fed up with her no-good husband coming home in the middle of the night, knock-kneed drunk. She met him on the front porch with her shotgun."

"Kill him?"

"Naw, she only used birdshot. Ruined his shirt and caused some bleeding to his shoulder. Might near put one of his eyes out. After it was over, she hitched up the buckboard and took him into town to Doc Baker's office, where he was tended to."

"So, what is it you figure we're supposed to do, arrest her and lock her up with those drunk cowboys we got sobering up?"

"Well, I don't know. You're the marshal."

"You talk to her husband?"

"He says he don't want to press charges and that he's done promised his wife that he'll never take another drink. They were bawling and hugging on one another when I left to come out here."

"So, maybe this is one of those sad stories with a happy ending we shouldn't be interfering with," Dalton said. "In fact, maybe I'll just sit and have me some more coffee, then go milk my cow. Want to stay for breakfast?"

The deputy shrugged, his excitement deflated. "Might as well," he said.

FOR SEVERAL DAYS thereafter, the story of Midge Akins shooting her husband, Buck, was the talk of Aberdene. The ladies of the church collectively agreed that Midge, a fine Christian woman, had been driven plumb to distraction and had finally done what she had to. They were organizing an around-the-clock prayer chain for her and putting together a petition urging Marshal Dalton not to charge her with any crime.

At the saloon, Buck Akins, sober and well on the mend, was too embarrassed to even show his face. The patrons enjoyed a good laugh when the story was told, then retold, often with a little something extra added. Even the marshal had to smile when he overheard someone suggest that the day would come when the incident would be recalled as "the Shootout at Akins Farm," and jokingly wondered if one of those big-city writers who produce dime novels might find the tale of interest.

His smile, however, would later vanish when a strange telegram was delivered to his office.

The face in his dream was calling out for help.

PART ONE

— ◇ —

THE CALLING

CHAPTER 1

T HE MARSHAL HAD tended to his farm chores well
before sunup and arrived at his office early. He sent
his deputy home to rest, then walked down to the café,
where he ordered two oatmeal breakfasts for the young
ranch hands who were still in jail, impatiently waiting for
their boss to come bail them out. Dalton greeted a couple of early-rising farmers who were waiting for the rebuilt feedstore to open, let Ima the waitress refill his
coffee cup, then made his way back to feed the prisoners.

While they ate noisily, he sat, put his scuffed boots
atop his desk, and gazed out at the dusty street, which
would soon awaken with activity. The café would fill,
wagons would arrive to haul away feed and groceries,
riders would visit the livery to have their horses shod,
and the teacher would appear on the schoolhouse steps,
ringing her bell to signal that class was about to begin.

Another day in Aberdene. And, barring an Indian
raid, a midtown gunfight, or a calamitous act of God—
events that had never occurred in the town's brief

history—Dalton would sit alone at his desk, twirling his worn-out hat on one finger, watching as his little part of the world passed slowly by.

If he could get rid of the jailed drunks early enough, he just might lock up and ride back out to the farm, pick up Poncho, the bluetick hound he'd raised from a pup, and go down to the creek and see if the catfish were biting. Poncho could amuse himself chasing squirrels until he realized it was a hopeless undertaking and decided to nap at Dalton's side.

On the off chance something did need attention while he was away, everyone in town knew where to find Deputy Blair. Odds were there would be no need. Never was.

By the time an ill-tempered foreman from the Two Aces ranch arrived, cussed out his hungover employees, and counted out bail money, Marshal Dalton had decided yes, it was a fine day for a brief fishing trip, as good a way as any to kill the remainder of a fine morning.

He was posting a notice to contact his deputy in the event of an emergency when he saw old Billy Sexton limping toward him, waving a yellow piece of paper. "Got yourself a telegram, Marshal," he called out, shielding his eyes from the sun with his free hand. "It just come in and I wanted to get it to you right away. Figured it might be important."

The marshal took a seat on the bench in front of his office and pushed back his hat before reading.

DESPERATELY NEED HELP . . . URGENT . . .
JOHN IN JAIL . . . PLEASE COME . . . ONLY ONE
I CAN TRUST.

The name at the end of the message caused him to struggle momentarily for breath. The shaking of his hand caused the paper he held to make a rattling noise. At the bottom of the message the sender's name was also typed in capital letters: *MANDY STEVENS RAWLINGS*.

Sexton was taken aback by Dalton's reaction. In his years working for Western Union, he had delivered countless messages bearing troubling news, most alerting the receiver that a friend or loved one was desperately ill or had passed, yet he hadn't expected someone like Ben Dalton to be so visibly shaken. Only as he viewed the look on the marshal's unshaven face did he finally remember a long-ago friendship between him and the sender. It was back in the days before the war, Sexton recalled. Ben was still a young man in those days and the sender of the message was the prettiest girl in town.

"You all right, Marshal?"

Dalton slowly folded the telegram and put it in his shirt pocket. "I'll be needing to send a reply," he said.

"Right now? You don't want to think on it a bit?" Sexton said as he took a small notebook and the stub of a pencil from his pocket.

"Just make it read, 'On my way.'"

The tone of his voice made it clear he needed no time to give the matter a second thought.

D ALTON COULDN'T REMEMBER the last time he'd felt so energized, so suddenly focused on a purpose, however nebulous it might be. His mind raced as he made a mental checklist of things he would need to do before being on his way.

Walking quickly over to J. R. Wheatley's livery, he sought out the young man who did chores in exchange for small pay and a place to sleep in back of the barn. Junior Atwood was one of Aberdene's lost souls, without family or history. He had simply ridden into town one day, hungry and sad-eyed, and looking for work. He'd never left. He was mentally slow but always smiling and excessively thorough at whatever task Wheatley assigned him. He had a well-earned reputation as someone who could be trusted and counted on, so long as his task wasn't too challenging.

In time, Junior and the marshal had become good friends, even fishing together now and then.

He was mucking out a stall when Dalton found him. "Need your help," Ben said. "I'm gonna be gone for a bit and want you to bunk out at the farm for a while. Continue your daywork here for J. R., but of a morning and evening see to the livestock and be sure and feed my dog regular. I'll pay proper wages for your caretaking. You'll find there's ample food on the kitchen shelves and my bed's a sight more comfortable than the hay you've been sleeping on. Be aware, though, that one side of it belongs to Poncho. He'll be glad for your company and easy to get along with as long as you scratch behind his ears now and then."

Junior was smiling and shaking his head. "I'll do it, Mr. Marshal. I surely will. How long you figure to be gone?"

"Can't rightly say. Go on out this evening and make yourself at home. I'll leave your pay hidden in the Dutch oven over the fireplace. Before you come to the livery in the mornings, be sure to milk the cow, feed the chickens, and gather the eggs. Poncho, he'll eat whatever it is you're fixing for yourself. If it's still light when you get home, pick the ripe tomatoes and okra out of the garden. You're welcome to them. That's about all I can think of that'll be needing done in my absence."

That matter tended, Dalton rode to Rolly Blair's cabin on the edge of town. He was pleased to see the thin white column of smoke rising from the chimney, indicating that the deputy was home and hadn't detoured by to see his lady friend.

Blair had just exited the outhouse and was buttoning his britches, whistling happily, when he saw Dalton arrive.

"What brings you this way so early in the day?"

Without speaking, Dalton dismounted, took the telegram from his pocket, and handed it to him.

"I'm leaving shortly," he said, "and wanted to let you know that as of this moment you are hereby and officially appointed acting marshal."

Blair was speechless for a moment. "For how long?" he finally replied.

"I've got no idea."

"You spoken to the mayor about this?"

Dalton shook his head. "Nope."

"What if he ain't happy with the idea?"

"I don't know. Maybe just shoot him."

For a moment, Blair wasn't sure whether his boss was joking.

A T THE FARM, he gathered a change of clothes and his straight razor and toothbrush and stuffed them into a saddlebag. He found his bedroll in the barn and, almost as an afterthought, located a box of cartridges for his Peacemaker, his favorite corncob pipe, tobacco, and matches. At the well, he filled a canteen, then knelt to scratch behind Poncho's ears, explaining to his wholly uninterested companion that he'd be in charge of the place for a while. "Don't be letting any squirrels sneak into the house or raccoons chase the chickens," he said. "And see you treat your guest—he's called Junior—with proper respect when he arrives or he just might forget to feed you."

Dalton rose and looked toward the house he'd called home all his life. Once warm and filled with life, it was now a lonely and uninviting place that had offered little comfort since his parents died in 1863, two years before he'd burned his Confederate uniform and returned to civilian life. If not for Poncho and the few daily chores that regularly demanded his attention, he would have little reason to spend much time at the place at all.

He unfolded Mandy's telegram and read her message again. Standing in a quiet disrupted only by wind ruffling the branches of the nearby pecan trees, he wondered what manner of desperation had prompted her to reach out after all these years.

In truth, it mattered little. All that did was that she needed him.

As Dalton rode away, heading north in the direction of Fort Worth, Poncho chose not to follow. His running days long past, he had already returned to sleeping peacefully in the shade of the porch.

CHAPTER 2

D ALTON RESISTED THE urge to hurry his mare, Dolly, along, choosing instead a leisurely pace that he figured would allow him to complete his journey in three or four days, if the weather held. Along the way he would be on the lookout for resting places that offered shade, tender grass, and streams running with clear, cool water. Knowing there would be a few way-stop towns—Brush Creek, Walnut Gap, and White Rose—along the way where he could purchase a meal and coffee for himself and a bucket of oats for his horse, he had brought no food or even a pot for brewing coffee. He had decided to travel light.

Alone on the trail, there is little for one to do once one is headed in the right direction. Ben knew that the route he was taking had no recent history of Comanche attacks, cattle rustlers, or thieving highwaymen to be wary of, so, mostly, it was thinking and talking to himself that passed the time.

It had been a while since he had allowed himself to take measure of his life, but Mandy Rawlings' telegram had set off a flood of thoughts, mostly memories of bygone days, back when his parents were still living, times were carefree, and there was no Civil War to be fought. As he rocked in the saddle to the rhythm of Dolly's steady gait, his mind drifted, one recollection offering a gentle reminder of another. And then another.

Woven through them all was the girl—now a woman, a wife, and a mother—who needed his help.

THOUGH TWO GRADES ahead of him in school, John Rawlings had been his best friend back then. Despite a dramatic difference in their backgrounds, they were bonded as if brothers. As he rode, Dalton recalled their spending summer nights on the bank of Loving Creek, sitting in the glow of a campfire, sharing stories and a half-full jug of moonshine John had slipped from the liquor cabinet in his father's office. They hunted rabbits and squirrels together, sat side-by-side in Miss Silverton's high school classes, and on Sunday mornings shared the same pew at the St. Gallagher church. They visited each other's homes regularly and once used Ben's pocketknife to cut small nicks in their thumbs and pressed them together. From that day, they were blood brothers.

Viewed from any vantage point, it was an unlikely relationship. John was the son of one of the wealthiest landowners in Central Texas, a tall, handsome young man of good fortune with every promise of a bright future. Ben, spindly then and always in need of a haircut and better-fitting clothes, was raised by a hard-working father who managed a hardscrabble living farming, raising a small herd of goats, and selling fire-wood to townspeople too busy or too lazy to chop their own. The only thing young Ben Dalton knew of his future, even if he had bothered to consider it, was that he longed for the day he would never again see or smell another goat.

There was never an indication, however, that he envied the status of John and his family. John, meanwhile, never looked down on the Daltons' station in life.

John was outgoing and gregarious. Ben was quiet and shy. Yet their friendship was steadfast and strong.

Until the Stevens family arrived in Aberdene.

ROLAND STEVENS HAD come from San Antonio to take over ownership of the local dry goods store. Blanche Wells, the previous proprietor, had begun to suffer with severe arthritis and increasingly poor eyesight and had announced her intention to retire as soon as she could find a suitable buyer.

Stevens, his wife, and his young daughter pulled their wagon to a halt in front of Miss Wells' store on the first day of spring 1858. By closing time, Blanche had handed over the keys, collected a few personal items into a wicker basket, and proudly walked out the front door. She never returned, even as a customer.

Just over a year later, she died in her sleep at age eighty-three. In her will, she left the money she had received from Stevens to the Aberdene library. Since it had no name at the time, referred to only as "the library," residents unanimously agreed it should henceforth be called the Blanche Wells Memorial Reading Room. Most townspeople, however, continued to refer to it simply as "the library."

One of its best customers was Mandy Stevens.

On most summer days, after working in her father's store in the mornings, she would sit on a wooden bench in the park, reading whatever new book she had discovered. John Rawlings and Ben Dalton quickly learned of her routine and set about to make sure that she was kept company and properly welcomed to town.

John always did most of the talking. *Are you enjoying our little community? What was it like, living in a big city like San Antonio? Are you planning to attend the Fourth of July picnic?* He mentioned that the book she was reading looked interesting and he'd like to read it when she was finished. He told her that he was planning to go off to college after graduation and study to become a lawyer. And, by the way, did she know that his prize calf had recently won a blue ribbon at the county stock show?

He showed off while his friend stood mutely by. But as Mandy replied, she always smiled at Ben as much as she did the talkative John. She liked them both and, in time, the three became good friends, daily spending time together as the boys helped her explore the community.

John was delighted to be seen in the company of the prettiest girl in town, never disputing anyone's suggestion that he and she might soon become something more than friends. Mandy, however, gave no reason to advance such speculation. Meanwhile, Ben, who had gradually become more at ease talking and being in her company, was never the subject of any such romantic rumors. Yet secretly he was feeling something that confused him. The more he was in Mandy's company, the less he wished to have his best friend around.

"You're always so quiet," she said to him one day as they stood together at the drugstore counter, trying to decide what flavor penny candy to buy. "It's like you're always thinking about something nobody else knows. Like you've got some deep, dark secret you don't want to share.

"On the other hand, John, he's funny, blabbering on a mile a minute about anything that comes into his head. Truth is, I bet he even talks in his sleep."

Ben just smiled. "It might surprise you to know that I talk to you more than anyone I've ever known. More even than John."

"Well, I consider that a fine compliment," she said as she paid for her candy. "Indeed I do, Ben Dalton."

Still, she had no idea what his hidden secret might be.

B EFORE THE YEAR was over, he would take it with him as he went off to war.

At his father's urging, he joined the Confederate Army the day after he graduated from Aberdene High. John also soon left, headed back East to enroll in college. Mandy dutifully saw them both off, tearfully wishing her friends well. In their absence, all that remained for her were shelves of unread books and her job stocking goods and ringing up sales at her father's store. A dark, lonely sadness swept over her like nothing she had ever experienced.

* * *

ASSIGNED TO THE First Texas Cavalry Battalion for
the next two and a half years, Dalton had little
time to think about anything but his and his fellow soldiers' survival. Waging war against the Union, he experienced a view of life he'd never imagined, filled
with blood, death, and a constant kill-or-be-killed
mindset. The pleasant dreams of his youth turned to
adult nightmares, and more than once he seriously
doubted he would live to ever see home—or Mandy
Stevens—again.

Only when word came that General Lee had surrendered, bringing an end to the madness and setting
soldiers on both sides free to resume normal lives, did
Ben dare consider his future.

The first thing that came to mind was to finally con-
fess his feelings to Mandy Stevens.

He never got the chance.

HIS FIRST STOP upon returning to Aberdene was
the dry goods store, where he hoped to find her
working. With news spreading of the war's end, he
thought she might even be expecting him. Instead, he
was met at the front door by her father.

"Welcome home, young man," Roland Stevens said.
"It's mighty good to see you so fit and well. God's
truth, we all worried about you while you were gone."

"I was hoping to say hello to Mandy."

Her father looked away briefly before he replied.
"She's not here, son. She moved away last year."

"Moved? Where?"

"I figured you knew, Ben." he said. "She and John Rawlings got married last spring. Surprised us all. He came home from college and asked her, plumb out of the blue, and she said yes. He's now practicing law in Fort Worth, doing quite well as I understand. Last time me and her mama got a letter, Mandy wrote that she was expecting. I'm now waiting to learn that I'm a grandpa."

Dalton didn't hear the last sentence. He had already turned and was hurriedly walking away.

After a brief stop at the livery to get his dog—J. R. Wheatley had looked after him during Ben's absence— he headed toward the farm with Poncho happily following. For the next month, no one in Aberdene saw the newly returned Dalton.

He passed his solitary days mending fences, putting a new roof on the barn, and clearing away brush. In the evenings, he sat with Poncho on the porch, smoking his pipe and listening to the peaceful night sounds of birds coming to roost and critters foraging.

He was well into his second month of self-exile on the morning that Saylor Edinberg's buggy came through the gate and stopped in front of the cabin. Aberdene's mayor was dressed in a black suit and his boots were polished to a mirror sheen. A new-looking bowler shaded his smiling face. "Fine, fine morning," he said as he climbed from the buggy.

Dalton nodded. "What brings you out this way?"

"Well, I've not had time to give you a proper welcome home," Edinberg said. "Folks tell me they haven't seen hide nor hair of you since you got back, so I decided to come looking. Wanted to let you know how proud I am of you fighting for the cause and returning in one piece."

The reply was silence.

Edinberg cleared his throat before his voice shifted to a more somber tone. "Truth is, I'm on my way to a funeral. Bill Thompson passed the other night after his tired old heart gave out on him."

"Sorry to hear."

The mayor looked over Ben's shoulder at the cabin, then out toward a clump of pecan trees under which new markers had been placed on the graves of Dalton's parents. He nodded his approval. "Looks like you've done a fine job fixing up the place. Your mama and daddy would be proud."

"Appreciate you saying so."

The mayor hadn't anticipated the difficulty he would face making conversation. "My friend, I'm not going to lie to you and suggest I know what you went through while you were gone. I'm sure it was something well on the other side of horrible. But, son, now that you're back, safe, it's time you started renewing your acquaintance with the world you've returned to. Time to get back to living." He gently slapped at Dalton's shoulder.

"Just so many fences a man can mend and roofs he can patch. A fella can't just sit on the porch with an old dog, letting the world pass him by."

Poncho lifted his head slightly and gave Edinberg a stern look and a brief show of teeth but wasted no breath growling.

Finally, the mayor got around to the real purpose of his visit. "With Bill Thompson going into the ground today, I'm urgently needing to hire a new marshal."

Rather than pausing to gauge Dalton's reaction, he hurried to his next thought. "You being a strong-minded young man with a fine reputation—and a war hero to boot—it's my sincere belief that you would be perfect for the job of seeing to law and order in our fine community."

He was surprised when Ben chuckled. "Mr. Mayor, I'm no war hero. I just got lucky and survived."

"Be that as it may, I'm here to offer you the job. Don't need to have your answer right now. Think on it a day or so and let me know. Meanwhile, I'll not offer the badge to anybody else until you decide."

A FTER A WEEK, Ben Dalton, cleanly shaved and wearing his best shirt, appeared at Mayor Edinberg's office and accepted the job.

Later in the day, as he sat in the café, marking the occasion with a plate of meat loaf and mashed potatoes, he overheard one of the local businessmen mention that Roland Stevens' daughter had given birth to a fine-looking baby boy.

For a moment, the new marshal considered arresting him for disturbing the peace.

That had been almost five years ago. During his time as marshal he had done his job well and received few complaints.

Mayor Edinberg was particularly pleased, mostly because Dalton had never once asked for an increase in pay.

CHAPTER 3

T HE SUN HAD just dipped below the tree line as Dalton began searching for a place to bed down for the night. If his guess was right, he could probably make it to Brush Creek in another hour, two at most, but Dolly was tiring and the idea of arriving in a strange town after dark didn't appeal to him. The sky was clear and the night promised to be warm, so sleeping under the stars would be fine.

They soon reached a sheltered meadow where the horse began nibbling at grass even before he could remove the saddle. From a spring on a nearby cliff, a small stream fed down into a pool of clear water. Ben was spreading his bedroll and regretting that he'd not brought the makings for coffee when he heard the shot.

It came from nearby.

Dolly's head jerked and she looked in the direction of the echoing sound, her brown eyes wide and searching. Taking his pistol from its holster, Dalton began carefully making his way up the side of the small cliff for a good vantage point.

Only a couple of hundred yards away he could see the faint flicker of a campfire and what appeared to be a man standing in its smoky shadows.

A half moon was on the rise, helping him find his way as he crept through the underbrush toward the campsite. As he neared, the figure of the man came into focus. Small and slump-shouldered, he seemed to be elderly. Despite the warmth of the evening, he wore a Mexican serape. His britches were well-worn, the bottom of the legs hidden by knee-high boots. Since he was hatless, Dalton could see that his wiry gray hair fell below his shoulders. His unkempt beard looked like a rat's nest.

In his hand was a gun.

As Ben slowly made his way closer, it appeared the old man was talking to himself. "Should oughta not done it," he kept repeating. On the opposite side of the fire lay a body, curled into a fetal position and motionless.

Dead, probably, Dalton thought as he stood and walked toward the man with the gun. He was behind him, only a few feet away, when he placed his Peacemaker to the back of the man's head. "I'd be much obliged if you would drop your weapon," he said. The old man didn't turn but let his pistol fall into the dirt. He continued his gibberish. "Wasn't meaning to . . . Should oughta not done it." And then he let out a volley of curses.

Dalton grabbed the man's shoulder and spun him around so he could see his face. What he saw were the anguished eyes of a man who was beginning to sob uncontrollably.

Once the crying stopped, the old man took a seat near the fire and grunted as he looked up at the puzzled stranger pointing a gun at him.

"I still got coffee in the pan here if you're wanting some," he said, his voice suddenly calm and friendly.

Dalton picked up the man's gun and put it in the waist of his britches, then turned his attention to the body. "He dead?"

" 'Fraid so. I shot him. Would have killed him more but I had only one bullet. Should oughta not done it, though."

"Mind telling me what happened?"

"Aw, we was just fussing, like we've been doing since back when we were kids. Finally had all of it I could stand. You can believe me when I tell you he was a no-good pain in the world's backside. Don't know why I didn't send him on his way a long time ago."

"He got a name?"

"Billy Joe . . . Billy Joe Barclay."

"And you are?"

"Name's Dee Wayne Barclay." He motioned toward the dead man. "Me and him, we're brothers."

Dalton found a ragged blanket and covered the body, then sat next to Barclay. The warmth of the campfire felt good. "I'm a marshal by profession," he said, "so I want you to understand that it's my duty to take you in. Where you from?"

"Just up the ways," he said. "Brush Creek, where we was born and raised. Me and Brother, we're gold searchers. We were on our way down to the San Saba River to do some panning. Heard that folks have been finding some big nuggets there. Big ones."

"How long you boys been looking for gold?"

"All our miserable lives," Barclay said. "And, I'm sorry to add, with scarce success. That's what we was fussing about when I shot him. He was saying there was no use for us to keep trying, that we wasn't ever going to find no gold." He waved a hand toward a pack mule grazing nearby. "He was saying we're such a sorry case that we even had to steal that ol' mule.

"I just got tired of his nagging. Took it all I could take."

Dalton let the man ramble. He talked of a deserted mine somewhere in the New Mexico territory, being chased by Comanches, briefly taking up with a gang of cattle rustlers, being jailed for a time somewhere in Missouri, and a red-haired lady he'd met in a Tascosa saloon. "I asked her to marry me before I even knew her name," he said.

As darkness fell, the stories became longer and increasingly incoherent. Dee Wayne's mind was wandering and he was obviously exhausted.

"You get some sleep," Dalton said, "At daylight, we'll head toward Brush Creek."

"What about my brother?"

"We'll take him with us."

A NSON KELLY, THE Brush Creek marshal, was standing in the doorway of the jail when they arrived. He spat an arching spray of tobacco into the street as Dalton dismounted, introduced himself, and explained what had happened.

The marshal's eyes went to the body tied aboard the mule, then the prisoner. "Howdy, Dee Wayne," he said. "I always figured this was gonna happen. Just didn't know when. Nor was I ever real sure who it would be shooting who."

Barclay was already walking up the steps to the jail as the marshal spoke. "Come on in and let's get you settled. Then I'll fetch the doc to tend to your brother."

The headquarters of Brush Creek law enforcement was a small but sturdy building made of bois d'arc logs. Inside there was barely room for a single jail cell and a small table that served as Kelly's desk. Once Barclay was locked away, the marshal turned to Dalton.

"I appreciate you bringing him in," he said, "though honestly I'd just as soon you had ridden on your way when you learned what Dee Wayne did. Both of those old coots are crazy as rabid skunks. Have been for as long as I've known them. Always talking about striking it rich, but truth is, they were so broke they couldn't pay attention."

From the cell came the rhythmic whisper of Dee Wayne's voice. "Should oughta not done it . . . should oughta not done it . . ."

After the doctor had come and taken the body away, the two marshals sat on the porch, away from the prisoner's body odor and his mournful chant. "I see you ain't wearing your badge," the local marshal said. "You get run out of town, or is it personal business that brings you this way?"

"Got a friend up in Fort Worth needing help," Dalton said.

"Then feel free to be on your way. I'll see to Dee Wayne's situation."

"What's going to happen to the old man?"

"Can't rightly say. If I get lucky, he'll try to escape and I'll have to shoot him."

* * *

A S HE CONTINUED toward his destination, Ben Dalton couldn't get the old man and his dead brother out of his mind. What terrible turn of events had triggered such raging insanity? How does a man sink to such lonely depths and lose all touch with reality and good sense?

He couldn't help but wonder if his decision to respond to Mandy Rawlings' telegram wasn't the first step toward his own kind of madness.

CHAPTER 4

MOST OF THE spring trail drives were over, weary wranglers and thousands of head of cattle having finally arrived in Fort Worth. It was called Cowtown for good reason. There, deals were struck and money changed hands to provide Northerners, Californians, and Indian reservations in the Midwest with a new supply of beef. Many of the cowhands, pay finally in their pockets, chose to remain for a few day to celebrate their journey's end. They generally did so in the part of town known as Hell's Half Acre, where liquor flowed, card games never ended, and the ladies all had smiling faces.

A group of drunken revelers who had all but destroyed a saloon they patronized were being escorted to jail when Ben Dalton entered the sheriff's office. Since Mandy's message had not included an address, he'd decided to first pay a visit to her husband and had a good idea where to find him.

"The sheriff don't like the prisoners having visits,"

the young jailer said, "even if they're from family." His tone was harsh and businesslike—until Dalton pulled a silver dollar from his pocket and placed it in his hand. "You'll be needing to make it quick," he said, suddenly more friendly. "Sheriff's gone to have him some supper and will be back soon."

He motioned Dalton past the large cagelike structure the drunk cowboys had just been locked into. They mingled, shoulder to shoulder, with other prisoners, as if trying to determine where they were and how they'd gotten there. There was loud cursing and the sound of some retching. A putrid odor came from a line of buckets that had been placed near the back wall. A fight was under way between two of the recently arrived inmates.

Once sober, they would be released after paying the sheriff whatever they had in their pockets. "Get-out" money, it was called. The more experienced cowboys had learned not to carry all of their pay with them when on a celebration toot, lest they leave Cowtown flat broke.

"Looks like business is good," Dalton said as the jailer directed him down a hallway leading to the rear of the building. At its end was a poorly lit row of three small cells, cleaner, quieter, and more strongly fortified. "This," the jailer said, "is where we keep those who are here for more serious reasons."

Two were empty. In the third, Ben could see a form stretched out on a wooden plank that served as a bed.

John Rawlings, shirtless and wearing no shoes, sat up and squinted into the darkened hallway when he heard his name called. His hair was disheveled and he obviously hadn't shaved in days. Only when he stood, wrapped in a thin blanket across his bare shoulders, and shuffled to the front of the cell did he recognize his visitor.

One of his eyes was swollen and there was a spot of dried blood on his forehead. It was obvious that someone had given him a beating.

"Good to see you, Ben," he said in a raspy voice. His bruised face was close enough to the bars that Dalton could smell his foul breath. He bore only slight resemblance to the boyhood companion his visitor remembered. "I really didn't figure on you coming."

Without speaking, Dalton found a stool in the hallway and moved it in front of the cell door. "If I'd given the matter a proper amount of thought, I most likely wouldn't have," he finally said after removing his hat and taking a seat.

"Ben, I didn't kill anybody," John said. "God's honest truth. You know such a thing's not in my nature. There's folks telling lies about me, and I don't know why." The semidarkness hid the tears forming in the corner of his eyes.

"And what is it I'm supposed to do?"

"I need somebody to prove I'm innocent and get me out of here. I need someone I can trust."

"That's me?"

"I'm begging you. Please . . ."

The desperation in Rawlings' voice made Dalton uncomfortable, and he was relieved when the jailer soon stuck his head around the corner and insisted it was time he leave. "Right now, mister. The sheriff will be coming back any minute," he said.

As the brief visit ended, John extended a shaking hand through the bars. Dalton reluctantly shook it.

"You're a good friend," Rawlings said, "the best I ever had. I want you to know I appreciate you coming. Mandy can explain the situation to you in more detail," he said. "We're living in an apartment over at the Langley Hotel. Go see her. She'll tell you I've done nothing wrong."

Dalton didn't reply. Suddenly, the idea of seeing Mandy again after all these years caused the knot that was already lodged in the pit of his stomach to grow. Or maybe it was the pain in his old friend's voice. He quickly walked toward the front of the jail, wondering what he'd gotten himself into.

He went in search of a place to stay the night, knowing full well that he would get no sleep.

T HE FOLLOWING MORNING, a bright-faced youngster opened the apartment door and smiled. "Who are you?" he asked.

Before Dalton could answer, the child's mother was standing behind him.

"Hello, Ben," Mandy said.

An immediate reply lodged in Dalton's throat as he nervously fumbled with his hat. What he saw in front of him was the beautiful woman he remembered. Her hair was cut a bit shorter but still glistened, forming a golden halo around her face. The grace and poise clearly remained. All that was missing was the smile. She leaned forward and lifted the youngster into her arms. "You've already met my son," she said. "His name is Alton."

A faint smile eased onto Ben's face as he reached out to the child and shook his small hand. "Proud to meet you, young man."

"I'm five," Alton said.

Mandy eased the boy to the floor and stepped to one side, waving her visitor inside. "Come in, come in and sit," she said. "It's good to see you. My lord, how long has it been? Let me get you some coffee." She, too, was nervous.

As he let his eyes roam the room, Dalton realized he still had not spoken to her. "Good to see you, too," he managed as he took a seat. He told her he had briefly visited her husband the previous evening. "He's doing fine and said to tell you not to worry."

It was the first lie he'd ever told her.

She was halfway to the kitchen when she called over her shoulder, "I appreciate you coming, you know. More than I can say."

L ITTLE ALTON SAT on the parlor floor, amusing himself with his toys, as Ben sipped at his coffee. Mandy repeatedly smoothed her dress and brushed a hand through her hair. "Well, tell me all about yourself," she said. "I understand you're now Aberdene's marshal. Daddy wrote me about it. Said you're doing a fine job. It's so good you came home from the war safely . . . Still living on the farm, I suppose . . . More coffee?" For several minutes she rambled on, asking questions before any could be answered, as if silence were an enemy.

Finally, Dalton interrupted her. "Mandy, why am I here?"

She took a deep breath and briefly looked to the ceiling. "Ben, I'm sure he didn't do it," she began, then told the story.

It was a Sunday evening. A busy day had tired them all. First, they had attended church, then they were invited to join friends for lunch at their home. "They have a son and a daughter, and the children enjoyed playing together until sometime in the middle of the afternoon," she said.

Later, they had stopped by John's office so he could pick up some papers he needed to read before meeting with a judge on Monday morning.

"When we got home, there was an envelope taped to the door. John waited until we were inside to open it. I could see it was a note or a letter, but he didn't read it aloud or tell me what it said. Thinking back, I know it upset him for some reason, though he tried to hide it. 'From a client,' was all he said.

"Shortly after, he said he needed to go out for a while. Didn't bother saying where he was going, just left—kind of in a hurry. I was bathing Alton, getting him ready for bed, when John got back. He didn't say anything that I recall, just sat here in the parlor, in the very chair you're sitting in now. He seemed to be troubled, but I was too busy to ask him what was wrong.

"I'd just finished reading Alton his bedtime story when there was a loud knock on the door. John answered it and there was the sheriff and one of his deputies. All I heard was 'You're under arrest.' They were out the door and gone before I could even ask what was going on."

Only later had she learned more details by reading a newspaper account. She took the torn-away front page from a folder and handed it to Ben.

Well-known Fort Worth bank president and civil leader Thomas A. Cookson, 52, was found dead in his

residence late Sunday evening. His body was discov-
ered by his younger brother, who had stopped by the
Cookson home to return a hunting rifle he had bor-
rowed. According to him, the elder Cookson had been
shot in the back of the head from close range.

The article then went on to list Cookson's achieve-
ments and pointed out that he had lived alone since his
wife died of cancer three years earlier.

It was the final paragraph of the story that got Dalton's attention. *The investigation is ongoing, according*
to Sheriff Otto Langston. However, a source says that
the prime suspect, a local attorney, has been arrested
and is now under lock and key in the city jail.

"At least they didn't use his name," Ben said.

"Not until the next day." She handed Ben a second
article. It quoted the sheriff saying he had the killer in
jail and that evidence had been collected, proving it
was John who committed the murder. He said that
Rawlings and Cookson had reportedly been longtime
enemies.

Mandy looked across the room, the color drained
from her face. "I never heard John so much as mention
Thomas Cookson's name," she said. "I don't think he
even knew the man. So, why, for God's sake, would he
murder him?"

Ben had no idea where to begin. He was no investi-
gator. Back home, he had never been required to actually solve the few crimes that occurred in Aberdene.
Everything was always pretty clear-cut. Someone did
something illegal, like stealing a horse, got caught, admitted to it, and he put them in jail. End of story. No
real investigation expertise needed.

He silently reread the articles, buying himself time to think before responding. "Did John have enemies?"

"He's a lawyer. It's hardly a popular profession, particularly when you represent bad people."

"Bad people?"

Mandy looked down at her young son for a moment, then slowly nodded. "People who have broken the law and are looking for someone to get them out of trouble. That's what my husband does for a living, and apparently he's quite good at it."

"So, for starters, the sheriff's not likely to be an admirer," Ben said. "Has John got one of his lawyer friends doing anything about his situation?"

"John doesn't have any friends, Ben, that's why I reached out to you," she said. "The people we went to visit that Sunday were church friends of mine, not his. It was the first time we've been invited to anyone's home since we've been here." Her comment was almost an apology.

"I've spoken to a few attorneys, but they all tell me they're too busy with other clients. We have the money to pay their fees, that's not a problem. Honestly, I think they just don't want to get involved. I think they're afraid."

"What's scaring them?"

"I don't know. But I'm scared, too. Except for when I went to see them and sent you the telegram, I haven't been out of the house. I'm afraid . . . for my son, for my husband, and for myself. I don't know what's going on."

For the first time since Dalton arrived, she cried. Not in great sobs, but silently, with small tears sliding down her cheeks. He felt a strong urge to somehow comfort her but stayed seated. Instead, it was Alton who went to his mother and gently laid his head in her lap.

She stroked her son's hair for a time, then shook her head. "I promised myself I wouldn't get emotional. I'm sorry."

He assured her no apology was needed. "Just so you know, I'm not sure I'm going to be of much help," he said. "But I'll try. First, I need a starting place, something or someone that might give me some idea of who would want to do something like this. Do you have the letter that was left on the door?"

"John must have had it with him when the sheriff came. Or maybe the sheriff took it. I've looked everywhere and can't find it."

"Is there anybody—doesn't have to be a friend—who can tell me what John's been up to lately, who he's been associating with?"

"I'm afraid I'm not the person to ask," she said. "John doesn't tell me much about his work. It's the way I've wanted it."

She thought for a moment, then went to her nearby writing desk and began shuffling through papers. After a few minutes, she returned with an address. "When we first got here," she said, "John worked for a little while with this man. Shelby Profer's his name. He's also an attorney, an older gentleman who has been around ages. He knows everybody in town. He and one of John's college professors were friends, and he apparently agreed to be John's mentor.

"For a while they really got along. Mr. Profer showed John the ropes, advised him, introduced him to people, even got him his first clients. Then something happened. I have no idea what, but they went their separate ways. Some kind of falling-out, I guess. I can only guess whose fault it was."

Ben took the address. "Good a place to start as any," he said as he bent to give Alton a pat on the back before leaving.

He was at the door, putting on his hat, when Mandy called his name.

"Ben, that telegram I sent," she said. "It wasn't John's idea, it was mine."

T HE INTERIOR OF Shelby Profer's office looked as if someone had tossed a stick of dynamite through the window. Law books were stacked so high on the floor that the piles had begun to topple. Open boxes of papers took up much of the room, leaving only a narrow trail from the doorway to a single chair for visitors. Piled on it were coats that had apparently been there since winter. Dalton could only assume there was a desk somewhere beneath the clutter of correspondence, more books, and a large bronze statue of a Longhorn steer. On one wall were numerous framed diplomas and citations, none of which was hanging straight. The only light in the room came from a small lamp leaning against the Longhorn statue.

Were it not for the loud snoring, it would have been all but impossible to know Profer was in and open for business.

"Excuse me," Dalton called out.

"Taking my midmorning nap," the aging lawyer said without apology. He groaned, then yawned before he said, "Come in and take a seat."

A head of snow-white hair emerged as Dalton wove his way toward the sound of the lawyer's voice. Profer stood and extended his hand. "I don't believe we've met," he said. Though he was somewhere in his eighties, his broad shoulders slumped only slightly and his grip was firm. He had an easy, inviting smile that could have fit the face of a kindly town doctor.

Dalton introduced himself and explained the purpose of his visit.

"John Rawlings," Profer said, drawing the name out slowly. "I hear he killed old man Cookson. Too bad. There's folks in town who would be happy to know it was the other way around." He chuckled to himself. "Honest truth is, it's probably fifty-fifty who was disliked more."

"So you figure John to be guilty?"

"Not saying I do. But it's been my professional experience that anybody, churchgoer or worthless as dirt, can go off the rails and find himself in a heap of trouble. Before we talk further, you need to know I no longer do criminal work. Don't have the energy or interest for it. Writing wills and settling the occasional tax dispute is my speed these days."

Ben explained he wasn't there to ask him to defend his friend.

"Well, then, mind if I ask your interest in this tragic matter?"

"I'm just trying to learn a little background on John Rawlings and am told that you were once his friend and mentor. His wife speaks highly of you. And she's convinced he didn't do it."

"Of course," the attorney said. "What loyal wife would think differently?"

He leaned back in his chair, searching for a spot on his desk to put his boots. "Yes, I liked John when he first came. He was smart and eager, though a bit too full of himself for my taste. A smart aleck, truth be known. It took me a while to convince him he didn't already know everything there was to know about lawyering and dealing with people.

"For a time, I thought he was making headway. I hitched him up with a few clients and he did them a good job. Was beginning to make a proper name for himself around the courthouse. Only problem was, he was in too big a hurry to get rich. Started looking for shortcuts. That's when he decided to throw in with a bad crowd. And that's when I figured I'd done all I could for him. We parted ways."

"What kind of bad crowd?" Dalton said.

"He started prowling the Half Acre, offering himself to clients I wouldn't have touched with a ten-foot pole. Outlaws. Thieves. A man known to be a gun for hire, con artists, you name it. Badder the better. If they had cash in their pockets and were willing to part with it, John Rawlings was willing to represent them. I decided I didn't wish to know anything about what he was up to. He was heading himself for real trouble. If I'd had to guess, it would have been him getting killed rather than him killing somebody."

Dalton wondered how much of what Profer was telling him Mandy knew.

"Only way of knowing what he was doing and who he was doing it with," Profer said, "is to spend some time walking in his shoes. And this is free advice—and my last word on the subject: You would be best not to try it."

CHAPTER 5

FOR THREE NIGHTS, Dalton wandered from one Hell's Half Acre saloon to another, searching for anyone who might have had dealings with John Rawlings. Lawyers, he quickly learned, were hardly popular in that part of town. Neither was anyone asking about them. One bartender had refused to serve him, and a cowboy who overheard a question he'd asked left his card game and approached with a stuttering suggestion that they step into the street for a fight. He'd been laughed at, been cursed, and had a glass of beer poured on his best shirt.

Leaving a loud and foul-smelling place called the Red Eye Palace and ready to call it a night, he made his way through the throng of people crowding the dusty street. He was on his way to the livery to check on Dolly when he sensed he was being followed. He made an abrupt turn into a darkened alley and waited for whoever it was to pass.

When a man who didn't resemble most of the Half Acre clientele walked by, Ben quickly fell in behind him. "You looking for me?" he said.

The follower turned and quickly put his hands in the air. "Oh my Lord," he said. "I thought you were somebody robbing me. Which would have been a major disappointment, since I'm quite without funds at the moment. Still, you near scared me out of my britches." The crooked grin that he managed indicated that he was pleasantly drunk. "From conversation I happened to overhear, I understand you're seeking information about a certain party I might know."

"Your name is . . . ?"

"Felton Winslow, Esquire. Attorney-at-law. Or used to be until I turned to rye whiskey and opium as my full-time profession."

"You know John Rawlings?"

"Might I suggest we have our conversation over some refreshment? If you're willing to buy a man a drink, there's a little saloon a few blocks over that I don't think you've visited. It's not a particularly popular place since the lady owner has seen fit to forbid card playing and the use of foul language. People can drink in peace and do their talking in a normal voice."

Dalton studied the little man. He wore a suit that was badly frayed and no longer fit. His eyes were hollow and watery and his hands shook as he nervously clenched and unclenched his small fists. He slowly danced from one foot to another like a man badly needing to relieve himself. His better days were clearly behind him.

"Lead the way," Dalton said.

*   *   *

T HE PLACE WAS a welcome contrast to the saloons he had been visiting. When they entered, the owner cast a wary eye toward Winslow, but her expression softened when Dalton pulled a gold piece from his pocket and placed it on the bar.

Winslow greedily gulped his drink after almost grabbing it from the bartender's hand. He let the whiskey warm his insides before he spoke.

"Not that John Rawlings and myself are friends, mind you," he said, "but from time to time he's been gentleman enough to purchase me a drink or two when visiting the establishments I frequent. To my best recollection, he started coming around about a year or so ago. Had himself one of those fancy cardboard business cards that he liked to pass around.

"It was pretty clear that he was always looking for the baddest cowboy in the place, someone who was most likely to be needing help to remain out of jail. I found it quite interesting to watch him work. Very confident, very outgoing. And he seemed to somehow know who needed help—and could pay to get it. If I'd had his knack for reading people, I might still be in good standing and practicing."

"You recall him dealing with anyone in particular?"

Winslow was silent for a moment, a signal that he was waiting for Dalton to order another round.

"There's a fella calls himself Colonel Abernathy. Wears a big white hat, has a diamond ring on his finger. He walks in a place, it gets quiet as a graveyard. Says he's in the cattle business, which I suppose is a true statement. He just doesn't bother saying whose cattle."

"So he's a rustler?"

"From my understanding—and realize that I'm hardly a part of the Acre's inner circle—it's a bit more complicated than that. From what I've deducted, his purpose in visiting the saloons is to hire out cowhands who are broke and down on their luck and have them do his stealing for him. They cut a few head from whatever herd they've driven to town, maybe take a few cows and calves from another herd or two, occasionally raid some of the small ranches out west of town, and see that they wind up on the Colonel's ranch, waiting to have his brand burned into their hindsides. Word is, he's got a big spread down south in the Glen Rose Valley. The Shooting Star, it's called, if I correctly remember."

Winslow drank more slowly this time. "I've seen him and John Rawlings with their heads together a number of times. Thick as . . . well . . . thieves, one might say."

"Has this Colonel been in trouble with the law?" Ben said.

"Not directly that I know of. I expect a man of his means wouldn't have himself any difficulties convincing certain folks, for a price, that he's an innocent and upstanding citizen. But now and again one of his hired hands, the ones thieving for him, don't show good sense and get themselves thrown in jail. Part of the Colonel's agreement with them is that he'll see to it they get out in a hurry and back to work. That, I assume, is why he would have need for a lawyer, one who doesn't ask him too many questions and keeps his workforce free to keep bringing him more cattle.

"And that, my good sir, is the absolute extent of my knowledge of Mr. John Rawlings' activities."

Dalton stood, tipped his hat, and slid a dollar across the table toward Winslow before leaving.

As he walked into the warm night, questions filled his head. What ugly level of greed had driven his old friend? How could he find out more about the activities of this Colonel? And was it possible what he had just learned was somehow tied to the murder of an apparently trustworthy banker?

TWO NIGHTS LATER, as he was leaving a café where he'd had a supper of red beans and corn bread, Dalton was attacked.

Dragging him from the street to the rear of a run-down laundry, two men, each outweighing him by thirty pounds or more, beat him into unconsciousness. Fists repeatedly pounded into his belly and rib cage. A tooth flew from his mouth and he thought he felt bones in his cheek crack after a blow to the face caused him to lose all sense of balance. Once he was on his knees, the attackers took turns kicking him. For good measure, one stomped his hat.

Amid their laughter and curses, they issued a warning: *Don't be asking about things that are none of your business. Go back where you came from, or next time you'll really get hurt.*

While Dalton lay in the darkness, ribs throbbing and blood oozing from his mouth, less than a mile away at the Red Eye Palace, Felton Winslow, Esq., was enjoying a second whiskey paid for by Colonel Abernathy. "Little man," the Colonel said as he placed an arm across the disgraced lawyer's skinny shoulders, "you did right by coming to see me."

Winslow nodded and sipped at his glass. "A man's got to earn his pleasure, am I right?"

I T WAS NEAR dawn before Dalton regained consciousness and another hour before he felt well enough to get to his feet. There was a taste of bile and copper in his mouth and he felt he might throw up. He had difficulty focusing. There was no part of his body that didn't hurt.

He was leaning against a wall that seemed to be swaying when one of the Chinese women who had arrived for work discovered him. She said something in her native language and rushed away, soon to return with a basin of water and a cloth. She gently bathed his swollen face. Another woman joined her and together they helped him inside where the heat from the fire and the steaming wash water helped clear his head. A little girl who had followed her mother into the alley had retrieved his crumpled hat and was trying to mold it back into shape.

He remained in the laundry most of the day, sleeping, waking, then sleeping again. He was vaguely aware of someone touching a dipper to his mouth, feeding him small drinks of water, then sips of hot broth. All around him was the muffled chatter of workers going about their jobs.

It was late in the afternoon when a customer arrived to pick up his cleaned clothes. Led to the back of the laundry by one of the women, he looked at Dalton and gave out a low whistle. "Mister," he said, "I hope you had yourself a good time last night, 'cause it appears you paid dearly for it."

He knelt beside Ben and looked more closely at his wounds. "I ain't no doctor, but it appears you've got a fair chance of living. Name's Jesse Stansberry. I run the hardware store down the street. Anything I can do to help you?"

For the first time since the attack, Dalton attempted to speak. "Livery . . ." he whispered. "To the livery . . ." The only clear thought he could manage was that he needed to check on his horse. He had to repeat himself several times before Stansberry understood.

"I'll gladly take you there," he said. "It's on my way home. I'll pull my buggy up out back and we'll figure how to load you up."

As the injured Dalton was being helped, the young girl who had earlier rescued his hat rushed to his side, a smile on her face as she held it out to him. With the help of the laundry's steam, she had managed to reshape it, almost to its original state.

Dalton nodded and slowly patted a hand to his heart, then pointed to her, wishing he could form the words to properly thank her.

D UKE KEENE, THE livery owner, had just made his rounds to refill oat buckets and finished grooming away knots from a horse's mane when Stansberry called out for help. "I got a fella—what's left of him— who asked that he be delivered here," he said.

Keene approached the buggy and immediately

recognized the barely conscious passenger. "I'm boarding his mare. Guess now I'm boarding him as well. There's a cot and some blankets back in the tack room where we can put him. Then I'll fetch a doctor."

Dalton moaned as the men eased him from the buggy. "I'm betting he could use a taste to ease his pain while we wait," Keene said. "I'll get my bottle."

A s soon as the doctor had cleaned the wounds, wrapped the damaged ribs, and stitched up a cut that ran across his nose and along one cheek, Dalton was again sleeping. Keene gently removed his boots and placed a blanket over him. He hung his new boarder's hat on a nearby wall peg. "Ain't much of a hat, is it?" he said.

"I'll stop in sometime tomorrow and check on him," the doctor said.

T wo lost days passed before Dalton felt well enough to get on his feet and slowly make his way across the livery to Dolly's stall. For several minutes he stroked her neck, pleased to find that she was being well cared for. Keene approached and stood next to him, holding a cup of coffee. "I'd say your horse looks a sight better than you do," he said. "How you feeling?"

"Better. Most likely thanks to you. You can rest assured I'll be paying for my care and keep, soon as I can get over to my hotel where I've got some money hid away. What I had in my pocket was stolen."

"Mister, I don't think it would be wise for you to try and go anywhere for a spell. You need to get yourself rested up. That's what the doc says. He patched you up and has been looking in on you. You're welcome to bunk here until you're mended. Truth is, I'll be glad for company that don't stand on four legs."

Keene asked if Ben felt like eating and before even getting an answer, he was on his way to the diner across the street.

Later, as he sat on the side of his cot, slowly sipping at a bowl of soup, Dalton tried to tell what had happened to him. His recollection was hazy except for darkness and pain, the faint images of three large men, then, later, a pretty little girl with his hat in her hand.

"Might be just as well you don't recall in detail," Keene said, "seeing as how you clearly took yourself quite a beating. I'd say you're lucky to still be among the living."

As they talked, a voice came from the livery entrance. "Anybody home?"

Keene turned to see Sheriff Otto Langston slowly walking along the stalls, examining the horses. A tall, rangy man known to favor bow ties and spit-polished boots, he wore a pearl-handled pistol on his hip. His mustache was finely trimmed and his hat rested low against his forehead.

"I've come to visit somebody who I understand was recently assaulted," he said. "My friend down at the hardware store made mention of helping him out."

Keene waved him toward the tack room.

The sheriff stood silently for a moment, as if assessing the damage that had been done to the man seated in front of him. "I'm mighty sorry about this," he finally said. "It displeases me greatly when I learn somebody's been mistreated in my town. Got any notion who done this to you?"

"I don't remember much," Dalton said. "Just that there were two of them and they were big and mean."

"You just visiting our fair city?"

Ben nodded and gave his name. "Can't say I've seen anything I'd be inclined to call fair since I got here," he said. "I come from Aberdene, down south, where folks act a bit kinder toward one another." He didn't mention that he was also a lawman.

The sheriff smiled. "Well, now, ain't that interesting. I'm told someone recently paid a visit to my jail, wanting to talk to one of my prisoners. A cold-blooded murderer, in fact, who I understand also once resided in Aberdene. Never heard of the place until he made mention of it.

"You're the man who was wanting to see John Rawlings, I'm guessing. Mind telling me what's your interest?"

"We were friends growing up," Dalton answered.

"And you come all the way from—what is it again?—Aberdene, just to say hello?"

Dalton felt an immediate dislike for the sheriff. "That's about the size of it."

As if thinking to himself, Langston shook his head and put a finger to the brim of his hat. "Well, I'll be going. Let me know if you think of anything that might help me find the men who did this to you. And I hope you'll feel better soon, so you can head on back home to Ab-er-dene." There was a hint of sarcasm in his voice as he strung out his final word.

Keene waited until the sheriff was gone before

he spoke. "Unless I'm badly mistaken," he said, "it sounded to me like you just got invited to leave town."

"That's the way I heard it, too," Dalton said as he picked up his soup bowl and resumed eating. As he did, he had a sudden flash of memory from the night behind the laundry. He remembered hearing one of his attackers tell him to "go back where you came from."

CHAPTER 6

Though the throbbing in his head had ceased and his mind had begun to clear, Dalton still struggled to make sense of the things that had happened to him in the days since his arrival in Fort Worth. It was obvious his presence wasn't welcome and the questions he'd been asking had displeased people. A picture, fuzzy and still without much shape, was slowly forming. Questions mounted and he had no real idea where to find the answers. Still, he was sure there was something amiss about John Rawlings being accused of murder, and it troubled him.

It occurred to him that he should talk to Mandy again and share his concerns, but he dismissed the idea of doing so immediately. In the first place, he really knew little more than he had when he first got to town. Second, he wanted his bruises to fade and be able to take a step without grimacing before he paid her another visit.

"Seems you're feeling better," Duke Keene said as

he watched his visitor brush Dolly. "Wouldn't advise entering no rodeos just yet, but I think you're soon gonna be good as new."

"I'm thinking of taking a ride over to the hotel so I can get my money and pay what I owe you."

"That'll be exactly nothing," the livery owner said. "Fact of the matter is, I'm thinking it don't make a lot of sense for you to be paying a dollar a day to stay there when my tack room and all its fine comforts are free for nothing as long as you need it."

"I can't . . ."

"Won't be no bother," Keene said. "Like I've done told you, it's nice having someone to talk to besides myself and the livestock. And it ain't likely you'll be here that long anyway since there's folks already wanting to run you out of town." With the last observation, he chuckled. "Now that's settled, we'll get you saddled up and you can ride over to that hotel and get your belongings, then come on back. I'll be expecting you to buy me some breakfast when you return."

Later in the day, Dalton thought, he also needed to pay a visit to the laundry and give the women there a proper show of his appreciation. He knew that it was quite likely they had saved his life. He asked Duke where he could buy some penny candy for the little girl who rescued his hat.

IN A SHABBY roadhouse several miles south of town, Sheriff Langston and Colonel Abernathy sat drinking tequila and talking in whispers despite the fact that they were the only ones in the place other than Luisa, the owner and cook. Scattered on the dirt floor around their table were discarded corn shucks from the tamales she had prepared for them.

"He looks like he was hit by a train," the sheriff said. "He's real beat up, limping around ol' man Keene's livery right now. My guess is that as soon as he's fit to ride, he'll be on his way."

The Colonel poured himself another shot and cursed. "He wasn't supposed to still be alive. And what about Rawlings?"

"Just sits in his cell, moaning and looking like his dog died. He's not causing any trouble. His wife—a pretty little thing—came to see him the other day, but I told her visiting wasn't allowed."

"What if the lawyer was to get so lonely and dejected he hangs himself in his cell some night? Or tries escaping, making it necessary for a guard to shoot him?"

The sheriff shook his head. "We've got to be careful about the way we do things," he said. "Trust me to handle it." He barely made eye contact with the Colonel as he spoke. The man scared him.

"Just be sure and see to it that you do," Abernathy said as he reached into his pocket, removed a pouch filled with gold coins, and pitched it across the table.

TEN YEARS EARLIER, Colonel Raymond J. Abernathy had come to Fort Worth from Brownsville and paid cash for a small ranch that immediately began to grow and expand until, in just a few years, it was one of the largest spreads in North Texas. Tall and robust with a head of snow-white hair and a carefully trimmed beard, he was a secretive sort, never making mention that his military rank had been attained as a Union

soldier rather than as a fighter for the Confederacy.
Nor was anyone aware of how he had accumulated the
money to buy his land. Some wondered if he might be
from a rich family. Others had suspicions that his
money had come by some illegal manner but kept the
notion to themselves. And for good reason.

Abernathy's younger days had, in fact, been spent
along the border, evading the law as he rode with a
band of Mexican cattle rustlers, robbed stage coaches,
and was involved in a number of gunfights that he always seemed to win. He was never one to embrace fair
play; it was said he once shot a man in the back after the
man had rightfully accused him of cheating at cards.

A frugal man, he had no interest in a wife and family and had already accumulated a sizable stake before
traveling north to join the Union. And by the time the
war ended, he was ready to chase his dream of becoming a man of substantial means. Purchasing the Shooting Star at a cheap price after threatening the previous
owner and his family was a start.

A familiar face around the Fort Worth stock pens
where arriving herds were kept, he occasionally made
legitimate purchases. However, when it came time for
the cattle he'd bought to be delivered to his ranch, a
willing and well-paid cowhand whom he'd quietly dealt
with would arrive with a dozen or more Longhorns
that the Colonel hadn't paid for.

In time, after the number of stolen cattle had grown,
he would order them driven back to the stockyards,
bearing his own brand, and sold. The scheme had added
considerably to the Colonel's growing wealth and en-
abled him to continue accumulating small farms and
ranches from frightened owners his men had threatened

and driven from their land. If it meant burning a barn or two or the midnight rustling of a small herd from time to time, such was the price of doing business.

So, too, were the payments that ensured that the sheriff could be counted on to look the other way.

Abernathy's philosophy was simple: Money meant power. And once he had enough of the first, the second came easily. Anyone who got in his way did so at great risk.

And this stranger from Aberdene was definitely in the way.

A S HE LEFT the roadhouse, Abernathy nodded to the men who had waited outside while he spoke with the sheriff. They were quickly on their horses, ready to escort their boss back to the ranch.

"I'm told that the man you boys paid a visit to the other evening is now up and about, mending nicely at Duke Keene's livery," the Colonel said. The tone of his voice left little doubt that he was not pleased.

I N TOWN, BEN Dalton waited while the hotel owner retrieved his saddlebag from the locked chest behind the counter. "Smart that you took advantage of our safekeeping service," the man said. "My woman who tidies up the rooms told me that you had visitors the other day. They had let themselves into your room and were looking around when she walked in to do her dusting. Said they weren't at all friendly and left in quite a hurry."

Dalton counted out what he owed for the room as

the man behind the desk stared at his bruised face. "I assume you're taking leave of our city," he finally said.

He got no reply. Dalton was busy digging in his saddlebag for something he'd placed there before leaving Aberdene. After locating it and polishing his badge on his shirt sleeve, he attached it to his belt. He knew full well that he had no jurisdiction in Fort Worth, but it felt good to be wearing it.

Back at the livery, he tried to help Keene muck the stalls but was of little use as sharp pains ran down his rib cage every time he lifted a fork. "Don't go taking this wrong," Duke said, "but you could be more useful if you was to just get out of the way."

Dalton retreated to a bench, silently watching as Duke completed his chores.

"Don't recall you mentioning you're a lawman," Keene said, pointing toward the gold badge. "For that matter, you've not said what it is you're doing in town, 'cept getting yourself beat up. Not that it's any of my business, of course."

Dalton briefly explained his purpose, leaving out the fact that he had been summoned by Mandy Rawlings.

"Done stuck your head in a wasp's nest, I reckon," Duke said. "This ain't the friendliest of places on its best of days, unless you've driven cattle here or are looking to make a fool of yourself over in the Acre. Strangers aren't commonly welcome, particular if they're poking around in another man's business. I've lived here all my life and know that to be God's truth. I've lived to this ripe old age by keeping my head down and tending my own knitting.

"I've got no personal knowledge of your friend, never having need for a lawyer myself, thank the stars.

But if he's got himself on the wrong side of Otto Langston, I'd say he's in a heap of trouble."

"What can you tell me about the sheriff?"

Duke turned his head toward the entrance of the livery, as if to make sure no one else was around. "He's crooked as a snake. Been wearing his badge forever, it seems, and has managed to keep the right folks on his side. Done right well for himself from what I'm told, able to afford things a man on his salary ain't likely to. You can figure that out for yourself.

"In Fort Worth, what Sheriff Langston says goes, no question asked. Cross him, and likely as not you'll be visiting his jail or on your way out of town. I think he's done given you your choice."

While Duke went to get them coffee, Dalton pondered what he'd heard. "Maybe me staying here isn't a good idea," he said. "I don't want you putting yourself in harm's way on my account."

Keene chuckled. "I ain't concerned," he said. "Man my age is no worry—or benefit—to anybody."

Two nights later, someone set fire to the livery.

CHAPTER 7

The sound of horses banging against their stalls woke Dalton, the smell of coal oil filling his nostrils. Even before he could get his boots on and find a bucket for bailing water, several neighbors had arrived and were beating at the flames with brooms and blankets. Ben, ignoring the pain in his rib cage, joined Keene in pumping water and splashing it against the large front doors of the building.

In short order it was over as only smoke lingered, floating lazily into the darkness and disappearing. The only damage had been to the entranceway.

While Duke thanked those who had rushed to help, Dalton busied himself calming the animals.

He returned to the front and found Keene sitting on a hay bale, dressed only in his long johns, his face buried in his hands. He looked up as Ben sat next to him and smiled. "First time my neighbors ever seen me without my britches on," he said. "Downright embarrassing."

"You okay?" Dalton asked, draping an arm across Duke's slumped shoulders.

"I'm fine, I'm fine. Been needing new doors anyway."

B Y FIRST LIGHT, Dalton was already dressed and had saddled Dolly. With tweezers he normally used for removing splinters from the legs of the horses, Duke plucked the stitches from Ben's nose and cheek. The bruises, once dark purple, were turning to the shade of river water.

"Danged if you ain't gonna be half handsome before this is over," Keene said.

D ALTON WAS SEATED on a bench in front of the sheriff's office when Otto Langston arrived, wearing a freshly ironed shirt and his trademark bow tie. He bent to smooth a pants leg and wipe dust from his boots before acknowledging his visitor's presence.

"Still here, I see," he said.

"Could have used your help last night," Dalton said as he stood, allowing Langston a good view of his badge.

"For what?"

"Somebody attempted to burn down Duke Keene's livery."

The sheriff's eyes were focused on the gold star on Dalton's belt as he replied. "Nobody hurt, I hope."

"Nope, I'm here. Fit as a fiddle."

"And that's supposed to mean what?"

"My guess is that their purpose was directed at me, to get my attention, just like the other night in back of the laundry. Doesn't seem I'm welcome here."

"Last time we spoke," Langston said with a thin smile, "you failed to mention that you're law. Got any suspects for these events you're describing?"

"Can't say I know who did it, but I've got a strong suspicion there's someone who does."

Langston ignored the not-so-subtle suggestion and walked past Dalton toward the door to his office.

"Lawman to lawman," Ben said as he moved to block the sheriff's way, "I was hoping you might share with me what kind of evidence you have that John Rawlings did the murder he's accused of."

"All I need," Langston shot back. "Plenty. But nothing I'm of a mind to share."

"You got an eyewitness? Was there a gun left behind? Somebody's footprints? Maybe Rawlings broke down and confessed. That why he hasn't even gotten himself a lawyer?"

The first signs of anger showed on the sheriff's face. "I'll ask the same thing I did the other day: What's your interest in a matter you've got no call to involve yourself with?"

It was Dalton's turn to smile. "Just interested in what's happening to an old friend. Any chance I can come in and say hello to him?"

Langston's attempt at a calm demeanor vanished. "You already did, against my instruction that he was to have no visitors. You need to know that your little stunt forced me to fire a fine young jailer. Now, why don't you move along before I think of something to arrest you for?"

Dalton tipped his hat and stepped off the porch. As he climbed into the saddle, the sheriff glared at him.

"One favor you can do for me," Dalton said. "Tell your friends the next time they think about sneaking up at night to burn down the livery, they might consider the risk of getting themselves shot."

"According to the law book I read from," the sheriff said, "that's an outright threat to commit bodily harm."

"Defending one's property's not a violation of the law where I come from."

"And I again suggest that's where you should be heading," Langston said as he entered his office, slamming the door behind him. Inside, he cursed and threw his hat against the wall.

IT WAS NOT difficult to learn the name of the fired jailer. At a small food stand just down the street from the sheriff's office, Dalton struck up a conversation with the elderly lady who stood behind the sweet-smelling strips of sizzling beef. He ordered breakfast and as she prepared it he explained that he was looking for the young man who used to work nearby. Recalling how he looked during their brief meeting days earlier, he attempted to describe him. She began to nod even before he'd finished.

"A nice young man," she said. "He ate here all the time. But I haven't seen him in the past few days."

"I'm told he was dismissed from his job," Ben said.

"Oh, poor Lanny . . ."

"You know Lanny's last name?"

"I think," she said, "it was Bailey . . . no, Butler. Lanny Butler. Such a nice boy. He lived on a farm with his mama and daddy."

*   *   *

D ALTON FOUND HIM, not back on the family farm, but drowning his sorrows in the first Hell's Half Acre saloon he visited.

The young man was not pleased to see the stranger who had caused him to be unemployed. "I'd appreciate your leaving me be," he said. "You've done enough to foul up my life. I can't even go home and face my pa, tell him I lost my job for taking a dollar bribe so somebody I didn't even know could visit a murderer."

"I offered, you accepted," Dalton said as he took a seat next to the boy. "If you can get yourself sober and presentable, I've got a paying job that might interest you."

Lanny Butler sat up straight and ran a hand through his hair. He wiped his mouth on a sleeve and cleared his throat. "I ain't really that drunk," he said. "Can't afford it. Sheriff didn't even give me my last wages. What's the job?"

Dalton explained that the owner of the livery needed someone to fetch new lumber and replace his doorway.

"I reckon I could do that," Butler said.

"And," Dalton said, "it'll give us a chance to talk."

L ANNY BUTLER PROVED to be a good carpenter. In short order he had replaced Keene's doors and, without prodding, set about tidying up the livery. Oat buckets were refilled, fresh hay was spread in the stalls, and the watering trough was wiped clean and refilled. Saddles and halters were lined up in a neat row and he had built a small fire in the forge to make fresh coffee.

"Looks to me your sign outside needs repainting," he told Duke. "I'd be glad to do it."

Dalton watched as Lanny climbed a ladder, paint bucket in hand. "Seeing as how I still can't pull my weight around here," he told Duke, "maybe I could hire the boy to help out for a spell. He seems to be hard-working and a pleasant sort."

"You're just feeling guilty for causing him to lose his jailing job."

"Not really," Ben said. "Truth is, I figure I might have done him a favor."

As soon as the KEENE'S LIVERY sign was repainted, Dalton offered Lanny the job. "You'll serve as the owner's assistant," he said. "Your new boss will instruct you about what needs doing. And he says you can bed down in one of the stalls if you're still not inclined to return to the farm and sleep in your own bed. Your pay will be fifty cents a day."

The youngster smiled and quickly accepted. "Didn't much care for working at the jail anyway," he said.

"Let's talk about that for a minute," Dalton said.

They walked outside and sat on a bench to enjoy the sun. The warmth felt good on Ben's aching ribs. "Can't even tell there was a fire," he said as he admired the new entrance doors.

"You're wanting to know about your friend," Lanny said.

Dalton nodded. "He being treated okay?"

Lanny dug his boot into the dirt before answering. "Mostly, he's just left alone," he said. Then, after a moment's hesitation, he added, "I seen the sheriff hit him upside the head with the butt of his pistol once. That was soon after he was brought in. Sheriff Langston was yelling and cussing at him. About what, I don't know. Likely trying to make him admit what he was supposed to have done."

"You ever have any conversation with Rawlings?"

"Only when I took him his dinner. He would always ask me to contact his wife and tell her he was innocent. Same thing every time I saw him. Kinda got me to believing him. That's why I let you go back and see him that evening, that and the dollar you gave me. To me, Mr. Rawlings just didn't look like a man who would do a killing."

"To me either," Dalton said.

W HILE LANNY WENT back inside the livery to see if Duke had any more chores for him, Dalton remained seated on the bench, closing his eyes as he lifted his face to the warm, cloudless sky. Soon he was dozing.

When he heard a woman's voice, he thought for a moment he was dreaming. Until he opened his eyes.

"That looks painful," Mandy Rawlings said as she reached out and gently touched his face. A brightly colored sunbonnet framed her face.

"How'd you know I was . . ."

"I didn't," she said. "I got so tired of being cooped up that I asked my neighbor to sit with Alton for a bit while I took a walk to the library."

"I see some things don't change."

"What do you mean?"

"I recall a time when you visited the library like it was your second home."

She smiled, silently pleased that he remembered.

"Anyway, I was just passing by, and there you sat. I wasn't even sure you were still in town."

"I've been meaning to pay you another visit," he said. "I just . . ."

Her expression turned solemn and she leaned closer. "Ben, I've recently learned some things that I'd like to discuss with you. But not here. Is there a chance you could come around this evening? Alton would be delighted to see you again, and I'll gladly cook you supper."

Ben stood and nodded. "As long as it's not rabbit chili and corn bread," he said. "That's about all I've been eating since I got here."

For the first time since their younger days, he heard her laugh as she turned to leave.

As he watched her walk away, he was unaware of Duke standing in the doorway until he heard his familiar chuckle. "A mighty fine-looking woman, if you don't mind my saying. I wasn't aware of you having made yourself a lady friend."

Dalton ignored the observation. "Reckon you could give me a haircut?"

"Going courting, are you?"

"She's just a friend, old man. In fact, she's the wife of John Rawlings."

"Still, sounds like courting to me," Duke said. "I can give you a haircut, but I got nothing sweet-smelling for you to splash on that beat-up face." His chuckle erupted to full-blown laughter as he walked inside to check on his new assistant.

M ANDY URGED HIM to have a second helping of her baked chicken and sweet potatoes before

leaving the table to put Alton to bed. To the youngster's delight, Ben had arrived with the same hard
candy he'd purchased earlier for the little girl at the
laundry. Obviously pleased to have a man in the house,
the child had pleaded with Dalton to play games and
read to him as he climbed into his lap.

"He seems quite taken with you," his mother said as
she returned to the dining room. "Even included you
in his bedtime prayers. Something about making your
face get well."

"Must be hard on him, with his daddy away."

Mandy only nodded as she began clearing dishes
from the table. "I've got pie if you're so inclined."

She waited until they had moved to the living room
before explaining her invitation. "A couple of days ago,
Shelby Profer showed up at my door. I hadn't seen him
in ages. He told me that you had visited him, asking
about John. Apparently, he was pretty guarded in his
response, which is his nature.

"But he told me your concern had made an impression on him, got him to thinking. Shelby's a lovable old
coot who likes to give everyone the impression that
he's something of a past-his-prime hermit. The fact is,
he still gets around and is on a first-name basis with
everyone of importance in town.

"He's been discreetly asking questions about Thomas
Cookson's murder and has heard things that he thinks
you should know. He asked that I pass them along
rather than him speaking with you directly and getting
more involved than he's comfortable with."

"Let me guess," Ben said. "Your sheriff's doing
some things that a righteous lawman shouldn't."

She seemed surprised that he already knew part of

what she was going to tell him. "There's more to it. What Shelby has been hearing is that Sheriff Langston's not the only one. A rancher named Ray Abernathy—people call him the Colonel—is apparently involved in all kinds of illegal dealings and has the sheriff on his payroll."

"But what does any of it have to do with John's situation?" Dalton said, hoping he was able to hide his sudden concern that Mandy might be aware of things that could threaten her well-being.

"Some of Shelby's lawyer friends have told him that the banker had become suspicious of some of the transactions the Colonel was making and got worried that he might be breaking the law himself. Apparently, he went looking for a lawyer to discuss the matter with."

"And wound up talking to your husband," Ben said.

"It looks that way. Shelby says he's never seen people so nervous about speaking with him about this matter."

"Did he say anything else?"

"He said I should tell you to be very careful, that these are dangerous people," she said. "Ben, I'm worried that I've gotten you into something I shouldn't have. I would think no less of you if you left this very evening and headed back to Aberdene. I'll find another way."

He was shaking his head before she completed her sentence. "We can't just leave your husband to rot away in jail. I'll be careful. Pass that along to Mr. Profer. Thank him kindly for the information and tell him I think it would be best if he doesn't involve himself further. You either.

"Just stay at home and tend to that boy. And tell

him I'll be back to see him soon—and when I do my
face will be all well, thanks to his prayers."

She walked with him to the door and her last words
were almost whispered. "Since seeing you the other
day, I've been wondering . . . are you happy?"

He thought for a moment before answering. "I get
by," he finally said. Honesty, he decided, was sometimes too painful.

As he walked into the quiet, cool evening, puzzled
by her question, he didn't notice the figure standing in
the shadows across the street, watching him.

CHAPTER 8

W HEN HE RETURNED to the livery, Ben was surprised to see Lanny still up. He had just put Keene's mule, Sister, in the corral out back.

"Take yourself an evening ride?" Dalton said.

Lanny nodded. "I'd have asked Mr. Keene if it was okay, but he was done in bed, asleep. I had an urgent purpose that we need to talk about."

"I'm listening," Ben said as he eased the saddle off Dolly and led her toward a stall.

"When you left earlier, I was up in the loft watching you ride off," Lanny said. "It appeared you were being followed by somebody. So I waited until he had distanced himself a bit, then trailed behind. After he seen you go into the hotel, he hid across the street, just watching and waiting. Stayed there, standing in the dark like a big statue, until he saw you preparing to leave."

"Was it anybody you've seen before?"

"I didn't get close enough to see his face, but the hat

he was wearing looked familiar. Like one of those that farmers like my daddy favor—brownish, with a big, floppy brim that covers the back of the neck and keeps the sun off when they're plowing. If it's who I'm thinking it is, he works for a friend of Sheriff Langston."

"Would that friend be a man who calls himself the Colonel?"

"Yep, that would be him."

T HE FOLLOWING MORNING, Ben was dressed and Dolly saddled before Duke poured his first cup of coffee. "They finally run you out of town?" he said.

"Not yet. I'm just thinking Dolly could use herself some exercise and fresh air, so we're going to take us a ride."

"Heading any place in particular?"

"Know of a rancher who calls himself the Colonel?"

Duke's eyes widened. "Whoa, what interest, may I ask, have you got in Colonel Ray Abernathy? He's somebody I'd strongly advise you to steer clear of. I don't even like having the man come here for me to shoe his horses."

"I understand he's got a big spread somewhere around here. Know where it is?"

"You right sure you want to know?" There was genuine concern in Keene's voice. "I'd admire to know what it is you're thinking."

Dalton told him what Lanny had seen the previous evening. "I'm just curious to know why somebody's tailing me," Ben said. "Just thought I'd pay a neighborly visit."

Duke pointed at Dalton's belt. "If you're planning

on wearing that badge, you ain't gonna appear very neighborly."

"Just tell me how to get there."

"Okay, okay," he said, "Head out south, toward the Glen Rose Valley. It's maybe a couple of hours if you pace your horse properly. Abernathy's place is called the Shooting Star, don't ask me why. Just look for a whole lot of cattle."

Seeing that Dalton was determined to make the trip, Duke filled a canteen and handed it up to him. "I'm not making light when I say to be careful," he said. Then he shook his head. "Just when I was finally getting you healed up."

D ALTON RODE PAST the jail to the food stand, ordered two sandwiches for the trail, and told the cook that he'd spoken with Lanny Butler. "He's doing fine. I'll see that he comes to visit," he said before heading south.

It felt good to be away from the city. The morning air was still crisp and the gentle breeze had a sweet smell. The open spaces and a quiet interrupted only by the rhythmic sound of Dolly's hooves against the caliche soil made Dalton homesick. As he rode, he found himself thinking about his dog Poncho and wondering how things were back on the farm.

Soon after he'd stopped to eat his lunch and allow Dolly to drink from a small stream, he reached a rise that gave him his first glimpse of his destination. In the distance, cattle mingled and smoke rose from the ranch house chimney.

At the entrance to the Shooting Star he was stopped

by a young man with a rifle resting on one shoulder. "I'll ask you to state your business," he called out as Dalton approached. When he saw the badge on the rider's belt, no further explanation was necessary. The guard tipped his hat and pointed to the road that wound toward the ranch headquarters.

Finding Colonel Abernathy wasn't difficult. Leaning against the rail of a holding pen where calves were being branded, he wore a pearl-handled pistol in a hand-tooled scabbard on his hip and was watching the activity intently. It was obvious that he was the man in charge as he puffed on a cigar and silently looked on while everyone else was busy with the task at hand. He only turned away when he saw Dalton walking toward him.

Flicking ashes from his cigar with one hand, he extended the other to shake the arriving visitor's hand. "Don't believe I've had the pleasure," he said.

Dalton introduced himself, noticing that the Colonel was also eyeing his badge. Before he asked, Ben explained that he was not there as an officer of the law. "I've got no jurisdiction in these parts," he said.

"Good to know you're not here to arrest me," Abernathy said. As he spoke, a couple of cowhands took their position a few yards away from their boss. One wore a hat that looked much like the one Lanny had described.

"So, what is it that brings you out to the Shooting Star?" Abernathy said.

"A bit of curiosity," said Ben, "and the need to get me some fresh air."

"Well, you're welcome to all the fresh air we've got.

The Good Lord has supplied us with plenty to spare. What is it you're curious about?"

Dalton turned from the Colonel and focused his attention on the cowhands. "Mostly, I'm wondering why it is I've been so tormented since I got to Fort Worth. Folks have been downright inhospitable. I've been attacked, beat up, and had my hat stomped. The place I'm staying was set on fire, I've been told to go back where I came from, and last night somebody—who's not too good at his job—wasted a good deal of time following me."

"Seems you've been having an unfortunate run of bad luck," the Colonel said.

"Ain't that the truth."

In the corral, a calf bawled as an SS branding iron burned into its hindquarter. "Always like hearing that sound," Abernathy said as he watched the young animal struggle to its feet and hurry away. "It tells me that little fella there now officially belongs to me."

The colonel again looked at Dalton's badge. "What is it brings you this way? Chasing down some outlaw on the run?"

"Nope, just seeing what I can do to help a friend."

"From what you're saying, it sounds like this friend of yours might be more trouble than he's worth."

Dalton tipped his hat and turned to walk away. "I best be on my way and leave you fellas to get on with your business," he said. Stopping after a few steps, he turned to the cowhand who had moved to stand at the Colonel's side. He was a big man, towering over his boss, with broad shoulders and menacing, coal-black eyes.

"Nice hat," Dalton said.

* * *

As HE RODE away, Ben patted Dolly's neck and bent to whisper in her ear. "Ol' girl," he said, "I think we got our message delivered. Now, let's hope we can make it back to the livery without getting me shot."

At the corral, Colonel Abernathy waited until Dalton was out of earshot before he spoke. "That's the last I ever want to see of that man," he said. He was glaring at the cowhands. "And if I can't depend on you boys to see to it, I'll find someone who can." He angrily tossed his cigar to the ground and crushed it with his boot.

From behind him came the plaintive bawling of another branded calf.

SHERIFF LANGSTON WAS standing in front of the dimly lit jail cell, hatless, his arms folded across his chest. He tried to ignore the stench as he watched John Rawlings sleep, inhaling and exhaling in short, quick breaths. The mind-numbing weeks of being locked up had taken their toll.

The stubble on his face was fast growing into an unkempt beard and as he lay shirtless, the outline of his ribs had begun to show. Even from a distance, his body odor was repellent.

"Time to wake up, Mr. Rawlings," the sheriff said. "We need to talk."

Rawlings jumped at the sound, coughed, then slowly pulled himself into a sitting position. He squinted toward the dark hallway at the form that had called his name. It took him a minute to recognize the sheriff. Though weak and ill, he remained defiant.

"Come to shoot me?" he said. "Or just beat on me some more?"

Langston ignored him, offering only a long silence. Finally, he shook his head and said, "I'm just here to see how you're doing, John. Want to be sure you're comfortable."

Rawlings lay back down, turning his face to the wall. "Go away," he mumbled.

"Not before we have us a conversation. I won't bother you for long. I've just got a question I need to ask."

When he got no reply, he continued. "I need you to tell me about this fellow Dalton. He's become a bother of late, snooping around, asking about things that ain't none of his business. Says he's here because of his concern for you. That sound right? You got a friend who carries a badge and sticks his nose in other folks' business?"

Rawlings turned back to face the sheriff. "I didn't ask him to come."

"Somebody did."

"I got no idea what you're talking about."

"Okay, John, I just felt the need to ask. I'll let you get back to your sleeping," Langston said as he turned to leave. "Oh, I meant to mention that your wife recently came by, asking to see you. I'm sorry to say that I had to inform her no visiting is allowed with murderers."

Rawlings spat across the cell toward the sheriff.

"Now, that ain't hardly polite," Langston said. "For acting out, I guess you'll be doing without your supper." His laughter echoed along the narrow hallway as he walked away.

In Langston's office, his newly hired deputy sat on the corner of his desk.

Dexter Wilson had been surprised when Colonel Abernathy informed him he would be taking a break from his duties at the Shooting Star. Instead, he was told to ride to Fort Worth and report to Sheriff Langston and be sworn in.

As Wilson had gathered up his belongings and was leaving the bunkhouse, Abernathy waited outside for him. "This won't be for long," the Colonel said. "Just until a certain matter gets taken care of." He slapped the cowboy on the back and broke into a wide grin. "I 'spect you'll find it fun to be wearing a badge.

"You're to do whatever the sheriff tells you. But bear in mind, I'm still your boss."

The chain of command had already been made clear to Langston. So had the job Deputy Wilson was to carry out.

CHAPTER 9

D EXTER WILSON HAD loyally served the Colonel
since he was a teenager. His parents had been
killed in a raid by Comanches and when Abernathy,
traveling north with plans to purchase a small ranch,
found the boy, wounded and cowering in the root cel-
lar, it was obvious he had also been left for dead. In
one of the Colonel's rare acts of human kindness, he
saw to it that the boy was nursed back to health, provided him a horse, and invited him along on his
journey.

In time, Wilson became the closest thing to a son
Abernathy would ever know.

A quick learner, he adopted many of the Colonel's
personal traits, few of them admirable, and rose to
second-in-command at the Shooting Star. It was Wilson who led the assaults on homes of struggling farmers whose land Abernathy coveted, rustled cattle with
great enthusiasm, and used his fists and the butt of a
pistol to keep discipline in the bunkhouse. If there was

a man meaner and more feared than Colonel Abernathy, it was Dexter Wilson.

He took quickly to his new role as a deputy sheriff,
breaking up fights in the Hell's Half Acre saloons and
giving notice to a number of local store owners that if
they wished to avoid damage and robberies they would
be wise to pay him a modest "protection fee." He even
arrested one of the Shooting Star cowboys after he'd
gotten wildly drunk one night and ridden back to the
ranch on another man's horse.

His primary duty, however, was to keep watch on
Ben Dalton.

Several times a day he would ride past the livery or
the café where Ben and Duke Keene were having
lunch. Once, he had watched Dalton enter the office of
a lawyer named Shelby Profer. On several occasions
he'd seen him slowly walk past the jail en route to visit
the lady who ran the food cart, usually accompanied
by the young helper from the livery.

Better at following someone without being noticed
than the cowhand the Colonel had originally assigned
the job, Wilson had soon memorized Dalton's routine.
Most interesting were his occasional visits to the hotel
apartment where John Rawlings' wife and son resided.

"Could be he's sweet on Mrs. Rawlings and taking
advantage of her husband's being locked up," he suggested to Sheriff Langston one morning as he prepared
to make his daily rounds.

A sudden realization caused the sheriff to slap his
hands together. "That's it. She's who got Dalton to
come here and start nosing around," he said.

Wilson failed to see that her role mattered. "This
fella's got everybody so riled up—you, the Colonel—

that I don't see why we don't just shoot him dead and be done with it. I'd be glad to oblige."

"We don't need any more killing," the sheriff said. "I've got me a position to protect and can't afford folks asking why people are suddenly dying on my watch. I want it seen to that nobody's harmed, you hear me?"

The new deputy smiled and turned away. He already had a plan, one he'd outlined to the Colonel at the same roadhouse where Abernathy and the sheriff regularly met. His boss had immediately embraced it. To set it in motion, he first needed to establish a friendship with the man he'd been shadowing.

DALTON WAS GROOMING his mare when Wilson walked into the livery. "Fine-looking horse," he said as he approached. "I'm the newly hired deputy and trying to get myself acquainted with folks in the neighborhood. I'm here looking for a man who's visiting from someplace to the south called Aberdene."

"I reckon that would be me. What can I do for you?"

Wilson moved closer and lowered his voice. "I got a message I've been asked to deliver," he said. "There's a fella in the jail who wants to know if you can come see him."

Dalton put his brush away and motioned for the deputy to take a seat on a nearby bench. "You would be talking about John Rawlings, I presume."

"Yeah, that's his name."

"I've already been told by your boss that no visiting is allowed. A while back, I got a jailer fired because he let me in for just a few minutes."

"Yeah, I know about Sheriff Langston's rules. But it

don't seem right. This man, Rawlings, he's in pretty bad shape. I know he's supposed to have killed somebody, but I can't help feeling sorry for him."

"What do you mean about him being in bad shape?"

"He ain't a pretty picture. You'll need to see for yourself."

"And how do you propose I do that?"

Wilson leaned closer and explained. If Dalton would wait until late at night, after the sheriff had gone home, he would let him in. "Things quiet down some by Mondays," he said. "That would be as good a time as any. There's a back entrance to the sheriff's office you could come through. Couldn't let you stay long, but . . ."

Dalton gave the deputy a puzzled look. "You're not concerned about getting fired if your boss finds out?"

"Hey," Wilson said. "I was looking for a job when I found this one. Bet I can find another. Besides, I can't say I care much for the sheriff. From what little I've seen, he don't seem to me to be a very fair sort of man."

"Will you still be up around midnight?" Dalton said.

Wilson smiled. "I will be if I know there's company coming."

THE NIGHT WAS moonless, so black that Dalton didn't even cast a shadow as he made his way along the narrow alley. In the distance, he could barely see the deputy leaning against the wall, smoking a cigarette. The only light shone dimly from a small lamp inside the sheriff's office.

Without a word, Wilson tossed his cigarette aside and signaled Dalton to follow him. They passed a large desk cluttered with wanted posters, a roster of the drunks still being held in the holding cage across the hallway, an ashtray overflowing and spilling onto an open law book, and a half-full cup of cold coffee. They made their way past the caged drunks, many of whom were either sleeping or passed out. Those still awake would have no recollection the next day of the two men who walked past.

When Wilson reached the door leading to the cells, he stopped. "I guess you can find your way from here," he said. "I'll wait for you up in Langston's office. Remember, I can't let you stay long."

Dalton nodded and slowly walked into the darkened hallway. It was hot and airless, ripe with odors that assaulted the senses. The silence was broken only by the buzzing of flies and the barely audible noise made by unseen rodents scurrying out of the way of the intruder. Feeling his way along the first set of bars, he whispered Rawlings' name and was surprised to hear an immediate response.

He made his way to the sound of Rawlings' voice, then felt a hand extended through the bars.

"I was told you would be coming," John said in a raspy voice. "Lordy, it's good to see you."

Were it not for the fact the prisoner was standing in the shadows, Dalton would have been able to see the recently administered bruises to Rawlings' face and the blood that had dried just below his hairline.

"They're gonna kill me, Ben. The sheriff's already told me as much."

"Why? What's this all about?" Dalton said. "Why are they claiming you killed this man Cookson?"

"Tom Cookson knew what they were up to. He told me, wanted me to help him. They had to shut him up.

They killed him and put the blame on me. Now they're intending to kill me, too."

"Who's 'they'?"

Instead of a reply, Rawlings began rambling, his words bouncing from one subject to another. He wanted to know how Mandy and his son were, asked about Aberdene, recalled some long-forgotten adventure they had shared as youngsters. "We had good times, didn't we?"

He laughed, then cried. He began pacing and beating his fists against the bars. "They're going to kill me for no good reason. I'm ashamed of things I've done, but I never did physical harm to anybody. You gotta believe that. Tell Mandy . . ."

Dalton fell silent, stunned by Rawlings' mental state. He made one last attempt to get him to tell who he thought was responsible for the situation he was in, but with no success.

"I'm tired, Ben . . . need to sleep," Rawlings said. "It was good seeing you, but I've got to lay down now."

Bewildered and saddened, Dalton turned to leave. As he made his way along the hallway, he heard his friend call out in a voice that was suddenly strong. "It was the Colonel," he yelled. "The Colonel's who wants me dead."

Standing at the entrance to the hallway, Wilson had eavesdropped on the strange conversation. As Dalton approached, he shook his head. "I told you he was in bad shape."

A S HE MADE his way back toward the livery, Dalton pondered the bizarre scene that had just played out. It had been nothing like he expected. His hands were shaking and his stomach was in knots and he felt as if he might throw up. He had just stood across from a friend-turned-stranger, a man on the ragged edge of insanity.

He took deep breaths, inhaling the cool night air and trying to clear his head. "I've got to get him out of there," he said to himself as he walked through the darkness.

For the first time in his life, he was contemplating doing something against the law.

S HELBY PROFER WAS standing in front of a full-length mirror, quite pleased that he had chosen the off-white vest to go with the dark suit he had last worn to a fellow attorney's funeral. If he was to go out in public, there to again ply his trade as a legal counselor, he wanted to do so in style. Though he had become a recluse, his vanity remained.

The reflection he saw brought a smile to his face. There was no way he looked eighty-eight years old.

The afternoon before, Ben Dalton had sat in his cluttered office, telling of his disturbing visit with John Rawlings, and it had troubled him. The concern, in fact, had weighed on him since he'd asked around earlier about the death of the local bank president and Rawlings' subsequent incarceration. His fellow attorneys' hesitancy to discuss the matter had seemed strange. Over time, thoughts of young Rawlings had developed into a bothersome itch, and Dalton's recent visit had convinced him it was time to scratch it.

With Duke Keene's help, the lawyer arranged for Lanny Butler to retrieve his buggy from the shed behind his office, bring a horse from the livery, and serve as his driver for the day.

Once outfitted and coiffed to his satisfaction, he left his office and took the short ride to the home of Mandy Rawlings. Omitting the details he'd been given regarding her husband's physical and mental condition, he explained that he had given his old friend's matter a good deal of thought and decided he would like to serve as John's legal counsel.

Mandy broke into a wide smile, stood on tiptoes, and hugged the white-haired man, then placed a kiss on his quickly reddening cheek. "I don't know how to thank you," she said.

"It's this fellow Ben Dalton you should be thanking," he said. "It was him who stirred my interest in your husband's difficulties and convinced me to pay you this visit."

He unbuckled his worn leather case, removed a document he had typed, and handed it to her. "By signing this," he said, "you give me permission to represent John in all legal matters. And, finally, to make it official, I will require good-faith compensation in the amount of one dollar."

"Mr. Profer, we have money," Mandy said. "I can pay you a proper fee for your services."

"One dollar will suffice," he said.

And with that he was off to the sheriff's office.

SITTING WITH HIS feet propped on his desk and puffing at his pipe, Otto Langston was at first speechless when the dapper Profer walked into his office and announced that he been hired as John Rawlings' at-

torney. "I'm here to see my client," he said. The booming sound of his voice and the thump of his cane against
the desk made it more a demand than a request.

The sheriff cleared his throat and got to his feet.
"I'm sorry, counselor, but I can't allow that. I have a
rule that prisoners being held for serious crimes—such
as cold-blooded murder—will not be allowed visita-
tions until a judge tells me so. And Rawlings hasn't
even appeared before Judge Blankenship yet. I've not
even permitted Mr. Rawlings' wife to see him."

"And this is a 'rule,' one that you, in some grand
flash of wisdom, pulled out of the thinnest of air? Sir,
you have no legal authority whatsoever to prevent me
from seeing this man. I demand—"

"Demand all you like, old man," Langston said,
"but you're not seeing my prisoner. I'll thank you to be
on your way. I'm busy." The sheriff's distaste for lawyers, young and old, was obvious.

Profer left, mumbling curses as he made his way out
to his buggy. "We'll next need to visit the courthouse
and find Judge Blankenship," he instructed young Butler. "I hope it's early enough in the day for him to still
be sober."

Inside, the sheriff summoned Deputy Wilson. "Ride
out to the ranch," he said, "and tell the Colonel we need
to meet."

"Is there a problem?"

"Could be," the sheriff said as he fumbled to relight
his pipe.

W E'VE GOT WAY too many people getting involved
in our business," Abernathy said as he poured

himself a shot of tequila. He was clearly in a foul mood. "We've got this out-of-town stranger, Rawlings' wife, and now that old fossil who calls himself a lawyer. I thought you said you could keep things under control."

"Don't worry, I will."

"When you figuring on starting?" the Colonel said as he slammed a fist against the table.

CHAPTER 10

DUKE KEENE WAS pacing from one end of the stables to another, wildly waving his arms. "It's a good way to get yourself killed dead," he said after listening to Dalton's plan. "Not that it makes me any matter, mind you, but young Lanny's taken a shine to you. You can't do this. I won't allow it." He stopped and kicked at the dirt.

"It's Rawlings who's going to be killed, whether it's fast or slow," Ben said. "He's dying a little more in there every day. What's being done to him is wrong. I've seen it. They're going to kill him, sure as I'm standing here."

"So why haven't they just put a bullet in his head and been done with it?"

"I haven't figured that part out yet, unless they're trying to make him tell something he won't talk about."

Duke took a seat against one of the stall doors and began to nervously draw circles in the dirt. "Craziest notion I've ever heard," he said. "Plumb crazy. A fine, upstanding lawman like yourself, breaking a man out of jail. And if you're able to do it without getting your fool head blown off, what then?"

"That's what I wanted to ask you about," Ben said, a hint of apology in his voice. "He'll be needing a place to hide out and I was hoping you might have a suggestion."

Keene rolled his eyes. "So I get to be involved, huh? Boy, it just gets better and better. Want me to stand lookout while you do your breaking in? Maybe fire a couple of warning shots at the sheriff? Hide your friend here in my loft?"

From the other side of the livery, Lanny listened to Duke's rant and laughed.

"It ain't funny," Keene said. "I'm serious as a grave-yard when I say this is a fool's mission that's being planned." The youngster hung his head. He decided against admitting that he'd already informed Dalton that the keys to the jail cells could be found in a small tin box on the sheriff's desk.

Keene was quiet for several minutes, continuing to draw his circles. Finally, he spoke. "Okay, there's this little cabin up to the north on Kenwood Creek," he said, "or, at least, there was. Haven't been there in ages. Me and my brother built it and used to go there for hunting and fishing before he passed. We kept the location our secret. I ain't been back since we buried him, but I'm guessing it's still standing. Best I can remember, it's about a ten-mile ride."

Dalton walked across the room and squeezed Duke's shoulder. "That sounds perfect," he said. "Only thing else I'll need is a map showing the way."

"When's all this supposed to happen?"

"Sooner the better," Ben said.

Had Dexter Wilson heard the conversation, he would be smiling. The enemy had, as he hoped, stepped willingly into his trap. As he assured the Colonel, once Dalton saw the condition John Rawlings was in, he would start thinking of a way to get him out. "I even showed him the best way to escape," he had said. "When they come out the back door, I'll be waiting in the alley. I won't have any choice but to shoot 'em both. Problem solved."

T HE MORNING FOLLOWING their discussion, Dalton found Keene busy loading up his mule with provisions. As Ben approached, he was doing an inventory. "A couple of blankets . . . coffee . . . jerky . . . cans of peaches . . . matches . . . a pan for cooking and boiling water . . . makings for cold-water corn bread . . . and a little taste of whiskey to warm his insides. I thought about it, but I ain't providing a firearm to a man who might be near crazy. Can you think of anything else?"

"You don't have to do this," Ben said.

"I'm just curious to see if the cabin's still there," Duke said. "I just need you to promise me you won't do anything until I return. I want to be sure we pick a good horse for your friend to be riding."

L ATE THE FOLLOWING day he was back. "It ain't like the luxury suite over at the Langley Hotel, but the roof's still standing. I had to run a mama fox and her pups out and kill a couple of snakes, but I think it'll do. Even chopped some firewood while I was there. When will you be leaving?"

"Tomorrow night." Ben removed his badge from his belt and handed it to Keene. "Wouldn't feel right wearing this while I'm breaking the law. Keep it for me until this is over."

T HE HOT WIND that had blown throughout the day had stilled and the streets were silent. Dawn was a few hours away when Dalton led the horses to the mouth of the alley. He could feel his heart pounding as he crept toward the back entrance to the sheriff's office.

He was surprised to find the door unlocked, taking it as a sign of good luck. Entering, he felt his way to Langston's desk and found the box containing the keys where Lanny had said they would be. The only sound he heard was a chorus of snoring coming from the nearby holding cage.

For a second he considered taking his Peacemaker from its holster but decided against it.

Feeling his way to the hallway, then along the bars, he reached Rawlings' cell and placed the key in the lock. The prisoner was lying on the bed motionless, and for a second Dalton feared he might already be dead. Only when he shook John's shoulder did he hear a soft moan that quickly developed into a fit of coughing.

"Get up and put your boots on," Dalton whispered.

"What the . . . ?"

"Hurry up. We're leaving."

Rawlings was still groggy by the time he was dressed and on his feet. "You're going to get yourself killed," he said as he was being helped toward the sheriff's office. His knees briefly buckled and for a moment he had to steady himself on the edge of the desk, spilling the leftover coffee.

K NEELING BEHIND A rain barrel, Dexter Wilson was waiting, his pistol pointed toward where his soon-to-emerge targets would appear.

He had followed Dalton from the livery, then watched him tie up his horses and disappear into the alley. The deputy had left the back door of the building unlocked so getting inside would be easy and had also made sure the key box on the sheriff's desk was in plain sight.

All that was left for him to do was wait for Dalton and Rawlings to step outside.

"I'm not sure I can make it," John said as they slowly made their way to the door. His legs, weak from not doing any walking for weeks, felt numb. With every step his breathing became more difficult.

"It's just a short way to the horses," Ben whispered, "then we're on our way."

As they finally reached the alley, they stopped for a moment to breathe in the night air. "I'd forgotten what open space feels like," Rawlings said.

Before they could take another step, Wilson stood and blocked their way. "You boys going somewhere?" he said, then laughed as he pointed his gun at Dalton. "You first," he said, "since I figure you to try running. Your friend, he don't look capable of any quick moves, so he'll be next."

They heard the click of his pistol being cocked.

As Wilson took aim, the wall on the opposite side of the alley suddenly shook with a thundering explosion.

There was a pained scream and the acrid smell of gunpowder filled the air. The deputy slowly went to his knees, then pitched headfirst into the dirt. His gun fell from his hand and bounced away toward the rain barrel.

Rawlings, his mouth agape, stared at the deputy's motionless body. "Is he dead?"

"Right now," Dalton said as he pulled John in the direction of the waiting horses, "that's not my main concern."

In the pitch-darkness, they couldn't see Lanny Butler, holding the smoking shotgun he'd borrowed from Duke Keene's tool cabinet. Earlier, from his perch in the livery loft, he'd seen Dalton following his friend and decided his help might be needed.

Now he was unaware of Ben and Rawlings riding away, since he was bent forward, hands on his knees, eyes closed, violently sick to his stomach. He had never shot a man before.

As dawn approached, it was a wandering drunk who first came upon Wilson's body. He quickly dug through the deputy's pockets and flashed a toothless smile upon finding a five-dollar gold piece. As he was happily staggering away, he tripped on the deputy's pistol, picked it up, and slipped it in the waistband of his ragged pants.

Minutes later, a shopkeeper on his way to open his store arrived and determined that despite the large amount of blood staining Wilson's shirt, he was still breathing. The man, his face ashen, raced around the corner and called out to the sheriff just as he was leisurely lighting his pipe for the first time of the day.

T HE SUN WAS on the rise, offering its warm welcome to the day, as Dalton and Rawlings rode northward. Neither had spoken since leaving Fort Worth. It was almost noon by the time they reached Kenwood Creek and began following along its bank. The rush of the water quickly got their tired horses' attention.

"According to the map," Ben said, "we're almost there. Let's let them get a drink while we stretch our legs a bit."

The fresh air seemed to have revived Rawlings. A touch of color was returning to the cheeks and he dismounted without needing help. He found a shady spot beneath a willow and stood, rolling his aching shoulders and holding his arms out wide. "I'm not sure what it is you're doing, Ben," he said, "but I'm deeply indebted. I'd about decided I was never going to get out of that godforsaken place.

"But we can't just keep running. I've got responsibilities back home . . . my family. And I need to clear my name. Want to share what you're planning next?"

Dalton admitted that he was thinking only one step at a time. "Up the way, we're going to get you to a place where you'll be safe and can get yourself healed up. Maybe when you're feeling better, you can explain to me how it is you got yourself into this mess in the first place. But for now you're going to be hiding—not leaving, not speaking to anyone—while I go back and try to sort things out."

* * *

THE CABIN WAS much as Duke had described it. A porch and a single room, built of native timber. There was a wood stove and two handmade beds where Keene and his brother had slept on their camping trips. The blankets Duke had brought were folded neatly on one. Against one wall, a short row of shelves held the food he'd stocked in, and on the small table that sat near the only window was the half-full bottle of whiskey.

On the porch, two fishing poles leaned against a stack of freshly chopped firewood. There was a rock-lined trail that led down to the creek.

"All the comforts of home," Dalton said. "Nary a steel bar in sight."

John let his eyes slowly roam his new home and made no reply.

"I'll be staying the night before heading back, so you might give some consideration to what you'll be cooking for supper," Ben said, attempting to lighten the mood. His real reason for remaining was to be certain that John was indeed well enough to be left to take care of himself.

"I think I'll take me a nap first," Rawlings said.

When he woke two hours later, he saw Dalton walking up from the creek, a fishing pole over one shoulder and holding a line of rope from which two catfish dangled. "Caught me some grasshoppers for bait and went fishing," he called out. His hair was still wet from the skinny-dip bath he'd also taken.

For the first time since they left the jail, Rawlings

smiled. He was remembering a time, long ago, when he and the man walking up the pathway had been regular fishing and swimming partners.

"I'll get a fire built," he said. "We'll eat us some supper, have a sip or two of your friend's whiskey . . . and do some talking."

THEY SAT ON the porch, watching a half moon slowly climb above the tree line. All around them were the soothing night sounds of the wilderness. "Peaceful," Dalton said, lifting his glass to salute the evening.

"Especially after you've spent night after night listening to drunk cowboys hollering and fighting and throwing their guts up just down the hall from you."

"Ready to tell me about it?"

Rawlings sighed and looked out into the darkness as if searching for a starting place for his story. And then, in a barely audible voice, he began:

"First, you need to understand that the people of Fort Worth aren't like those we grew up with in Aberdene," he said. "There's a lot of them crazy for money. For them, it's what defines success and power and self-worth. I know, I let myself get drawn into it. I chased it to places I shouldn't have gone, building a reputation as someone who was ready to help bad people out of bad situations. I was good at it, Ben, and it became like opium or good whiskey. The more success I had, the more money I made, and the more I wanted.

"Then this man who had struck it rich in some silver mines over in New Mexico came to me. He was looked up to, lived in one of the biggest houses in town, had a lot of high-ranking city people in his pocket. Word was he would likely be the next mayor, maybe even governor some day.

"He walks into my office, lays an envelope full of money on my desk, and says, 'I hear you're the lawyer who makes things go away.'"

Dalton could sense the difficulty Rawlings was having but said nothing.

"He'd gotten himself in a drunken rage and killed his son, a little boy the same age as my Alton. He'd hit him and thrown him down the stairs. When he realized he was dead, he buried him out in a pasture. And he came to me, asking my advice on how to be sure he didn't go to jail and have his reputation ruined. He was more worried about his reputation than what had happened to his son.

"And, Ben, I helped him come up with a lie that made it go away, even earned him sympathy from everyone in town. Half the people in town, me included, attended the funeral. And from that moment on, I've hated myself. I hated what I had allowed myself to become."

He got to his feet and moved to the edge of the porch, wrapping his arms across his chest as if the evening had suddenly grown cold. At that moment, he again looked like the hopeless man Dalton had visited in jail on his first evening in Fort Worth.

"Does Mandy know about this?" He regretted the question even before he finished asking it.

"We've always agreed that we'd never discuss my business," John said. "But yes, I'm sure she has an idea that the work I've done has been less than honorable. And I hated that, too. It was like lying to her in silence. She deserves better—someone more like you."

The observation made Ben uncomfortable and he quickly urged his friend's story along. "I still don't understand how it is you wound up charged with the murder of that banker," he said.

"I needed to tell you the first part of the story so you could better understand the difficulties I made for myself. This is the second part:

"Thomas Cookson gave me a chance at a little bit of redemption," John said. "A decent and honest man, he came to me, asking me to help him avoid getting involved with some things that he knew to be wrong. I can remember to this day what he said to me: 'You're a fine lawyer. You could be an asset to this town if you get on the proper side of the law.'

"He said some bad people were threatening him. A rancher named Ray Abernathy—calls himself the Colonel—was the main one."

Dalton nodded. "We've met."

"Then I expect you're already aware of him being a ruthless individual. He's one of those I mentioned earlier who worships wealth and all the power that comes with it."

Rawlings was getting tired, his voice weak and drained. "I need to get some sleep," he said abruptly. "We can continue this in the morning."

The two men rose and walked into the cabin, where a lone lantern cast dim shadows against the walls. Rawlings sat on the edge of his bed, struggling to pull off his boots. "Ben," he said, "that man in the alley. You think he's dead?"

"I guess we'll find out soon enough," Dalton said. The question that concerned him more was who had fired the shot that had saved their lives.

* * *

EARLIER, IN FORT Worth, Sheriff Langston had been at his wits' end long before Ray Abernathy burst into his office. "Where is he?" the Colonel yelled. "Is he still alive?" The deputy whom the sheriff had sent to the Shooting Star to pass along the news hadn't been able to tell him much, only that Wilson was shot while attempting to stop a jailbreak. In exchange for his lack of more detail, he had received a staggering slap to the face.

"He's over at Doc Thorndale's," Langston said. "He's alive, but not doing too well. They say he's still unconscious."

Abernathy stormed out and headed for the doctor's office. He slammed the door so hard that the few remaining prisoners in the drunk cage jumped at the sound.

Wilson, bare-chested, was still lying on a table when the Colonel entered. The patient's eyes were open, as if he were staring at something far away.

"I've managed to keep him alive," the nervous doctor said, "but that's about all. He was most likely shot with a twelve-gauge. Ripped away all the hide off one shoulder and damaged some muscle. Looks like some ribs might also be broken. What I'm most concerned about, however, is his face. I'm still trying to remove all the buckshot and determine if any of the pellets went into the brain. And I'm afraid he's going to lose sight in his left eye.

"How long it will be before he regains consciousness, I couldn't say. Maybe in a day or two, maybe never. He's lucky he's not dead."

Abernathy's eyes were ablaze with anger. "See to it you keep him alive," he said. "And I'll be wanting to know when I can take him back to the ranch."

"Any idea who might have done this?" the doctor said.

"Don't need an idea," the Colonel said as he stormed away. "I know. And there'll be nothing you or God himself will be able to do to keep him alive once I'm done with him."

S HERIFF LANGSTON WAS dreading Abernathy's return to his office. He still had to tell him that it was John Rawlings who had escaped.

When he did, the Colonel's curses echoed through the building. "Get him back . . . hang him, shoot him, I don't care which," he said. "I just want something done about this . . . now . . . including arresting the man who helped Rawlings get free."

"But we're not even sure who it was," Langston argued, despite also being relatively certain it was Ben Dalton. "I got to have some proof before—"

Abernathy raised a hand to stop him. "I don't want to hear more excuses. You've caused me grief enough and I'm tired to my bones of it. Just do what you've got to do," he said. "If you can't, I'll find somebody else to wear that badge."

T HE SMELL OF brewing coffee woke Rawlings. Dalton was cooking turkey eggs he had found in a nest under the porch. "You still snore like you did back when we were kids," he said.

John laughed. "I can't recall the last time I slept so well," he said. "Aside from my rear end being sore from all that riding, I feel better than I have in a long time."

"I've got to head back and face some music shortly," Ben said, "so, if you're okay with it, I'd like to finish up our conversation when we're done eating."

Rawlings agreed.

After breakfast, they walked along the pathway to the bank of the creek and found a fallen log to sit on. "I got something to ask first," John said as he tossed a rock in the direction of a surprised egret. "In the jail, you saw me at my worst. I was scraping the bottom. Do you think I'm crazy?"

Dalton chose to be honest. "I think you were headed in that direction," he said, "but, no, I don't think you're crazy. Wouldn't consider leaving you here by your lonesome if I did."

"Good. That's settled. I'll admit to being a fool, but I'm not crazy. You saved me from that."

And with that he returned to his story:

"It was before my time," he said, "but from what I've been told, Colonel Abernathy started taking over folks' land as soon as he got here. At first, he would offer them far less than their property was worth, and then if they turned him down, he used threats and violence. Barns got burned, cattle got rustled, warnings of physical harm were made. Today, he owns half of the county and still isn't satisfied.

"Now, he's wanting to take over Fort Worth, at least the Hell's Half Acre part. There's a lot of money to be made in the saloons and gambling houses, and the Colonel wants what he considers his share. He's already managed to buy out a few of the little cafés and a dry goods store."

"How's he planning on taking over the drinking and gambling places?" Dalton said.

"For that, he needs the bank's help. Cookson told me it started with the Colonel asking him to sign some papers that weren't truthful. Thomas declined to do so and thought the matter was settled. But then Abernathy came back, asking him to begin foreclosure proceedings against some of the Acre businesses. When Cookson declined and ordered him out of his office, threats were made. On the next visit, Abernathy brought the sheriff with him."

Though hardly a businessman, Dalton had to admire Abernathy's devious plan. Have the bank take possession of an establishment, no matter whether it was thriving or not, then turn it over to the Colonel for a cheap price. The sheriff's role would be to apply pressure that would convince nervous owners to choose an early retirement or leave town.

"Cookson told Abernathy that there was no legal way to start foreclosure proceedings if owners were paid up on their loans and their businesses were doing well. For the Colonel, the solution to the problem was simple. The bank could raise interest rates on their notes so high that they would be impossible to pay. Meanwhile, the sheriff would start raids and make arrests that were sure to cause harm to business. More threats were made and deliveries of whiskey and beer were being delayed.

"You saw how many Langston's got crammed into that drunk cage. Every night, his men make more and more arrests on his orders, sending a message. After a while, a patron feels it wise to take his drinking and card playing down the street to another spot. Soon, however, it's also a target. Business keeps going down, the cost of operating goes up, and pretty soon the Colonel's got folks where he wants them."

John tossed another rock at the stubborn egret that was now strutting along the opposite bank. "Actually, it's a pretty good plan. But to make it all work, he needed Thomas Cookson as a partner. And Cookson continued to balk. Then threats were made against his family.

"That's when he came to see me, asking what I could do to help. I told him that to protect himself he needed to put everything he told me in writing and give it to me for safekeeping.

"A few days after he delivered it, I got a message tacked on our door, saying he needed to see me. Said it was urgent, so I immediately went to his house. He was dead when I got there."

The picture was getting clearer for Dalton. "I'm guessing somebody tried to get him to tell where that document was and when he wouldn't, he got himself killed. Then the sheriff blamed you, locked you up, and has been trying to get you to talk."

Rawlings nodded. "That's about the size of it. A few nights ago, he stood in front of my cell and started talking all friendly about how much my wife and son must be missing me, how it would be a shame if something bad happened to them when I wasn't in a position to do anything about it. I had decided to tell him what he wanted to know . . . and then you broke me out."

The last of what John said escaped Dalton. His thoughts had shifted to Mandy and her son. If, as he feared, they were in danger, he needed to be nearby.

"I better be getting on back," he said, watching as the egret finally flew away.

CHAPTER 11

HE WAS STILL in the doorway when Mandy began rattling off questions. "Is it true? Did John really get out of jail? Is he okay? You helped him, didn't you?"

After Rawlings told him of the none-too-subtle threat Sheriff Langston had made, the safety of Mandy and her son became Ben Dalton's main concern. He had ridden straight from the cabin to them, ignoring the danger he was sure awaited upon his return to town. He had decided that rather than hide, he would meet the matter head-on. First, however, he needed to be certain that Mandy and Alton were safe.

The youngster stood at his mother's side, smiling, hoping that his new friend had again brought candy. Ben reached out and picked him up. "I'll bring you a surprise next time, little man," he said as Mandy closed the door. "Today, I was in a bit of a rush."

Alton's mother took him from Dalton's arms and suggested he go to his room and find a book they could read later. The smile she'd given him faded as soon as he left the room.

"I can't answer a lot of your questions," Ben said, "except to tell you that John's okay and in a safe place."

"Where? Why isn't he here?"

"He said to tell both of you that he sends his love. That's all I can say for now. The less you know, the better it will be, for the time being." He paused, took a deep breath, then said the words he'd been dreading. "I think you could be in danger, both of you."

He was surprised by her reaction. "Did you see a couple of men down in the lobby when you came in?" she said. "One of them is big enough to lift a wagon. The other's so mean-looking he scared Alton. Shelby Profer brought them over when he came to tell me he'd heard John escaped."

That she already had bodyguards watching over her and Alton resolved one of the worries Ben had during his ride back.

"Things are going to be okay," he said as he prepared to leave. "John's done nothing wrong, he's innocent. It might take some time, but we're going to prove it." He considered giving her a reassuring hug but decided against it.

P ROFER WAS IN the lobby, talking to the men Mandy had described, when Dalton came down the stairs. "Good to see you, Ben," he said. "I trust your trip went well."

When he got no reply, he smiled. "That's the last question I'll ask," he said. "In my experience, too much knowledge isn't always a good thing. Come and let me introduce you to my friends."

Brent St. John was almost as wide as he was tall, weighing at least two-fifty, maybe more. His biceps looked like melons and his knuckles were crisscrossed with scars. B. J. Wong, half Chinese, half something else, was short, stocky, bald, and as mean-looking as Mandy had said. His nose appeared to have been broken more than once.

Both wore firearms on their hips.

"These fine gentlemen," Profer said, "earn their livelihoods ring fighting in exhibitions held regularly down by the stockyards. They take on all comers, mostly visiting cattle herders foolishly hoping to prove their mettle, sometimes uninformed locals who have had a bit too much courage to drink. Neither, I'm assured, has ever lost a bout. I know I've never lost a wager I made on their talents. I've made arrangements with them to see to the safekeeping of Mrs. Rawlings and her son. This will be their home, day and night, for the foreseeable future.

"When Otto Langston visited yesterday to see if John Rawlings might have returned home after his escape, Mr. St. John kindly escorted him to the apartment and waited while he checked."

The men silently nodded as Dalton shook their hands and thanked them.

"You know," the elderly attorney said, "in my younger days I, too, was rather handy with my fists. I recall a time when—"

Dalton smiled and cut him short. "I'd like to hear about it, but some other time. Right now, I need to get over to the livery."

"Of course," Profer said. "There's just one more thing. In the event you're visited by anyone wishing to place you under arrest or threatening harm, advise them that you have quite aggressive legal counsel at your service."

Dalton turned and looked at the old lawyer.

"Mrs. Rawlings was kind enough to pay your retainer fee," he said.

"S HERIFF LANGSTON'S DONE been by a half-dozen times," Duke said as he watched Ben lead Dolly toward an empty stall. "I don't guess it's any surprise that he's figured out what it was that took place."

"Does he have proof, a witness?"

"Last I heard, Deputy Wilson was unconscious and might not pull through."

"Do they know who shot him?"

"That, apparently, is a mystery nobody's been able to solve."

As Keene spoke, Lanny appeared, a mucking rake over his shoulder. He broke into a smile when he saw Dalton. "Good to see you back," he said as he took Dolly's reins. "I'll see she gets unsaddled and has a good brushing. She'll probably be wanting a bucket of oats as well."

As the young man led the mare away, Duke wiped a bandanna across his forehead. "That's the first smile I've seen on that boy's face since you hightailed it. He's been worthless, moping around, not talking. I couldn't even get him to eat the chili and rice I cooked up last night."

"I'll talk to him."

"Speaking of talking, did you get a chance to have a conversation with our friend up at the cabin?"

"I did. We talked for quite a spell."

"And . . . ?"

"Things aren't good. Has anybody made you an offer on the livery lately?"

"No, but I'm expecting it," Keene said as he reached into his pocket and withdrew Dalton's badge. "I think it might be a good idea for you to start carrying it again," he said.

THE COLONEL HAD not only demanded that Dexter Wilson be transported back to the Shooting Star but made it clear that he expected the doctor to accompany him. When Doc Thorndale argued that he had other patients to look after, Abernathy had responded with sarcasm. "Any of them been shot and near dead?" he said. "You're coming and you'll stay until you get him well and back on his feet. The quicker you do that, the faster you can get back to handing out pills and powders to sick old ladies."

At the ranch, Wilson was gently lifted from the back of a wagon and carried into the main house by a couple of cowboys who had been waiting on the porch. A maid had already put clean sheets on his bed and pulled the Colonel's favorite chair close. The nervous doctor was assigned a next-door room.

Late into the night, Abernathy kept vigil, sipping from a bottle of whiskey as he watched Wilson's shallow breathing. "You've gotta wake up, boy," he whispered. "I need you to say who did this to you. I just want to hear his name."

If Wilson was unable to provide it soon, the Colonel already had another person in mind who could. If it was hellfire his enemies wanted, he was more than ready to oblige them.

D ALTON WAS SITTING with Lanny, mending a halter, when Otto Langston paid another visit. As soon as the sheriff walked through the livery door, the young man got to his feet and hurried off to tend to more chores. Ben kept his seat.

"I need to speak with you," Langston said as he approached. Though he attempted to display his gruff, all-business manner, it was obvious he was harried. His shirt looked as if it had been worn for several days, he hadn't shaved, and his shoulders slumped ever so slightly.

"I've got a missing prisoner and was wondering if you might have knowledge of his whereabouts."

Dalton lifted his head to look at the sheriff but remained seated. "Yeah, I heard that John Rawlings escaped," he said. "Seems everybody in town is talking about it. But no, I've got no idea where you might go looking for him."

Langston huffed. "I've also got a deputy who was shot and is near dead. Know anything about that?"

"Nope, but I wish him the best."

"Where've you been of late?"

"Had my craw full of city life and wanted some open space," Dalton said. "On a whim, I decided to just ride off west for some peace and quiet for a couple of days, breathe some fresh air and sleep under the stars. It was good getting away. You might want to try it, Sheriff. It'll do wonders to calm a man."

Langston rested a hand on the butt of his sidearm and glared. He was tired of the game playing. "Reckon why old man Profer just came to my office, waving his fancy cane around, telling me he was now your lawyer if all you've been doing lately is taking a trip to get yourself some fresh air?"

Dalton shrugged, then got to his feet. "If there's nothing else I can do for you, Sheriff, I've got things to tend to. I wish you luck finding your escaped prisoner."

"We'll talk again," Langston said as he stormed away, muttering curses as he left.

D UKE KEENE EMERGED from a nearby stall, Lanny at his side. "For an honest man," he said, "you make a mighty fine liar. Not that the sheriff believed a word you said, but you bluffed him real good. That man's worried as a rodeo goat and I, for one, am proud to see it."

He cleared his throat and moved closer. "Seeing as how you're in a talking mood, there's something else we need to discuss." He reached out to Lanny and motioned for him to take a seat.

"It was the boy here who saved your hide the other night," he said.

In a halting voice, Lanny told of taking Keene's shotgun and following Dexter Wilson to the alley. "I shot him," he said. "I was scared he was going to kill you and your friend and didn't know nothing else to do."

Surprised, Dalton was silent for a moment, then said, "So I owe you my life. As does John Rawlings. I thank you for it, and so will he. What you did took a great deal of courage."

"I'm glad to hear he ain't dead," Lanny said.

"Me, too," Ben replied. "Now that we had this talk, it's never to be spoken of again. Understand? Whatever fight's going on, I don't want you part of it."

Lanny's relief was obvious. "I understand," he said as Keene slapped him on the back and told him to get back to work.

Dalton waited until Lanny was out of earshot before he spoke to Duke. "I'd feel more comfortable if we sent him up to the cabin for a while. You can provide him a map and tell him he's to take added provisions to Rawlings. He can also let John know that his wife and son are being well cared for. I'll convince him I need him to stay for a few days and keep watch over John."

"I reckon I can tend the chores by myself," Duke said. "Did it before he came along. Of course, if you're inclined to pitch in . . ."

Ben smiled and shook his head. "Won't be able to for a couple of days," he said. "I've got another trip I need to make."

He had decided help might soon be needed if the Colonel decided to go to war. And he had an idea where he might find it.

PART TWO

SATURDAY NIGHT DANCE

CHAPTER 12

DALTON HAD AT least been honest about enjoying being away from the city. As he rode toward the rising sun, letting Dolly set her own pace, he hoped the time came soon when he would never have to set foot in Fort Worth again.

It was nearing noon when he saw the community of Brush Creek in the distance.

He found Marshal Anson Kelly in the café, finishing a large slice of blueberry pie. "All your outlaws taking a dinner break?" Dalton asked.

"Wasn't expecting to see you again," Kelly said. "Have a seat and tell me what you've been doing." He hardly anticipated the story his fellow marshal laid out over the next half hour. Or the favor Dalton had come to ask.

"Sounds like you've stuck your head in a beehive," Kelly said. He pushed his empty plate away and wiped crumbs from his mouth. "Let me see if I've got this right: You've got a rich rancher who wants to be richer and don't mind breaking laws, even killing folks to make it happen. He's got crooked friends in high places and a whole bunch of dumb cowboys working for him who are willing to do whatever he asks, including ganging up on folks in alleys and setting buildings on fire. Am I missing anything?"

"That about covers it."

"And on your side is an escaped convict, a lawyer who's older than dirt, a livery owner who doesn't even carry a gun, and two hired bodyguards you met just a couple of days ago."

"And you, if you're willing."

"Don't sound like a fair fight to me. But I reckon this is the sort of thing we signed up for. As it so happens, I've been planning a visit to Fort Worth anyway." He explained that Dee Wayne Barclay, the man Dalton had earlier taken into custody after he murdered his brother, was still sitting in the Brush Creek jail. "All day long, he just talks to himself and imagines that snakes are climbing up the walls. I'm getting mighty tired of having him around and there's no way a man like him can ever be tried, even if he did murder blood kin."

With the help of the local doctor, Kelly explained, he had exchanged telegrams with a lock-in mental institution in Fort Worth that was willing to take Barclay off his hands. "They say they'll take custody and lock him up if I deliver him. They want to study him.

"So, as long as I'm heading that way . . ."

Dalton was shaking his hand before he even completed his sentence.

"I've got a young fella in town who I occasionally deputize," Kelly said. "He's no Doc Holliday, but he'll agree to watch out for the chicken stealing and bar fights if I give him a badge."

Dalton was still pumping his hand as he spoke. "One other thing you need to know," Kelly said.

"What's that?"

"I ain't a very good shot."

"Me neither," Ben said.

The following morning as they were loading up to leave, Dee Wayne, shackled and straddled atop a mule, was singing at the top of his lungs. On the porch, the young hardware store janitor stood, proudly admiring the badge Kelly had just pinned to his shirt.

The Brush Creek marshal climbed into his saddle and looked over at Dalton. "We ain't much of a posse, are we?" he said.

Ben could do nothing but laugh as he pulled at the reins to point Dolly back toward Fort Worth.

I N THE HEADQUARTERS of the Shooting Star there was no such levity. Doc Thorndale slowly pulled a blanket over Dexter Wilson's face and turned to the Colonel. "He was just too shot up. I did everything I could."

Abernathy stared at the bed for several minutes, angrily chomping at the last stages of his cigar. "We'll bury him in that grove down by the duck pond," he finally said. "Then, once that's done, I'm gonna go kill somebody."

The funeral was held on a gray, rainy morning as Shooting Star cowboys gathered beneath a canopy of giant cottonwoods. Though none had liked Wilson and his arrogant, bullying manner, they were there at the Colonel's insistence. Several struggled to mask their surprise at the kind words their boss, hat in hand, head bent, spoke.

Then, even as dirt was being shoveled into the grave, his mood abruptly changed.

"Until we find John Rawlings and get rid of this fella from out of town, I'll not be happy," he said. He called out a half-dozen names, ordering each to begin regular visits to the Half Acre saloons to see what they might learn. "You'll be there to look and listen, not get yourselves drunk," Abernathy said. Another ranch hand was assigned to keep watch on Dalton. "I'll expect you to do what our worthless sheriff can't seem to."

Two others, the same men who had carried out the attack on Dalton in back of the laundry, were summoned to the Colonel's office. He had another plan he wished to discuss in private. It had come to him late one night as he'd kept vigil at Wilson's bedside.

D ALTON WAS EAGER to look in on Mandy and Alton as Kelly continued on through Fort Worth, en route to deliver Dee Wayne Barclay to officials at the mental facility. They agreed to meet later at the livery. "I've got a friend there who cooks a fine bowl of chili," Ben said, "and he'll see that your horse is well cared for when you get there."

Though his stay in Brush Creek had only been overnight, he felt he'd been gone for days. Even with bodyguards in place, the mention Sheriff Langston had made to Rawlings about his family—obviously a thinly disguised threat—had gnawed at him. He would feel better seeing that all was well. Only when assured of that could he turn his thoughts to dealing with Langston and the Colonel.

As he approached the hotel, there was a flurry of activity outside the building. People mingled on the sidewalks and in the street, sharing whispers and pointing toward the upstairs window of the Rawlings apartment. Several women appeared to be crying. A deputy Dalton didn't recognize stood near the front door, talking quietly with Shelby Profer. The bodyguard was sitting on a bench, next to the sheriff. Both silently stared at the ground.

Dalton left Dolly at a hitching post and raced toward the crowd, not even bothering to breathe. Profer saw him and waved him over.

Ben struggled unsuccessfully to form the words to the question that was racing through his mind.

"The boy's been taken," the attorney said. He was pale and shaking as he spoke.

"Where's Mandy?"

"She's upstairs. A neighbor lady is with her. She's pretty upset. I'm so sorry . . ."

Dalton rushed toward the door, briefly glaring at the sheriff as he passed. "We'll talk later," he said.

Doc Thorndale yelled out to him from the sitting room as he passed but got no response. Ben was calling Mandy's name even before he reached the top of the stairs.

She was sitting on the sofa next to her neighbor, her face buried in her hands.

"It's my fault, Ben," she said as he gently placed a hand on her shoulder. "All my fault. What are we going to do?"

"We're going to find him."

After several false starts, each interrupted by fits of
crying, she managed to tell Dalton what had happened
just hours earlier. She wanted to pick up some new
books at the library and had asked her neighbor, Jennie Dawson, if she would briefly sit with Alton while
she was gone. Miss Dawson was already aware of the
tense situation in the Rawlings home and understood
the need for the two bodyguards.

"Jennie came over and Mr. St. John was already
here. He told her he would be downstairs if they
needed him for anything. Mr. Wong insisted on accompanying me to the library, even though I wasn't
going to be away very long," Mandy said as she began
to cry again. "When we got back, Alton was gone. We
found Jennie locked in the storage room, her hands
tied and her mouth covered with a cloth."

"There was an envelope over there by the lamp,"
she added, pointing toward a small table. "I couldn't
bear to read it and gave it to Mr. Profer when he arrived. That's all I know. I wasn't gone but a short
time . . . and this happens." She stood and wrapped her
arms around Dalton. "First John, now this," she said.
"What am I going to do? Please . . ."

For a moment, Ben feared she might faint and eased
her back onto the sofa. "I'll be back in a few minutes,"
he said. He wanted to see the note that had been left.

Before he reached the bottom of the stairs, Doc
Thorndale appeared in the lobby and was pointing in
the direction of the adjacent sitting room. "You need
to see this," he said.

Sitting in a chair, his head bent forward as if he
might be dozing, was Brent St. John. The blackening
bloodstains that covered the front of his shirt and the

jagged wound beneath his chin told a gruesome story. The huge bodyguard was dead, his throat cut. His side-arm was still in its holster.

"No sign that there was a fight," the doctor said. "Somebody just slipped up behind him and . . ." He made an exaggerated sweeping motion with his right arm. "The man was dead before he could say a prayer."

Shelby Profer came up behind them. "I feel responsible for this," the attorney said. "Brent didn't sign up for this kind of madness. Big as he was, he was as kind and gentle a man as you'd ever hope to know. Only people he ever got mad at were those foolish enough to get in the ring with him. And that lasted only until the fight ended."

The old lawyer was obviously shaken.

"Mandy told me you've got a note," Dalton said.

Profer took the single piece of paper from his vest pocket and, without bothering to put on his spectacles, read the message.

YOUR DADDY HAS SOMETHING I WANT. WHEN HE GIVES IT TO ME YOU CAN GO HOME. THIS NEEDS TO HAPPEN FAST.

"Of course, it's not signed," Profer said, "but I don't think there's any room to argue who it comes from."

"The Colonel," Ben said, spitting the words.

"If not him, his people."

Dalton rushed from the room and out to where Otto Langston was standing. He grabbed the sheriff by his lapels and pulled his face close, knocking off his hat. "Tell me what you know about this," he said.

The sheriff made a weak attempt to brush his aggressor's hands away, and then his shoulders slumped and his arms went to his side. "This is none of my doing," he said, "I swear to God."

"If I find out you're lying—and my guess is you are—your life's not going to be worth a plug nickel. If that boy gets hurt, so help me I'll kill you. That's a promise." With that, he shoved the sheriff away as onlookers silently watched the confrontation.

B ROTHERS CLAUDE AND Calvin Sloan came to work at the Shooting Star as soon as they had been released from the Brownsville jail. They were still teenagers, with little talent for anything but trouble, when Colonel Abernathy offered them jobs on a ranch he planned to soon buy. Getting away from the Texas border and moving north, he explained, would offer smart young men like them a chance for a fresh start. In truth, he saw them as worthless and simple-minded and had hired them for their muscle and willingness to do anything he ordered.

Including kidnapping a five-year-old boy.

Sitting behind the desk in his office, Abernathy had given them simple instructions, making them repeat his words back to him several times to be certain they knew every step of their assignment. They were to enter the Rawlings apartment where there would be only the woman and her son. They were to tie her up and take the child, riding directly to Miss Luisa's roadhouse. There, in a small back room where she lived, she would look after the child until the Colonel's problem was solved.

Though unaware that bodyguards had been hired,

he nonetheless told Claude and Calvin to arm themselves. "Just in case," Abernathy said.

Fʀᴏᴍ ᴛʜᴇɪʀ ʜɪᴅɪɴɢ place behind a row of shrubs, they watched a pretty young woman and a strange-looking man leave the building and walk quickly down the street. Inside, they could see another man, sitting in a chair.

"How we gonna get past him?" Calvin whispered. "Even sitting down he looks big enough to lift a cow."

They crept closer and could see that a side door led from the sitting room into a small fountain garden. It was directly behind where the man sat. Claude smiled and told his brother to give him time to make his way to that door, then go in the front way and strike up a conversation. "I just need you to get his attention for a few seconds," he said.

It was their first deviation from the Colonel's carefully laid-out plan.

Inside, Calvin was smiling broadly as he approached Brent St. John. "Howdy, my friend," he said, "You live here or just resting?"

The bodyguard looked up but didn't reply. Neither did he hear the door open slightly behind him, nor the liquid sound Claude's Bowie knife made as it sliced across his neck. His body was still violently quivering as the two intruders raced up the stairway toward the Rawlings apartment.

Bursting through the door, they found a woman and a little boy sitting on the living room rug, sorting out a large pile of toys. Both screamed at the sight of the men. Claude hurried to put his hand over the struggling woman's mouth while Calvin picked up the boy.

In only a couple of minutes, the woman they presumed to be the mother had been bound and gagged and locked away. Though kicking wildly, the child was unable to escape the grasp of the man who lifted him onto a shoulder and hurried toward the door.

They were well on their way to the roadhouse before Alton stopped crying.

"That was pretty dang easy," Claude said as they rode southward. "I reckon we ought to treat ourselves to a beer or two at Miss Luisa's when we get there."

W HEN DALTON ARRIVED at the livery, Duke had already made Anson Kelly welcome, handing the visitor a second helping of chili and refilling his whiskey glass. It was the livery owner who first noticed the troubled look on Ben's face.

"If I couldn't see that's Dolly you're leading," Keene said, "I'd guess someone stole your horse."

Dalton ignored his friend's attempt at humor and went straight to the point. "The Rawlings boy's been kidnapped," he said. The other two fell silent as he related the events that had occurred. "And they killed a man named Brent St. John. He was there to guard Mandy and Alton. They cut his throat."

With every sentence, his voice grew louder, his anger boiling. Even Dolly lifted her head and pulled against the halter.

Kelly put his bowl aside and was about to approach Dalton when another man appeared in the doorway. Otto Langston was the picture of defeat, minus his hat, his hair unkempt, and his body language that of a schoolboy getting ready for a whipping from the teacher.

"We need to have that talk," the sheriff said as he took an unsteady step toward Dalton. "I stopped to have me something to drink before coming, thinking it might settle my nerves. All it did was make me drunk enough to say I'm sorry for what's happened. When I told you the taking of that youngster was none of my doing, that was the truth. Same with the killing of Brent St. John."

Dalton was hardly in a forgiving mood. "But those things were done by the lowlife people you're in cahoots with. In my mind, that makes you as responsible as they are. You're the sorriest excuse for a lawman I've ever seen."

"You're right," Langston said, his head hanging. "I ain't here to make excuses, nor do I expect you to accept my apology. I'm here to admit I've done a lot of bad things—though I ain't killed nobody—and to tell you I want to help make things right. I just don't know how to go about it."

The livery went silent except for the movement of the horses in their stalls. The sheriff still stood near the doorway, waiting for some reply. Finally, Duke approached him and held out a tin cup. "Hair of the dog," he said as he handed Langston a shot of whiskey. "And if nobody else has a suggestion, I got one to offer."

Langston gulped down his drink. "And what's that?" he said.

"First, help us find the boy and get him home to his mama, then join us in taking care of Raymond Abernathy so I never again have to look at his face or shoe another one of his horses."

"I'm turning in my badge first thing in the morning," Langston said.

"There'll be a lot of folks, shopkeepers in particular, who will pleased to hear that," Dalton said. "No more having to pay protection money, no more bail costs after being jailed when it wasn't called for, no more money slipped to you under the table by Colonel Abernathy. Am I leaving anything out?"

Marshal Kelly got to his feet and approached Dalton. "Seeing as how I've been invited into this mess you've got," he said, "I think it earns me the right to state my opinion. If not, I should just ride on back to Brush Creek."

He got no argument and continued. "Seems to me if the sheriff has actually gotten religion and is sincere about wanting to help, he could best do so by staying right where he is. He could keep on doing things just as he has been. In the meantime, he could keep an eye on this Abernathy fellow and alert us to what he's up to."

"Like having us our own spy," Keene added as his face lit up.

All eyes turned to the sheriff, who had buried his hands in his pockets and was kicking at the dirt. Finally, he replied, "It could work. Won't be hard for me to continue what I've been doing. God knows I've had plenty of practice. If it'll help to get that little boy back and bring some peace to folks in town, I'll do it."

Still with reservations, Dalton was the only one who didn't shake Langston's hand. He needed to see proof that it wasn't just the whiskey talking.

Before turning to leave, the sheriff gestured toward Ben. "A couple of things you ought to know," he said.

"I've stationed a trustworthy deputy at Mandy Rawlings' door and told him to shoot anybody who attempts to get in who's not welcome.

"And," he added, "be aware the Colonel has done told me he wants you dead. Sooner the better, he says."

As LANGSTON EXITED the livery, he had to weave his way through a group of men who were gathering in the street. There were at least a dozen of them, maybe more. They were mostly young cowboys who had at one time or another been defeated in the ring by Brent St. John.

With them was Shelby Profer, leaning against his cane.

The attorney ignored the sheriff and approached Dalton. "These men are interested friends of the late Brent St. John," he said. "There are a couple of others who have gone over to the hotel to stand guard with Mr. Wong. To a man, they want you to be aware they stand ready to do anything and everything necessary to see that whoever murdered their friend and kidnapped the Rawlings child is properly dealt with." He turned to the gathering. "You'll note that they are able-bodied and wearing sidearms," he said.

Marshal Kelly stood next to Dalton and leaned to whisper in his ear. "The posse's looking better," he said.

CHAPTER 13

Frustration showed on the Colonel's face as he stepped onto the porch and squinted into the morning sun. He had not slept well despite consuming a large amount of tequila before going to bed, and the skin beneath his eyes sagged and was turning the color of ripe plums. Leaning against the railing, he let his gaze wander from the barn to the corral, the orchard, and the well-kept garden out to the distant pastures where hundreds of cattle appeared as brown dots on the landscape. And he wondered to himself: *With all this, why does my head feel like it might explode and my stomach hurt like somebody set fire to it?*

He was waiting for the arrival of Sheriff Langston. Earlier, he'd sent a messenger to tell him they needed to talk, but at the Shooting Star instead of Luisa's roadhouse. No need for the law, however friendly and easily manipulated, to be nosing around their usual meeting place with the Rawlings youngster being hidden there.

"Too early for hard liquor," Abernathy told his Mexican maid. "Just bring coffee, strong and black, por favor."

She was on her way to the kitchen when the sheriff stepped onto the porch. "Morning, Colonel," he said, lightly touching the brim of his hat.

"A time of the day I could gladly do without," Abernathy replied, setting the tone for their meeting.

"Troubles?"

The Colonel frowned. "I think you know the answer to that. Tell me what the mood is in town. I've had some of my men hanging around the saloons, but all they're coming back with is hangovers and promises on God's bible they didn't do any drinking."

Langston shook his head. "I saw one of them take a pretty good beating, just because it was known he works for you," he said. "Folks are riled up. That little boy disappearing and Brent St. John getting his throat cut has angered a lot of people."

"I sent idiots to get the boy. Idiots. There was no need for killing," the Colonel said.

Langston didn't bother to agree. "Those who aren't angry are scared," he said. "They've been coming to my office in droves, demanding that something be done."

"It'll blow over," Abernathy said as he poured coffee from his cup into a saucer to let it cool. "The scared ones will outnumber those who are angry before long. Then things will return to normal."

"But until they do. . . ."

There was a sudden sharpness to the Colonel's voice. "Until then . . . I want John Rawlings found and brought to me. The other man we've talked about still needs killing. And if you can't do it, I'll use every man on this place to get my satisfaction. But if I'm forced to do it that way, things might get a little unpleasant for a worthless town sheriff."

"I can take care of it," Langston said. "It just might take a little time."

Abernathy threw his china cup against the wall and erupted in curses. "I don't *have* time," he said.

The sheriff waited until he calmed before passing along his last bit of news. "Getting back in touch with the Rawlings boy's mother won't be easy. They've put more guards on her place. There must be a dozen or more, working in shifts. And they're armed."

"Who's responsible for that?"

"The old lawyer named Shelby Profer. He's suddenly taken quite an interest in these matters."

For the first time since they had begun talking, Abernathy smiled. "Then it's him I need to send a message. Be something, wouldn't it, if his office was to go up in flames tomorrow night?" he said.

Hoping he had successfully managed to mask his fear of the Colonel, Langston took his leave and rode back to Fort Worth.

Later in the day he and Ben Dalton visited Profer's office.

ANYONE WHO SO much as considers pouring kerosene or coal oil on the walls of this building can expect to be sued to within an inch of his life, not to mention a lengthy list of criminal charges that will be brought," Profer bellowed. "I've officed here for a good half century and plan on breathing my final breath sitting behind this very desk. Should we ride out to the ranch and advise Mr. Abernathy of the consequences his proposed action will bring?"

Dalton shook his head and offered an alternate plan. "I think those volunteers you rounded up can provide adequate protection for your property," he said. "We can post them around the building, all with lanterns so they can be seen, and I'm guessing anybody the Colonel sends to set a fire will quickly rethink their plan."

"And what harm will it do to them?" Profer said.

"I'm guessing there will be enough of them who ride into town," Dalton said, "that there won't be too many left to look after the ranch. We can get coal oil, too. Maybe it's time we send a message of our own."

"Ah, yes," the attorney said, slapping an open hand down on his desk, "we fight fire with fire, as the saying goes. I think it's a marvelous plan. Marvelous indeed."

THE FOLLOWING EVENING, Marshal Kelly sat astride his horse on a rise south of town, looking through his spyglass. In a canyon below were a half dozen of Brent St. John's friends. Each had an unlit torch, a canteen filled with coal oil, and matches in his pocket.

It was nearing midnight when the flickering of the Shooting Star torches appeared on the horizon, moonlit shadows moving in the direction of Fort Worth, just as the sheriff had said they would. Ten, maybe a dozen, Kelly thought before riding into the canyon.

"They'll be past us shortly," he said. "Then we'll be on our way."

True to his word, the Colonel had ordered his men to set fire to Shelby Profer's office. He told the ranch hands he'd been sending into the saloons to find the building's location and they had returned with a hand-drawn map. Torches were passed out to everyone and four of the men were assigned to carry fuel. Abernathy's final instructions were simple, military-like: "Do it quickly and get out."

When one of the cowboys asked what they were to do if there was indication someone might be inside the building, the Colonel only glared at him and repeated himself. "I said, do it quickly and get out."

He would remain at the ranch, awaiting word of the mission's success.

Inside the livery, Dalton's planning was somewhat more elaborate. With Profer's help, he had assembled those who had expressed their anger at St. John's murder. He told them what Sheriff Langston had learned. "We'll send a message of our own," he said. Half of those in attendance would accompany Kelly. The others were to arm themselves and join him in protecting the lawyer's property.

As he spoke, Duke was passing out torches and the canteens filled with coal oil. He was still miffed that Dalton had flatly refused to allow him to participate more. He, Profer, and the sheriff were told to remain in the livery.

Kelly was standing next to his fellow marshal as the meeting ended. "I don't even want to think how many laws are gonna get broken tonight," he said.

"This isn't about the law anymore," Dalton said. "It's about right and wrong."

* * *

ABERNATHY'S MEN WERE boisterous, almost giddy, as they headed toward town. Their mission was nothing more than a game, and each was eager to play. But as they neared their target, they were surprised by what they encountered. All around the perimeter, men stood in the glow of lanterns placed at their feet, each pointing a rifle.

Even as the ranch hands reined their horses to a stop, several shots broke the night silence, bullets humming over their heads and disappearing into the darkness. "Be advised our aim's better than that," Dalton yelled from his position on the front steps of the building. "Come any closer and we'll gladly prove it."

Torches began falling to the ground and were soon extinguished. Canisters of fuel oil were abandoned. Horses were abruptly turned and were heading south. Behind them, a cheer broke out.

AT THE SHOOTING Star, Colonel Abernathy had fallen into a drunken sleep in his office, snoring loudly and unaware of the activity playing out less than a hundred yards away.

At Sheriff Langston's suggestion, Kelly and his followers had entered the ranch from the east, near the big stand of cottonwoods, and slowly advanced toward the barn. Two of the men had dismounted and gone ahead on foot to check inside. "We've got no cause to kill livestock," the marshal said. "If there's cows or horses inside, quietly lead them out before we arrive."

Nearby, the empty bunkhouse was dark and the only light in the main house came from a flickering lantern located by a window in the Colonel's office. Aside from the normal night sounds, all was quiet until Abernathy's cook was awakened by the splashing of liquid against the barn walls.

By the time she had shaken Abernathy awake, torches had been lit and an orange glow was coming from the barn. Smoke was already climbing into the night sky as the Colonel staggered out to the front porch. He was frozen in place for a moment, then rushed inside to get his pistol. By the time he returned he heard only the distant sound of horses galloping away.

Abernathy could do nothing but watch in stunned silence as his barn was consumed in flames.

The message had been delivered.

DUKE KEENE HAD paced nervously while he awaited everyone's safe return. The guardians of Profer's office were the first back, some expressing disappointment that things had begun and ended so quickly. "They hightailed it out before things even got interesting," one said. "Cowards," said another as he accepted a whiskey bottle that was being passed around.

Shelby Profer was shaking every hand he could find. "Your efforts are greatly appreciated," he said over and over. Dalton told him that a few men had remained at his office on the off chance the arsonists decided to return. "It's not likely, though," he said. "At least not tonight."

It was almost dawn when Kelly and the others returned. "Not a shot fired," he reported. "But the Colonel will be needing to build himself a new barn."

Sheriff Langston watched the celebration in silence. He could only imagine the fury Abernathy would display once his unsuccessful employees returned. Failure, he knew, was not something for which the Colonel had any tolerance.

Aside from money and power, the only thing that drove Raymond Abernathy was revenge, the more ugly and violent the better.

"This," Langston finally whispered to Dalton, "is gonna start a war."

CHAPTER 14

AN UNSETTLING QUIET fell over town in the following days as Dalton's focus returned to finding the
kidnapped child. At his request, Doc Thorndale had
looked in on Mandy and, finding her in a high state of
anxiety, prescribed medication to calm her. Outside
the apartment, guards continued to rotate in shifts.

In his office, Sheriff Langston attempted to give the
impression that he was going about business as usual.
A few drunks had been arrested and jailed and he'd
visited a local farmer who had reported his milk cow
stolen. He also tried to show concern that the whereabouts of escaped prisoner John Rawlings, and now
his son, were still unknown. He'd even announced a
reward to anyone who aided in their return. But he'd
heard nothing from the Colonel.

Aside from wagons arriving in town every few days
to pick up loads of lumber, there was every indication
that all was quiet at the Shooting Star.

"What's the chances of Abernathy telling you where the boy is?" Dalton asked as he entered.

"Not good. My guess is he's already looking for a reason to suspect I had something to do with his barn getting burned. If I start nosing around, it'll lead to no good."

"I've got half a mind to ride out there and put a gun to his head," Ben said. "If he won't tell me what I want to know, I'll just shoot him and be done with all this."

"I doubt you would even make it to the front door. He's already made it clear he wants you killed, and I 'spect he's got everybody working for him on the lookout. Wouldn't surprise me if there's a bounty on your head. He all but offered me one."

W HEN DALTON RETURNED to the livery he found Duke filling saddlebags with staples—jerky, cold biscuits, coffee, sugar, peppermint sticks, and a half-full bottle of whiskey. His horse was already saddled. "Whiskey's for me," he said.

"Where you headed?"

"I'm feeling a bit stove up," Keene said, "so I'm going to take me a ride up to the cabin and check on Lanny and your friend." He was pleased when Ben offered no argument, only a suggestion.

"I think it would be best if you didn't make mention of anything about John's boy . . . or the man Lanny shot dying," he said.

"Wasn't planning on it." There was a sharpness to Keene's reply. He was still not completely over having been excluded from the confrontations earlier in the week. "I may be old and look it," he said, "but my mind ain't yet gone.

"I'd appreciate your seeing to things in my absence. There's another bottle on the shelf in the tool shed, so you shouldn't have any trouble getting some of Profer's boys to come help out."

T HE WARM, FRESH air and winding miles of peace and quiet gave Duke's mood a needed boost. Things that had occurred since Ben Dalton's arrival had gone from bad to worse. And they weren't likely to get better anytime soon. His world, once a grinding routine and staying a safe distance from any trouble, had changed. And he had to admit it wasn't all bad. For once, he was feeling involved in something energizing and worthwhile. His bones still ached when he got up each morning after fitful sleep, his eyesight made his eyeglasses necessary, and the task of lifting bales of hay, something he'd once been able to do all day, had become a challenge, yet he felt more vibrant and alive than he had in ages.

He made his way through a tangle of wild grapevines, forded Kenwood Creek, and rode into a clearing that gave him a good view of the little cabin. "Hello the house," he called out. "Don't be alarmed, I'm bringing provisions . . . and sipping whiskey."

Lanny Butler was first to appear on the porch, waving as the livery owner approached.

"I believe you've growed since I last saw you," Duke said as the smiling young man took the reins of his horse. "Fresh air here must be agreeing with you."

"It sure is good to see you."

"Where's John?

"Down at the creek, fishing."

"He doing okay?"

"Seems to be, but he don't say much. He catches fish, I cook 'em. Every day. Then in the evenings we sit out on the porch for a spell and look up at the stars. We agree that it's another pretty night, then get ready for bed. That's about it."

"It's good you're keeping him company," Duke said.

As he spoke, Rawlings was making his way up the pathway. His beard was now full and bushy, his hair grown down to his shoulders. He was tanned and there seemed to be a slight bounce to his step. He smiled when he saw Duke.

"Nice to have company," he said as he helped with the saddlebags. "I've been hoping to hear news."

On his ride to the cabin, Duke had rehearsed what he would say. "There's still considerable interest in your whereabouts," he said. "Your sneaking away like you did caused the sheriff a good deal of embarrassment. Your friend Ben Dalton told me I should assure you he's still in the process of sorting things out and hopes to soon prove your innocence. He's now got ol' Shelby Profer helping him."

Before Rawlings could ask, he added, "I was also told to pass along that your wife sends her love and looks forward to you coming home soon."

Duke was relieved when Lanny approached and interrupted. "Come on inside and let me fix you something to eat," he said.

"I reckon you're serving catfish, right?" Duke said. His familiar chuckle delighted his host.

For most of the day, Keene managed to dodge

Rawlings' questioning, claiming ignorance of what Dalton might have learned and honestly saying he had not had any direct conversation with Mrs. Rawlings. He did know for a fact that she was unaware of where he was. "Ben tells me that's for her own good," Duke said, "and I can understand that. All he's told her is you're safe and being well taken care of. Being here today, I can attest to that and will report it soon as I get back."

"How much longer do you figure I'll need to stay here?"

"That's not for me to say. I just run the livery and do occasional errands. Too old for much else."

Seeing that he was unlikely to learn more, John ended his questioning. "I need to chop some wood," he said, "so I'll let you go eat your dinner in peace. It's good to have you here."

For much of the remainder of the day, Duke roamed the nearby woods and walked along the creek bank, remembering long-ago days spent there with his brother. "Took me a sentimental journey," he said when he returned to the cabin. "Me and my brother, Jake, had us some good times here when we were still young and full of beans."

When night fell and supper was done, they did exactly as Lanny had predicted, sitting on the porch and looking up at the stars. Concerned that Rawlings might again begin questioning him, Duke took control of what little conversation there was. He was still in a nostalgic state of mind. "There was a time," he said, pointing into the darkness where he knew there was a thick stand of trees, "when we considered building us a still over yonder. Just for our own pleasure, mind you. But that's one of the things we never got around to. Jake fell sick and we didn't come up here as often, then hardly at all. After he passed, I just lost interest in the place. Until today, I didn't realize how much I missed its peacefulness."

With that, he fell silent. So did John and Lanny. Long into the evening, they were content to quietly sip whiskey and look at the stars.

D UKE WAS UP early the next morning, preparing to head back to Fort Worth. "I'll leave you to your fishing," he said as he shook Rawlings' hand. He nodded to Lanny, then gave him a quick hug. "Y'all take care. I'm proud that I'll be able to report back that you're both doing good," he said.

He was already in the saddle when Rawlings handed him an envelope. "Think you can see that my wife gets this?" John said. "I just wanted her to know I'm okay. I didn't mention where I am."

As Keene rode toward home, his thoughts were of fond memories of his late brother and of the two men he'd left behind in the best hiding place he could imagine.

W HERE YOUNG ALTON Rawlings was being hidden was neither peaceful nor pleasant. In a shack behind the isolated roadhouse, he was locked in a small room Luisa usually used for storing bags of corn and flour for making the tamales and tortillas she served to the infrequent customers who stopped in. The boy's makeshift bed was a pile of soiled blankets, his only companion a stray dog that Luisa had recently taken in. The nameless dog would whine and scratch at the storeroom door until she unlocked it and allowed him to enter.

Lately, she had begun allowing it to sleep with the child. And when Alton would cry, as he had done often since the Colonel's men brought him there, the dog would gently lick away his tears.

The only thing Luisa disliked more than children was the responsibility of holding one hostage, but the money the gringo rancher paid her each time he visited wasn't to be ignored. She had never bothered to learn the boy's name.

An obese woman of middle age, she was always chewing on a plug of tobacco and rarely bothered wiping away the brown juice that crusted on the corners of her mouth. A devout Catholic who decorated her own tiny bedroom with cheap paintings of Jesus, she prayed and cursed with equal enthusiasm. She terrified Alton.

Once a day, after any noontime customers had left, she would fill two small plates with tamales and deliver them to the boy and the dog. There would also be a pitcher of water for them to share.

Alton's only escape from the room came when she would lead him on a visit to the outhouse, cursing if he cried for his mother. She had yet to raise a hand to the child, but if things didn't improve soon, that might have to change.

If the boy's distraught mother had known any of this, she would have killed Luisa with her bare hands.

CHAPTER 15

T HE IRREGULAR CADENCE of Ben Dalton's snoring amused Duke. It was late in the day and he'd just returned to find his livery in better shape than he'd left it. The floors were swept clean, troughs filled with clean water, and oat buckets tended to. Dalton was seated on a hay bale, his back to the gate of Dolly's freshly mucked stall, hat pulled down on his face. Keene waited a few minutes before he spoke. "If you're guarding this place," he said, "you ain't exactly doing a bang-up job."

Dalton grunted and quickly got to his feet. "Everything okay at the cabin?"

"Except for eating catfish for breakfast they seem to be doing fine." After he'd had his chuckle, he provided Ben a detailed account of his brief visit. "All I can say about Lanny is he's highly bored and wanting to come home," he said. "Physically, John Rawlings looks really good, and he seems to have all his wits about him. If I have any worry at all, it's how much longer we can

keep him there before he demands to come visit his
family. He's getting lonesome. He sent a letter to his
wife."

"You didn't mention anything about . . ."

Keene turned and started removing his horse's
saddle before the question was even finished. "I'm going to cook up some chili to see if I can get the fish
taste out of my mouth," he said. "You hungry after
your nap?"

Dalton was about to tell him it was the first sleep
he'd had in two days when a shot was fired.

Keene hurried into a vacant stall and Dalton knelt
behind the hay bale he'd been sitting on.

"Come out and show yourself," a slurred voice from
the street called. "I'm here to kill you, Ben Dalton, so
we just as well get it over with." The words were loud
but slurred.

"He's drunk," Ben said.

"He's also shooting at us," Duke replied.

Already drawing a crowd, the cowboy the Colonel
had earlier assigned to keep watch on Dalton stood
with his legs wide apart. Still, he swayed as he struggled for balance. He fired another shot that ricocheted
off Duke's new door and into the loft floor. "I'm not
leaving until I kill you dead," he said, "and then I'm
going to get my pay for doing it."

The next voice they heard was that of Sheriff Langston, urging onlookers to go home or take cover inside
one of the nearby shops. Then he called out a warning
to the shooter. "Holster your gun," he said, "or I'll be
forced to do something I don't want to."

The cowboy waved his pistol in the sheriff's direction and started cursing. "I've got me a job to do," he

said, "and I ain't waiting any longer to get it done." He turned and fired another shot toward the doorway to the livery.

Sheriff Langston, his gun drawn, began slowly walking toward the shooter. "Unlike you, I'm sober as a judge," he said, "so my aim's a lot better. The law says I've got every right to shoot you, but I don't want to do that." His voice was calm yet forceful.

For a moment, the drunk cowboy stood silently, weighing his choices, then slowly let his gun fall to the ground, where it made a small puff of dust as it landed. A deputy who had just arrived took him into custody and led him off to jail.

Langston rushed into the shadowy livery. "Everybody in here okay?" he said.

Keene stood up and looked out from his hiding place, and Dalton walked toward the sheriff. His hand was extended. "That," he said, "was as righteous a display of what a good lawman's supposed to be as I've seen in a long time," he said. "I was impressed."

Duke disagreed. "I was wishing you woulda killed the fool," he said.

Dalton and Langston smiled and shook hands.

"What are you going to do with him?" Ben asked.

"I'll wait until he's sobered up, then send him out to tell Colonel Abernathy that no one from his ranch is welcome any longer in our saloons."

Dalton gave him a nod of approval. "Can you legally do that?" he said.

"I reckon we'll see." He turned to leave but after a few steps stopped and turned back to Dalton. "I told you there was a bounty being offered, didn't I?"

"That you did . . . Sheriff."

* * *

T HERE WAS AN expectant look on Mandy Rawlings'
face as she swung open the door, hoping to see
that her son was being returned. The light disappeared
from her eyes when she saw Ben standing alone in the
hallway.

"We're still looking," he said. "We're going to
find him."

"I'm sorry for making you stand there. Come in,"
she said. "I heard there was some shooting downtown.
You okay?"

"Just some drunk blowing off steam."

He held the envelope out to her. "I was asked to
deliver this from John. Like I've mentioned before,
he's been told that you can't know where he is, but I
can assure you he's safe and doing well."

She walked to the sofa and sat, her hands trembling
as she opened the letter.

"I'll leave you to it," Dalton said, suddenly feeling
he was intruding.

"No," she said, "stay for a bit. Just let me read this,
and then I'd like to talk for a while."

She immediately recognized her husband's handwriting and put one hand to her mouth, muffling a sob
as she read:

My Dearest Mandy,
There are no words to express how much I miss you
and little Alton, so I'll just use this letter to tell you I am
feeling fine and hope to be home very soon. For your
safety, I can't tell you where I am, but know it is quiet
and peaceful here. It would be wonderful if you could
be here with me.

Hiding out like this makes me feel like a criminal at times, but I assure you I'm not. I am innocent of what happened to Thomas Cookson.

If you see Ben, please tell him how much I appreciate everything he has done. He's a good man and will help you with anything you need in my absence. You only have to ask. He is the best friend I've ever had and I credit him with saving my life.

There were a lot of things I wanted to say when I sat down to write this, but now the only thing that is really important is that you know I love you very much.

Your husband, John

P.S.—To pass the time I have been doing a lot of reading. Great Expectations *by Charles Dickens is a very interesting book. I suggest the next time you visit the library you borrow it. You might also recommend it to Ben and my old friend Shelby Profer.*

M ANDY WIPED TEARS from the corners of her eyes and looked across the room at Dalton. "He says he's okay," she said, folding the single piece of paper and returning it to the envelope. Ben was relieved that she hadn't offered it to him to read.

She patted a space on the sofa beside her. "Come and sit for a minute before you go. I've been thinking a lot about the times back when we were kids, you and John and me," she said. "Life was so good then, so sweet and simple. And now look at us, things all crazy and ugly. I just can't understand it."

She looked at her lap and idly twirled her husband's letter as she spoke. "There's one thing about what he wrote that puzzles me. He says he's been doing a lot of reading. I've never known him to even look at a book that didn't have something to do with the law.

"Now, suddenly, he's suggesting I look for *Great Expectations* the next time I go to the library. I read it months ago and returned it. Oh, and he said you and Mr. Profer might also find it an interesting read.

"That's not the John Rawlings I know."

W HEN DALTON RETURNED, Shelby Profer's buggy was parked outside the livery. One of the cowboys helping watch his office had driven him over so he could learn what the earlier shooting had been about. Ben explained what had happened, then told the attorney about Keene's visit to the cabin. "In fact, I just delivered a letter from John to his wife," he said. "He even mentioned you in it. Something about a book he thinks you should read." It took him a moment to recall the title and author.

"*Great Expectations?* Charles Dickens?" Profer said as he slowly twirled his cane. "I'm going to need to see that letter," he said. "I think young John may be trying to tell us something."

CHAPTER 16

THE ELDERLY LIBRARIAN peered at them over wire-rimmed glasses, a forced smile on her face. One of the men didn't impress her as someone likely to spend much time in search of a book. The old man, on the other hand, looked and sounded well-educated. She was surprised that he hadn't already read *Great Expectations*.

She led them toward the fiction section and the row of books whose authors' last names began with D.

"Dickens . . . Charles Dickens . . . Mis-ter Dickens," she said to herself as her finger passed along the leather spines. "I'm sure we have it. It's not one of our more popular titles, mind you, but it does occasionally get borrowed." She returned to her desk and looked through files. "Nope, it's not out. It must have been put on the wrong shelf."

The two men watched as she frittered about, humming to herself as she happily searched.

"Found it," she finally called out as she hurried

back to them, clutching the book to her breast. "Who on earth could have put it in the section for family histories? Such carelessness is embarrassing."

"I'd like to borrow it if I may," Profer said, showing her a card that identified him as a member of the Fort Worth Lawyers Association.

He waited until he and Ben were outside before he opened the book and began flipping through it. Halfway through the three hundred pages were several loose papers that fell out and fluttered to the sidewalk. Dalton collected them and handed them to Profer.

As the lawyer read, a smile broke across his face and he began to nod. "This is what it's all about," he said, "what someone has been willing to kill for. These are the notes Thomas Cookson gave to Rawlings for safekeeping. I told you he was a bright young man, didn't I?

"John hid them in the library of all places."

I T HAD BEGUN like this:
     John Rawlings was surprised when Thomas Cookson appeared in his office that afternoon, shortly after the bank had closed for the day. The young lawyer had his account at Fort Worth Bank & Trust but had met the owner and president only once. Cookson had appeared from his office just long enough to shake his hand the first time he made a deposit and thank him for choosing to do business with his institution.

Short and portly, Cookson hardly looked like a man with great expertise in financial matters. His suit, though obviously expensive and well tailored, seemed always wrinkled and fit a bit too snugly. Though almost bald, he refused to wear a hat. The constant smile he had for his customers seemed genuine, though there was always a slight hint that his thoughts were elsewhere. All in all, however, he was viewed as a pillar of the community and more than once it had been suggested that he consider running for public office. And each time the subject came up, Cookson would laugh and say he was busy enough, thank you, seeing to the financial needs and well-being of the farmers, ranchers, and business owners who patronized his bank.

On the day he visited Rawlings there was no smile on his face.

"There is a somewhat delicate matter I wish to discuss," he said, "and I'd prefer to do it in the privacy of my own home. Could I persuade you to come to the house this evening, perhaps after you've had your supper? Bring whatever papers you need me to sign to officially become a client and I'll write you a check."

To a lawyer, the last sentence included the magic words. They agreed to continue their conversation at eight o'clock and the banker quickly exited the office.

That evening, after he and Mandy had put their son to bed, John went to the Cookson residence, where Thomas' wife cheerfully greeted him at the front door and escorted him to her husband's home office.

"Close the door, please," Cookson said. "I keep few secrets from my wife, but this is a matter I don't wish her to worry over." He poured his visitor a glass of brandy and, after being assured their conversation would not leave the room, went straight to the matter he wished to discuss.

For the next hour, he described a problem that had been aggravating his ulcer and robbing him of sleep. "I consider myself an honest and law-abiding man," he

began, "but I fear I may have stepped beyond a line I
don't want to cross. To have done so goes against all I
believe in, but the safety of the lady who just ushered
you in is at stake, and her well-being is my foremost
concern.

"After coming to the conclusion that I needed counsel
and deciding today to speak with a lawyer, I chose you."

Rawlings took a sip of his brandy but said nothing.

"So that all of our cards are on the table, I should
say that you are hardly the first man I would have chosen under more normal circumstances. I know of your
dealings with some of the, shall we say, less reputable
of our citizens. On one hand, I don't approve of the
career path you seem to have chosen, despite the fact I
see you have done quite well for yourself. On the
other—and this is of greater importance to me at the
moment—you are clearly an aggressive and fearless attorney, one who seems to have accumulated considerable knowledge of undesirable individuals and the way
they think. That, Mr. Rawlings, is why I've asked you
here tonight.

"I have come in contact with a grossly undesirable
man who now threatens everything I hold sacred."

Far from comfortable with the shaded compliment
he had just been given, John leaned forward and
cleared his throat. "Do you want to tell me who this
person is?"

"He is Colonel Raymond Abernathy, a local rancher
of considerable means. He's a customer at my bank.
My largest depositor, in fact. There was a time when I
was so enamored of his financial success that I welcomed him as a shareholder and even offered him a
place on our board of directors."

Cookson sighed deeply and rubbed his temple before continuing. "In time, I began to hear rumors that, I'm embarrassed to admit, I chose to disregard. We're all, in one way or another, greedy people, Mr. Rawlings, and I allowed it to blind me to the truth."

He told of suspicions that the rapid growth of Abernathy's herd was due to his stealing cattle that belonged to others. Cookson had personally signed off on land transactions that were troubling. Too often, small farmers had sold their property to the Colonel for far less than it was worth. But if people were being forced from their homes, none said so.

"It's sad to say that ignorance is, indeed, bliss," he said.

"He was doing the same thing with some of the local businesses, particularly those down in Hell's Half Acre. A shop owner would begin to struggle to make payments on his loan—a situation I sometimes helped create—and soon had sold out to Abernathy. It seemed he was trying to own everything in sight.

"But I guess things weren't moving fast enough to suit him. You learn in my business, Mr. Rawlings, that greed too often begets greed. I'm guessing you've experienced a taste of that yourself.

"At any rate, that's when the Colonel paid a visit to my office. He was quite friendly at first, saying all the right things about the economic future of the city and how he wanted to do his part. It seemed a fair enough reason for his purchases. Or at least one I could deal with.

"But on later visits, he began outlining a plan: There were those too stubborn to hear him out and give up their farm or grocery or whatever. There was a way, he suggested, that they could be convinced to reconsider their position.

"That's when he mentioned the idea that the bank increase interest rates on loans to a level that would be impossible to pay. Bankruptcy would be the next step, that or selling out cheap to the Colonel.

"I reluctantly carried out his plan a couple of times but felt terrible about it. Thus, I later made it clear to him that not only would I no longer consider such actions but that, in all likelihood, they would be in violation of any number of state and federal banking regulations. Basically, I threw him out of my office.

"The next time he came back, he had several of his men with him, including our fine Sheriff Langston. In retrospect, it was to make sure I was aware that he had muscle as well as high-ranking city officials in his corner. He came in, all smiles, and said he just wanted to know if I had reconsidered my position.

"I told him I hadn't and he quickly left. Foolishly, I thought it was over.

"He waited a couple of days before returning earlier this week. He talked about what a nice house I had, how pretty my wife was, what a good life we were living—and what a shame it would be if all that were to suddenly end. It was a threat, pure and simple."

Cookson fell silent, leaning back in his chair and locking his chubby fingers together, waiting for the lawyer to respond. When Rawlings said nothing, he continued.

"I had one of my clerks pull our records of Abernathy's financial dealings," he said, "and I think they clearly show he has dealt unfairly with a number of people. Whether it rises to the level of criminal activity is for someone like you to say. But even if it could be proved, I don't know what I can do."

Neither did Rawlings, in light of the fact that the Colonel and local law enforcement were obviously on a friendly basis.

John knew Cookson expected a response, so he got to his feet and began pacing around the room, thinking. "As I see it," he finally said, "your primary concern is keeping your wife and home safe and protecting the integrity of your bank. To do the latter, you need to find a way to avoid being accused of any illegal activity."

"Exactly."

Rawlings shook his head and continued. "What you need is a way to protect yourself, something that will give Colonel Abernathy reason to back away. It's pretty clear there's no use alerting Sheriff Langston to your concerns. A judge would do nothing without proof. I've never dealt with banking authorities or federal law enforcement, but I'm afraid anything they could do would take forever and a day."

For the first time, Cookson's voice was shrill, pleading. "Then what can I do?"

"I need to sleep on it," John said. "And I'll try to have an answer for you when you come by my office in the morning."

He walked into the cool of the spring evening, contemplating the bank owner's dilemma. It was complicated, potentially a matter of life and death if the Colonel's threats were to be taken seriously. He'd never dealt with anything similar before and was frustrated in the knowledge that he had no good answer.

John knew that once home he would get little sleep.

* * *

WHEN HE ARRIVED at his office the following morning, Thomas Cookson was waiting. "I hope you got more sleep than I did," he said.

"Not much. Come in."

The banker didn't even bother to sit. Neither did Rawlings.

"I think it would be a good idea," he said, "for you to put everything you told me last night in writing. Then give it to me for safekeeping and, if Abernathy continues to bother you, tell him what you've done and warn him that you'll see it made public if necessary."

"Aren't you concerned that telling him might put you in jeopardy as well?"

"That's what lawyers do," John boasted with a strained laugh. "Of course, it might be wise at this stage if you didn't reveal the name of your attorney."

Shortly after Cookson delivered the detailed document and copies of the Colonel's financial records, there was yet another confrontation in the banker's office. Abernathy's patience had disappeared as he cursed and jabbed a demanding finger at the banker's chest. The shouting could be heard all the way into the bank lobby.

When Cookson told him what he had done on advice of counsel, Abernathy stormed out, yelling a threat over his shoulder. "This isn't over," he said, shoving a customer from his path.

Two days later, Rawlings had found the note on his door, asking that he visit his client immediately. When he arrived, Thomas Cookson was dead.

Hurrying back to the apartment, he barely had time

to hide the pages in a book Mandy had set aside to return to the library before he was arrested and taken to jail.

A LL THIS IS finally beginning to make sense," Shelby Profer said as he folded the notes and stuffed them inside his jacket. "Thomas Cookson got himself killed because he wouldn't give up the notes he'd written. Rawlings was blamed for the murder once they figured out that he had the incriminating information. When he went to jail and very nearly died without telling where it was, they next decided that by kidnapping the youngster they could get somebody, maybe even Mrs. Rawlings, to tell them what they wanted to know."

"Where does it end?" Ben said.

"I haven't the slightest idea," Profer said as he turned to go back inside.

"Ma'am," he said to the librarian, "I've changed my mind and wish to return your book. As a man who genuinely admires the adventurous plots of dime novels, I fear Charles Dickens might be a bit too dense for my taste."

CHAPTER 17

THE RAISING OF the new barn at the Shooting Star was progressing swiftly, but Colonel Abernathy showed scant interest. Most days he sat alone in his office, brooding, drinking, and talking to himself. The recent string of mishaps and shortcomings, coupled with the growing resistance of the townspeople, gnawed at him.

If he didn't soon get his hands on Thomas Cookson's damaging exposé of his business dealings, all he had worked for could be destroyed. No effort—threats, bribery, arson, murder, and now kidnapping—had proved effective. He realized that the growing list of crimes he had orchestrated were enough to put him behind bars for the rest of his life.

As he viewed the situation through the bottom of his tequila glass, he saw nothing but dismal failure from those he had assigned the task of protecting him and his fortune. His inept hired hands had failed him; so had the sheriff. And the troublesome banker.

Abernathy's mood was more dark and foul than usual when Raff Bailey entered his office to admit his recent foolish behavior. "I got myself drunk and fired some shots at the livery," he said. "Nobody got hurt, but the sheriff said I was to tell you we're all now barred from setting foot in any Half Acre saloon."

The tipsy Colonel was on his feet, preparing to take a swing at him, when Bailey quickly pulled two torn pieces of paper from his hip pocket and laid them on the desk. "Sheriff Langston also said to tell you that he's arranged for an exchange," he said.

Abernathy fell back into his chair, put on his glasses, and slowly read the pieces of paper. One was the top of the first page the banker had written, describing his belief that the Shooting Star's herd had been built on cattle rustling and shady dealings at the local stock pens. The other was the bottom half of a final page where Cookson wrote that he had financial documents proving his claims and was willing to swear everything he had written was the truth. His signature was attached.

The Colonel cursed under his breath. He didn't have to guess what had been written on the missing pages.

Bailey, still feeling the effects of his daylong bout with cheap rye, struggled to remember everything he'd been told to say.

"You are to deliver the boy to the front steps of St. John's Catholic. If he is unharmed and there is no shooting, you will get what it is you're wanting and can ride away free."

"And when is this to take place?"

"Noon Sunday, just as church services let out."

"They're wanting to do it in front of as many witnesses as possible," Abernathy said. "I assume you're to report my response."

Bailey nodded. "As quick as you have an answer."

"Tell them the boy will be delivered," the Colonel said.

THE PLAN WAS Dalton's and at first Profer had balked. "We'll lose all of our leverage," he argued. "Giving up the details Cookson's notes have provided us lets Abernathy go scot free. I absolutely forbid it. It's totally foolish and in no way addresses the demand for justice in this matter."

"I've always been a first-things-first kind of thinker," the marshal said in a calming voice. "If there's a way to see that little boy back home safe with his mama, to get the Rawlings family back together, I say we've got an obligation to do it. Then we can get back to figuring out how to deal with Colonel Abernathy. I promise you, he'll still pay for what he's done. I just can't tell you exactly how or when. What I can promise is I'm not leaving until it happens."

"Okay, okay," the old lawyer finally said, "we'll see to first things first."

THE CHURCH BELLS were chiming as members of the congregation exited into the sunlight, shaking hands with the priest and chatting noisily among themselves. Children dressed in their Sunday best rushed away to play for a few minutes before heading home. For most in the crowd, the only thing to anticipate was

Sunday dinner and afternoon naps. Along the edges of the sidewalk, however, were a number of men who had neither heard the sermon nor joined in the singing. They had been summoned to their posts by Shelby Profer, who sat nearby in his buggy. Other guards mingled with the crowd while Dalton and Anson Kelly stood on the steps, shoulder to shoulder with Mandy. Sheriff Langston was alone, watching intently from the shade of a grape arbor.

Though the day was warm, Mandy began to shiver as she watched a half-dozen horses slowly approach.

Dalton squinted in their direction and was pleased to see a small child riding in front of the man who had earlier fired shots into the livery. Mandy, too, recognized the small figure and gripped Ben's hand. As the riders got closer, he recognized several of the horsemen as Shooting Star cowboys he'd seen from time to time in Half Acre saloons. Colonel Abernathy, however, was not among them.

"Too cowardly to show his face," Kelly whispered. "That, or he feared being arrested. Or shot."

Profer was stepping from his buggy, a satchel under his arm, as Raff Bailey gently lifted the child from the saddle and helped him to the ground. Still wearing the same clothes he'd had on when he was taken, he had a frightened look on his face when he saw the large crowd. Then he began to smile and threw out his arms as he heard his mother's voice and saw her running toward him.

As she lifted Alton into her arms, both were crying.

Profer approached Bailey and handed him the satchel. "I was hoping your boss would come for this himself, so I could give him a message," the attorney said.

"I'll pass it along," Bailey said as he looked inside to be sure it contained what the Colonel was expecting.

"Fine, fine. You can tell him that in my eighty-eight years I've never seen a more cowardly act than him taking this child from his mother. There's a special place in hell for men of his kind, and I'll make it my final mission in life to see he gets there. I'd appreciate you passing that along, if you'll be so kind."

As the cowboys rode away toward the ranch, the churchgoers began to crowd around, at first silently watching the moving mother-son reunion, then bursting into applause. "This," Mandy whispered to Dalton, "is the miracle I've prayed so hard for. Thank you. Thank you all." Ben gently placed an arm across her shoulders and reached out to touch Alton's hand.

Nearby, the dog that had befriended the child lay in the grass, panting. He had followed along from Luisa's roadhouse and was exhausted. Alton, still in his mother's arms, reached out for him. "They appear to be friends," Dalton said. "I'll take him back to the livery and see he gets fresh water and something to eat." For a moment he found himself thinking of Poncho back on the farm.

People had begun to disperse when another group of riders approached. Three men soon joined the celebration: Duke Keene, Lanny Butler, and a clean-shaven, wide-smiling John Rawlings. Duke had traveled to the cabin and alerted the others that there was no longer a need to hide.

Dalton shook John's hand, then watched as he and his wife embraced. Alton then climbed into his daddy's arms.

Shelby Profer was standing near his buggy, watching, as Dalton approached. "You were right," the law-yer said, "and I admire your wisdom. First things first. I'll remember that." He slapped Ben on the back. "To be honest, I can't recall the last time I felt this good."

The dog joined them, wagging his tail as Dalton knelt to stroke his fur. "I'm feeling pretty good my-self," he said.

"We should embrace this joyous occasion," Profer said as he climbed into his buggy, "but there is still much to be done."

At the Shooting Star, where the Colonel read the papers Bailey had delivered to him, then hurled them across the room, there was little evidence of joy.

D ALTON WAS GROOMING Dolly and talking with An-son Kelly when Rawlings entered the livery. He had his son in his arms. It had been three days since the events in the churchyard.

"Alton's been asking about 'his' dog," John said, "so I thought we'd best come pay a visit."

Dalton whistled and the dog appeared from Dolly's stall, where he'd been sleeping since his arrival. His ears pointed upward, his brown eyes were bright, and he had obviously been bathed. When he saw the boy, he gave out a single bark and hurried toward him. He was licking Alton's smiling face even before the young-ster's feet reached the ground.

"How's everybody doing?" Ben asked as he watched them play.

"Adjusting," John said. "The little one has some nightmares, so he's been sleeping with Mandy and me. But he's getting better, happy to be home. Mandy, she still cries some, though she can't explain why. Says she's just happy we're a family again. So am I."

He said that his wife would be inviting Ben over for dinner as soon as things have settled. "She wants everyone to come—you, Duke, Lanny, Mr. Profer . . ." He glanced over at Marshal Kelly and smiled. "You'll be invited, as well."

"You might suggest she not plan on cooking catfish," Kelly said. "If she does, I seriously doubt Duke will be able to make it."

John laughed, then turned serious. "The real reason I'm here, Ben, is to tell you how much I appreciate everything you've done for us. Putting it in the proper words is impossible, but I owe you a debt I can't possibly ever repay, for your help and a lifetime of being a good friend."

Dalton quickly turned his attention to Alton, kneeling next to him to scratch behind the dog's ears. "I realize he's your friend, and you're welcome to come visit him anytime you want," he told the boy, "but since I couldn't just keep calling him 'dog,' I gave him a name."

"What?" Alton said.

"I call him Too."

John interrupted. "Too?"

"Yep," Ben said, "he's now known as Poncho Too."

CHAPTER 18

"IT's YOU SHOULD be getting thanked," Ben said to Anson Kelly as the two sat on the edge of a narrow stream, watching their horses drink. With Duke and Lanny busy mending the broken axle of a farmer's hay wagon, they had decided to take a pleasure ride into the countryside. "You come up to Fort Worth at the request of a total stranger, asking nothing more than a bed to sleep on and a few bowls of Keene's chili, and find yourself involved in all this."

Kelly was no more comfortable receiving plaudits than Dalton. "Hey, you gave me good reason to get myself shed of crazy ol' Dee Wayne Barclay," he said. "That's payment aplenty. And the fact is I don't see your pockets getting any fuller either."

They sat watching the water rush past, occasionally tossing pebbles at a turtle sunning on a fallen log. Too, who had accompanied them, was busy upstream, frantically pawing at an armadillo den.

It occurred to Dalton that he knew little about the

man he'd reached out to for help. "What was it caused you to want to be a lawman?" he said.

"Needed work when I got home from the war."

Dalton shook his head. "Naw, there's a lot of ways to earn more than a marshal's pay," he said.

"My pa was the Brush Creek marshal before me. In his day, things were a bit more exciting than breaking up an occasional bar fight," Kelly said. "Back then, the Comanches were raiding farms, highwaymen were robbing innocent folks and needed to be chased down, and every now and then there would be a shooting. We once had a stagecoach robbed no more than thirty minutes after it left town. My pa solved it pretty quick when he learned the robbers were actually two half-wit farm boys he knew. They'd just swiped their daddy's shotgun, climbed on their mules, hid their faces with kerchiefs, and set out one day to be bandits.

"Papa was a good man and a fine marshal, tougher than nails but fair as the day's long. He had folks' respect. As I was growing up, watching him, wanting to be like him, that's what most impressed me—the respect he got; the respect he worked hard every day to earn. I made up my mind that was what I wanted. No amount of end-of-the-month wages can buy a man that.

"It's too bad Sheriff Langston lost sight of that," he said.

"I think maybe he's trying to find a way to set things right."

Kelly fell silent for a minute, tossing another pebble. "I'm guessing you get respect from your people back in Aberdene."

"Hope so," Dalton said.

"I got no business bringing it up, but since we're having this conversation, it seems to me you must have a powerful good reason for leaving that behind to come up here and involve yourself in this ugly business. I'm guessing there's strong feelings that must have called out to you."

Ben quickly changed the subject. "Is your pa still living?"

"Ten days before the war ended and I was to be heading home," Kelly said, "he fell dead on the porch one morning as he was leaving for work. The doc said his heart just gave out on him. Mama waited to have him buried until I could get back."

"So you lost your daddy and got his badge," Ben said as he got to his feet and pulled a knotted bandanna from his saddle horn. Inside it were a half-dozen cold biscuits they shared, and for a while the morning quiet was interrupted only by the soft sound of rushing water and Too's distant barking.

T HEY WERE WELL on their way back to the livery before the subject on both men's minds was brought up.

"You realize," Kelly said, "this Colonel fellow isn't going to quit, don't you?" The observation needed no reply from Dalton. "What's been done to him is the worst thing that can happen to a man short of being broke or shot dead. I expect his pride's worth more to him than all the cows he's got on his ranch, or money he has in the bank, and it has been sorely damaged. Only way he can get it restored is by fighting back."

"What do you expect he'll do?"

"If I was to guess, he'll be coming after you since you're who came to town and stirred things up."

Dalton had already considered the possibility, but hearing it from someone else added a new level to his concern. He needed a way to confront Abernathy and bring things to an end, without getting any of his friends hurt in the process. Doing so, he had already decided, would force him to become the aggressor.

"I find him particularly dangerous," Kelly added, "because of his being such a cowardly man. He may pose as a bully, even talk a big game, but he's not likely to confront you man-to-man. His sort sends others to fight their battles. And that, as I'm sure you know, will make it more difficult to recognize your enemy."

Weary from his digging earlier, Too lay limp across the front of Dalton's saddle, peacefully snoring to the rhythm of Dolly's steady gait. "Since it comes down to that," Ben said, "it might be just as well if you head on back to Brush Creek. You've already done more than was asked."

Kelly didn't even look over as he replied, "I'm staying to see it ended."

Ben smiled. "I've got to respect that," he said.

RAYMOND ABERNATHY, MEANWHILE, was taking stock of his situation. He'd stopped drinking as much in the evenings and would leave the main house early each morning to ride the fences of the Shooting Star. Clearheaded and alone with his thoughts, he weighed his pluses and minuses.

His massive ranch was still intact and money was

certainly no problem. The barn had been rebuilt, better than before, and the fact that he had finally recovered and destroyed the affidavit Thomas Cookson had written relieved him of any immediate worry that he might be charged with any crime.

On balance, things seemed good—until he began to mentally list those things that kept him awake nights. Mostly, they were people who had recently entered his life, spoiling plans and refusing to show proper respect for his hard-won power and position. As he rode, he would spit their names like curses: the stranger named Ben Dalton, the old lawyer Shelby Profer, and the young one, John Rawlings. These men had managed to turn the entire town against him. He was no longer feared and respected. The few businesses he had taken ownership of in Hell's Half Acre were virtually without customers and he had considered burning them to the ground. Shop owners who had once routinely paid for protection were keeping their money in their pockets. And there was the group of young men in town who had banded together like soldiers, standing guard and burning his barn. Also, he'd become certain that Sheriff Langston, though he pretended otherwise, was betraying him.

He counted too many minuses, too many enemies.

To turn away the rebellion, he needed to do something that would restore his image and return fear to the hearts of the townspeople. By nature an impulsive and impatient man, he vowed to take his time planning what he would do next. Whatever the route back to his glory days would take, it would likely be as bloody and violent as anything he had encountered in wartime.

"That's my God's honest promise," he said to

himself as he spurred his horse through a verdant pasture of grazing Longhorns.

I T HAD BEEN almost two weeks since any of the Shooting Star crew was seen in town. With the new barn completed, no wagons arrived at the lumberyard, and the cowboys seemed to have taken the sheriff's ban on their patronizing the saloons seriously. Not a single employee of the Colonel's was locked away in Langston's jail.

Things seemed to have returned to normal as people went about their daily lives, shopping, attending socials and prayer meetings, and allowing their children to play in the park after school let out. In the minds of most, the reign of Colonel Abernathy had ended that Sunday morning in front of St. John's Catholic when the Rawlings boy was safely returned.

Lawyer Profer was even having difficulty convincing the young men he'd hired that any new danger might be on the horizon and kept them alert only by promising higher wages. At the livery, business had returned to a steady pace.

When Mandy Rawlings hosted her promised supper, it was Duke Keene who was the first to voice his concern. "This," he said, "feels like that calm before the next storm. I know Abernathy's planning something no good. You can make a bet on it. And here we sit, eating this fine roast beef and these tasty mashed potatoes, just waiting."

He was saying what everyone seated at the table was thinking.

"Could be he's finally gotten the message to stay

away and leave folks alone," John said. His attempt at optimism fell on deaf ears and he waited until Mandy left the room to check on Alton before finishing his thought. "If it was left up to me, I'd like to see the man dead and buried. What he did to my son, to me and my family, isn't something I can just forgive and forget."

"Nor should you," Profer said. "Nor should any of us."

The conversation ended and the mood lightened as Mandy returned to the dining room with Alton at her side, dressed in his pajamas and holding a favorite stuffed animal. "He wants to tell everyone good night," she said.

As the little boy hugged his father before heading off to bed, Ben Dalton watched and forced a slight smile. The look on his face didn't escape Anson Kelly, who was seated beside him.

"I'll be serving pie as soon as I get this little guy tucked in," Mandy told her guests.

A T THE SHOOTING Star, Colonel Abernathy was sitting alone in his office, the only light coming from the red glow of his cigar. He was again mentally going through his checklist. His revenge plan, he'd begun privately calling it.

He had turned the ranch into a virtual fortress. Half of the beds in the bunkhouse were empty as his men were ordered to alternate shifts, standing day and night guard around the perimeter. One wrangler was positioned in the loft of the barn, sweeping the horizon with a spyglass. A new gate and guardhouse had been built at the entrance. The Colonel kept his rifle within reach and had begun wearing his pearl-handled side-arm anytime he ventured from the house.

As the days passed, his mounting anger increasingly focused on Ben Dalton. For reasons that still weren't clear to him, this outsider had become the driving force of those in town who had chosen to declare war against him. All logic suggested that if Dalton disappeared, the other troublemakers would soon fade away.

Logic, however, was no longer in the Colonel's grasp. He would summon his ranch hands to a meeting after breakfast and lay out his plan.

The best way to inflict pain on his enemy, he had decided, would be to first harm those around him. He would save Dalton for last—and deal with him person-ally.

CHAPTER 19

LANNY BUTLER WAS still haunted by that night in the alley. Only after he returned from the cabin and overheard a conversation between Duke and one of his customers did he learn that Dexter Wilson had died. And with that knowledge, the nightmares returned, the roar of the shotgun blast and the smell of gunpowder and smoke, and then the cold darkness as he fled.

Now, he rarely left the livery, even to visit the food stand and chat with the lady who owned it. Staying busy was his only escape. Even when the stalls were clean and filled with fresh hay, he cleaned them again. He arranged, then rearranged Duke's tools. He made sure a fire was kept and fresh coffee brewed throughout the day. And though he continued to believe he had done the right thing that night, the act of taking another person's life, even to save others, was rarely out of his thoughts.

One night, as another bad dream played out, he was jolted awake by the restless braying of Keene's mule out in the corral. Slipping into his pants and boots, he went out to check. The full moon was bright and high in the sky, so he knew it must be well past midnight when he saw the solitary figure sitting atop the fence railing. Silently moving closer, he realized it was his boss.

"You okay, Mr. Keene?" he said, moving out of the shadows.

For a moment, Duke seemed not to hear him, then turned and waved him over. "Come and sit," he said. "It's a fine night."

"What are you doing up so late?"

"I'm having trouble sleeping. It comes with age. Come on up and sit. I'm tired of trying to have me a conversation with this ol' mule."

Lanny pulled himself up onto the fence. For a while they silently sat side by side, admiring the white moon and breathing in the fresh night air.

"I know you're bothered, boy," Keene finally said. "You've had something on your mind for a good while and I'm wondering if maybe it's time we talk about it. Though there's some who won't agree, I can be a pretty good listener."

"Duke, I'm fine."

Keene chuckled and said, "Oh, yeah, you're fine and folks are always referring to me as the most handsome man in all of Fort Worth. Lying won't do neither one of us any good, son. Won't make things right. I've been watching you mope around with that hangdog look on your face. I was hoping maybe that visit up to the cabin would help, but you came back the same as you was when you left. What can I do to help?"

There was a long silence before Lanny spoke. "You ever kill anybody, even if it wasn't on purpose?"

For a few moments, nothing was said until the young man slowly walked toward the livery. Duke called out to him. "I never answered your question," he said.

Lanny turned and looked back.

"Once," Duke said. "I was even younger than you. Just a boy. My daddy was a hard-drinking man, a mean and hateful drunk. He beat up on my mama something fierce, and I got tired of watching it. One night he knocked her against the wall—she was crying and bleeding bad from her mouth—so I picked up his Peacemaker that was laying on the kitchen table. And I shot him. Killed him.

"To this day I can still see it all in my mind, him laying on the floor, his dead eyes open, and hear Mama crying. A thing like that you never forget. You just find a way to make your peace with it.

"So now you know my secret. And I'll thank you to keep it between you and me."

A S USUAL, JULY arrived in Fort Worth with a vengeance. However, despite the wilting gardens, dusty streets, and temperature near one hundred degrees, there was always an atmosphere of excitement as townspeople looked ahead to the annual Saturday Summer Festival. The men would barbecue, the women would bake, and the children would anticipate wearing themselves out playing games and running races. When it got dark and a cooling breeze would finally arrive, there would be fiddle music and dancing.

"This will be the first festival that Alton will really enjoy," Mandy told her husband as she rolled dough for the pies she would take. "Instead of just sitting and watching the other children, he's old enough to run and play with them."

Even over in Hell's Half Acre there was a feeling of anticipation. Saloonkeepers stocked extra kegs of beer, the little cafés added special items to their menus, and B. J. Wong promised to take on all comers in a boxing exhibition to be held in memory of Brent St. John. His earnings would be donated to pay for a headstone for his friend's grave. Young cowboys could get wildly drunk without worrying that they would be hauled off to jail, since Sheriff Langston had instructed his deputies to ignore everything but gunfire and stealing.

If one's intent was only to celebrate with eating, drinking, and into-the-night card games, he could expect no trouble from the law.

In the livery, Duke was giving Lanny a haircut. "Might find you a gal willing to do some dancing if you look presentable," he said. Nearby, a pot of his chili was almost done. Only at his insistence had Dalton and Kelly agreed to look in on the festivities. "Even old man Profer says he's coming, and I don't ever recall him showing up at the Summer Festival before."

It would, indeed, be the largest attendance in the event's history. Farm families came from miles around, businesses closed so their employees could join the celebration, and volunteer wagons delivered the elderly to a special tent erected for them on the edge of the park.

"How many cows you figure gave their lives to make this event successful?" Kelly said as he breathed in the sweet aroma wafting from the barbecue pits. John Rawlings was walking toward him, heard the question, and laughed. "My guess is that somebody's herd is considerably smaller," he said.

Standing in the shade of an ancient oak, the two men were together alone for the first time. They silently watched the crowd mingle and the children at play and laughed as they saw an oversized farmer make a return visit to the pie table.

"I want you to know that your volunteering to come here and help Ben—and the rest of us—is much appreciated," John said. "When will you be heading back to Brush Creek?"

Kelly's reply was a noncommittal shrug.

"You and Ben don't think we've seen the last of it, do you?"

"Not by a long shot, most likely," Kelly said.

Seeing that his answer disturbed Rawlings, he followed it with a quick smile. "Let's go get us some of your wife's baking before that big ol' boy cleans her plumb out." He slapped the lawyer on the back. "Today's not meant for worrying."

THE PACE SLOWED as night approached. Families settled onto blankets, many of the youngsters dozing peacefully after a tiring day. Young couples walked hand-in-hand in search of privacy and the fiddlers began tuning up.

Dalton was sitting on a bench beside Shelby Profer, petting Too, whom he had brought to say hello to Alton.

"If it wasn't impolite in mixed company," the attorney said, "I'd let my belt out a notch or two. A man living alone doesn't often have the opportunity to enjoy such delightful food. This feast, on top of Mrs. Rawlings' fine supper the other evening, has spoiled me no end. Next thing you know, I'll be dealing with the gout."

As soon as the music started, couples, young and old, began moving toward the bandstand.

"Sadly, I have justifiable cause for not dancing, being of an advanced age and quite arthritic," Profer said. "What's your excuse?"

Before he could answer, Mandy appeared from behind their bench. "I might ask the same question," she said. "John has left to put our son to bed and told me I have his permission to ask you for one dance. He also said I should see if you would be a gentleman and accompany me home afterward."

Dalton was quickly on his feet, following her to the area roped off for dancing. "You probably don't recall," he said, "but I was never much of a dancer."

"Oh, I recall," she said, smiling. "I have a very good memory."

When the music resumed, he took her hand and stiffly began his best imitation of two-stepping. He held her at arm's length and kept his chin high, as if the whole world were watching. "You know, this isn't a cotillion, Ben. It's just a barn dance with no roof. Relax."

She moved closer and rested her head against his shoulder. Suddenly his world was filled with the magic scent of shampoo, lilac water, and fresh apple pie, and he wished the music would go on forever.

THE NIGHT HAD cooled and thunderheads were rolling in as they stopped at a table where bags of penny candy were being sold. "For Alton," Ben said. "I promised him."

Then they began their walk to the apartment as Too followed. "I warned you I wasn't much of a dancer," Ben said.

She laughed and leaned her shoulder into his arm. "No," she said, "you really aren't. But I enjoyed it just the same.

"I've thought about you over the years, you know. You're still very special to me. I asked you a question when you first got here and you didn't really give me an answer."

"What?"

"I asked if you're happy," she said.

Ben struggled for a reply. "Right this minute," he finally said, "yes . . . I'm happy." With that he turned to leave. "Thank you kindly for the dance. And tell John and the little one I said good night."

For several seconds she stood on the porch, holding the small bag of candy, watching the man and his dog walk away. Only when the rain began to gently fall did she go inside to see if her son was still awake.

CHAPTER 20

SITTING IN HIS office, Sheriff Langston reluctantly accepted Dalton's invitation to take a day ride out to Glen Rose Valley. Since Kelly had told Ben of his brief conversation with John Rawlings, the idea of seeing what the Colonel was up to had consumed his thoughts. It was time to make the owner of the Shooting Star aware that he had not been forgotten.

"We'll not be welcome," the sheriff warned as he unsuccessfully argued against the idea.

"We won't trespass," Ben said. "I just want to get close enough to have us a look through your spyglass."

As he spoke, Langston had tapped out his pipe and was already taking two rifles from the gun case behind his desk. "If we're going," he said, "let's get it over with. I know a little roadhouse along the way where we can have us some dinner."

They rode in silence as the day quickly warmed. Finally, the sheriff spoke. "What good do you anticipate coming from this trip?"

"Can't say. None, probably, but I'm tired of waiting for Abernathy to make the next move. You got any thoughts on what he might be thinking?"

"It won't be nothing good, that I assure you." As he spoke he was pointing toward the faint chimney smoke rising from a small adobe building in the distance. "Yonder is Miss Luisa's place. She's unfriendly as a woke-up copperhead but makes real good tamales."

Her ill-tempered greeting lent credence to Langston's warning. She eyed the two men warily before nodding toward a table. "Is your other friend coming?" she said.

"Nope, just us. We'll not be needing tequila today." Langston didn't bother explaining that this had long been his and the Colonel's private meeting place.

They ate quickly, washing their meal down with day-old sweet tea. Luisa was hurriedly wiping the table even before they left their chairs. "When you see Señor Abernathy," she said, "tell him he still owes me money for watching that boy," she said. "And somebody should pay me for my dog that's gone missing."

Dalton glared across the table at the sheriff.

"I didn't have any idea," Langston said. "Swear to God."

"If I ever find out you did . . ." Ben ended his threat in midthought, gritting his teeth as he walked away.

After a short ride they reached a mesa that afforded them a good view of the ranch. They tethered the horses in a stand of oak trees and stretched out on a large rock formation. The sheriff handed his gold-plated spyglass to Dalton.

In the distance he could see the newly built gate and guardhouse. In every direction he looked, men were riding along the fences, rifles across their saddles. They would occasionally stop and take long looks into the distance, then continue. In the compound, however, there was little activity. The corral was empty except for a half-dozen goats and a few chickens, and the doors of the new barn were shut. Focusing on the main house, Dalton could see no activity.

"They've hunkered down," he said. "There's not much ranch work going on that I can see. Everybody's standing guard, like they're expecting a raid. It makes no sense."

"That's just the Colonel taking extra care," the sheriff said. "All he's worried about is his own sorry hide. He's built a fort around himself. You seen enough?"

"Let's wait a little longer and see if he shows himself."

It was almost two hours before Abernathy finally stepped out on his front porch, flanked by two armed ranch hands.

Dalton watched as the Colonel lit a cigar, talked briefly with his men, then slowly paced the length of the porch. "He looks nervous, like he's expecting someone to jump out of the bushes and shoot him."

"If that happens," the sheriff said, "I'll be wanting my glass returned so I can see it for myself."

"Let's head back," Dalton said. "I've seen what I came to see."

He was untying the horses when there was a rustle in the nearby bushes. Then one of the ranch hands stepped into view, pointing a cocked rifle. He had been alerted to their presence by the guard keeping watch from the loft of the barn. There was a slight tremor in his voice as he ordered the intruders to raise their hands. "And they best be empty," he said.

Though he couldn't recall his name, the sheriff recognized the young cowboy. He'd spent some time in the jailhouse drunk cage. "You've got no cause for this," Langston said. "We're not trespassing on Shooting Star property."

"But you're spying on it, ain't you? I figure that's just as bad. I'll thank you to let your gun belts fall to the ground and get on your horses. Head them down to the main gate."

As the sheriff climbed into his saddle, he glanced over at Dalton. "I told you this was a bad idea," he said.

Ben just nodded. "And turns out you were exactly right."

T HEY WERE USHERED into Colonel Abernathy's office, where he sat smiling. Two men stood by the door, another at his side.

"The governor don't get this amount of protection," Dalton said.

" 'Cause he doesn't have the money I do," Abernathy shot back. "Tell me what it is you boys are doing out this way, spying on my property."

Neither replied.

"I'm of a mind to just have you both shot and be done with it. I suspect a stranger from out of town and a betraying, lying sheriff wouldn't be too greatly missed. Besides, you were trespassing as far as I'm concerned." He removed his Colt from its holster and placed it on the desk. "First, though, I want to offer a suggestion that just might provide a way to see your sorry lives spared."

The sheriff was no longer attempting to hide his apprehension. "What would that be?" he said.

"First of all," the Colonel said, "Mr. Dalton here gets on his horse and rides back to wherever he came from, promising never to show his face in these parts again. I'll thank him to take that prissy lawyer, Rawlings, with him as well. Second, things go back to the way they used to be. I get full cooperation for my business dealings." He pointed toward the sheriff. "Starting with you."

One of the cowboys standing behind him cleared his throat. "Oh, and my men will again be welcomed to whatever drinking establishment they choose."

Dalton leaned forward and placed his palms on the corner of Abernathy's desk, convinced he had only a few seconds to live. "You think people are just going to forget the things you've done? The people you've killed and robbed and run off their land?" he said. "Just today I saw where you kept that little boy and it made me wonder what kind of a man could even consider such a thing. You've got no right to even be breathing."

The Colonel was reaching for his pistol when a series of explosions rattled the windows and shook the floor. His gun slid from the desk and the guard standing nearby lost his balance and fell to his knees.

Having no idea what had just happened, Dalton and the sheriff were quickly on their feet and out the door, running toward their horses.

EARLIER, ANSON KELLY had argued against the proposed trip as strongly as the sheriff. There was nothing to be gained from it, he pointed out, but if

Dalton was so stubbornly determined, he would go with him. Ben had declined the offer, saying it would be best if Kelly remained in town and looked after things at the livery.

His horse was saddled and waiting as he watched Ben and the sheriff ride away. After making a quick purchase at the feedstore, he tracked them to the road-house, then on toward the Shooting Star. He then hid in a shallow gully to watch as his friends were ultimately captured and escorted to the ranch.

Lighting the corncob pipe he had borrowed from Keene and hiding his sidearm in his saddlebag, he casually rode toward the entrance to the Shooting Star. When a cowboy emerged with a raised rifle, ordering him to stop, Kelly gave a look of mock fear and lifted his hands. "I've just come looking for work," he said. "I mean no harm."

The weary guard lowered his rifle and turned to announce a "stand down" to another hand who had remained in the guardhouse, napping. The short diversion allowed Kelly time to slip two sticks of the feedstore dynamite from beneath his shirt sleeve and put their fuses to the bowl of Duke's pipe. He then tossed them into the doorway.

The explosion and fire caused his horse to rear, but Kelly quickly got him under control and pointed him toward the compound. As he galloped past the splintered remains of the guardhouse, the only remaining evidence of its former occupants was a lone hat lying nearby, flames rising from its brim.

As Dalton and Langston spurred their horses and hurried toward him, Kelly tossed another stick of dynamite in the direction of two men who were taking aim. Only one got off a shot before they were engulfed in a blanket of smoke and dust.

By the time they reached where Kelly waited, the sheriff was slumped in his saddle, the back of his shirt damp with blood. There was a pained look on his pale face as he gripped the saddle horn in an effort to stay astride his horse. Dalton reached out to steady him as they joined Kelly en route to safety.

In the distance, the Colonel stood on his porch, fanning away the smoke, insane with rage. "Go after them," he yelled. "Kill them."

No one made a move.

D UKE AND LANNY joined them as they sat in the waiting room of the doctor's office, anticipating word on the sheriff's condition. There was a wash of relief when they saw Doc Thorndale enter with a smile on his face. "The bullet entered his lower back and exited just above his belt line," he said, "leaving him with a couple of busted ribs and all internal organs functioning and in good shape. He's in a great deal of pain, but he'll survive."

Relieved by the news, Duke listened as Dalton described their bizarre rescue. "I've never heard of such a thing," he said, looking at Kelly. "However did you even imagine such?"

"A few years back," Kelly said, "we had this young fella who set out to be a bank robber. Said he was tired of working at the feedstore. Anyway, he didn't own a gun, so he used dynamite instead. And it worked pretty good for him. He robbed two or three banks in neighboring towns before I finally caught him."

"How'd you catch him?" Lanny said.

"He forgot to bring along matches to the last bank he figured on robbing."

Keene slapped his knee and was still chuckling when he stood to leave. "Another thing that amazes me is Ben here apparently has himself a guardian angel. If I'm remembering correctly, this is the second time somebody's kindly pulled his bacon out of the fire."

Duke gave Lanny a wink as he walked away.

B Y THE TIME Finis Jacob, editor of the *Fort Worth Record*, learned of the shooting, the sheriff was already up and about, reporting to his office daily. He still moved gingerly and wasn't up to riding a horse, so he was making his daily rounds in a buggy.

His trips along the Fort Worth streets, tipping his hat to those he passed, looked more like a victory parade than carrying out any peacekeeping duties.

To the readers, Otto Langston had become a hero, even to many who had long viewed him as just another corrupt politician, woefully unqualified for his job. Jacob's first story, headlined "Sheriff Wounded in Shooting Star Gun Battle," had redeemed him. The next, "Heroic Sheriff Already Back on the Job," suggested he was deserving of a medal.

The *Record* account said Langston had fought off *three rifle-wielding assailants, killing them all.*

"Reckon the sheriff owns the paper?" Duke said after reading the second article. "This reads like he wrote it himself. Him or one of those dime-novel dandies from back east."

The truth of the matter was that Jacob, who spent much of his time gathering information from a bar stool in the Half Acre's Red Eye Palace, had heard vague rumors about the Shooting Star incident but had not even interviewed Langston to hear his version. Nor had he ever visited the Colonel's ranch. Bored with writing about the Summer Festival, school plays, and ladies' garden meetings, he had simply decided to provide his readers some excitement and give his circulation a boost, never mind facts.

Only Jacob and the sheriff would know that the stories were the product of unbridled imagination. And it was highly unlikely Sheriff Langston would be inclined to speak out against anything that praised him so highly.

When the issues of the newspaper were delivered to the Shooting Star, the maid wisely saw to it that they were tossed into the trash bin before the Colonel could see them.

CHAPTER 21

ONE TRUTH THE editor had managed was the fact that three of Abernathy's men were killed, two at the ranch's entrance and one as he attempted to get off a shot at the fleeing riders.

"I read in the news that our sheriff performed rather heroically," Shelby Profer said as Dalton entered his office. Ben didn't bother setting the record straight.

"It seems the Colonel's decided we're fixing to attack his ranch," he said after describing all the armed guards he and Langston had seen on their ill-fated trip.

"Could be the man's losing his faculties. Which would be no great surprise, considering the bad luck he's been experiencing of late. A man with his sizable ego often has a fragile mind. I'd suggest you not read too much into what you saw. What he was thinking a few days ago might not be what he's planning today."

"That's what I figure," Ben said. "I still believe the danger to be here in town. Anson feels the same and thinks we should post guards around the livery."

"Those we've assembled are willing and appear quite able, but I wonder if there is a crack shot among them," Profer said as he arranged papers on his desk, then leaned back in his chair. "Certainly I am no military tactician, but a good guess is that the most vulnerable spot is wherever you might be at any given time. We're in agreement that you are the Colonel's primary target. The less seen of you the better."

"I can't run," Dalton said.

"Not suggesting it. Not at all. Indeed, we need you here. I'm only saying you should go about your business with heightened awareness. I've rather come to like you, as have others in town, and wish you no harm."

R AYMOND ABERNATHY HAD been reflecting on his days fighting the South. The old lawyer in town might lack knowledge of military strategy, but the Colonel didn't. He hadn't even bothered to attend the burying of his three men, choosing instead to remain alone in his office, poring over maps of Fort Worth and devising a plan of attack.

When Raff Bailey answered a summons to the ranch headquarters, he was surprised to find his boss dressed in his old Union uniform. For a moment, he wondered if he was expected to salute or surrender.

"If my counting is correct," Abernathy said, "we have fourteen able-bodied men capable of putting up a good fight. If well-armed and deployed properly, that should be enough manpower to achieve our goal."

Bailey watched as the Colonel paced, arms behind his back, his recently polished riding boots clicking against the floor. His hurried thoughts seemed to collide as he stopped talking only long enough to light a cigar.

"You will be my second-in-command," he said.

Raff was stunned, recalling when he had stood in the same room, being severely chastised for his drunken assault on the livery. Then, the Colonel had spoken to him like a witless child. Now, he was being promoted to a field general, hearing a plan for an insane maneuver.

"Sir," he said, "we could get a lot of people killed. We've already lost—"

"Casualties are to be expected," Abernathy said. "They are the price to be paid for victory." There was a maniacal look on his face as he spoke, and Bailey suddenly felt a growing sense of discomfort. He and the others in the bunkhouse had signed on as cowboys, not soldiers.

Abernathy moved to the maps he had tacked up along the office wall. "They will anticipate our arriving from the southern part of town," he said, pointing to the route he had marked in ink. The jagged lines looked as if they had been drawn with a feeble, unsure hand.

"We'll not disappoint them, sending a small group in from that direction. But"—he smiled before moving a trembling finger to the top of the map—"our strength will come from here. Our main force will come from the north, behind the stock pens, and travel down through Hell's Half Acre.

"Of course, they will expect us to attack under the cover of darkness. Instead, we will arrive at first light. By then they will be tired from standing in wait throughout the night."

As the Colonel raved on, Bailey slumped into a chair. "And when is all this to take place?"

"Soon. Perhaps in a few days. We'll need to sort out our weapons and ammunition, select our best horses, and determine who will ride with each detail." Abernathy's enthusiasm seemed almost childlike.

When Bailey returned to the bunkhouse to pass along to the others what he had learned, his face was ashen. "We have hired ourselves out to a madman," he said.

PART THREE

— ◇ —

COUNTING DOWN

CHAPTER 22

Normally, hell's half Acre was a hotbed of rumor and false information. Lips loosed by whiskey told secrets they had vowed not to, and stories—like the ones Finis Jacob had printed in the *Record*—were so embellished from one telling to the next that they had scant resemblance to the first whispered version.

With none of the Shooting Star cowboys visiting the saloons to offer even a remotely accurate account of what had taken place, Sheriff Langston's image grew. In one version, he and Colonel Abernathy had faced off against each other in a quick-draw confrontation. Cheered on by his workers, the Colonel got off the first shot, wounding the sheriff. Bleeding badly and in considerable pain, Langston steadied himself, took careful aim, and shot the ranch owner squarely between the eyes. In one account, he had used his Peacemaker; another had him firing a rifle one-handed.

Those who knew Otto Langston immediately recognized the absurdity of such a tale, many assuming that the sheriff himself had been the first to tell it. Others, however, took it as gospel and spread the story of Colonel Abernathy's demise from one barroom and card table to another.

Editor Jacob had even considered publishing an article in the *Record* eulogizing the late Colonel but sobered and came to his senses just in time to salvage what little credibility he had remaining.

Among those who deemed the story ludicrous was Duke Keene. He'd heard it while having breakfast in the café and responded with his trademark chuckle. "I wish he was dead, with buzzards happily picking at what's left," he said.

Most shared his sentiment but remained skeptical. "Even if it is true he's dead," one customer suggested, "I'm guessing his evil ghost will still come around to haunt us, just out of pure meanness. I don't figure this town will ever be rid of Raymond Abernathy."

"I guess we'll see," Duke said as he walked out the door.

THOUGH CERTAIN THE worst was yet to come, Shelby Profer believed it was in the town's best interest that life continue as normally as possible. "There's nothing positive that will come from just sitting and waiting. Every day we hide our faces and refuse to carry out our civic duties is a day won by Abernathy."

He was talking to John Rawlings, whom he had invited to his cluttered office.

After asking about the welfare of Mandy and little Alton, then how Rawlings was recovering from his nightmare time spent in jail, Profer turned to the purpose of the meeting.

"My frankness," he began, "is well-intended when I suggest your career in the legal profession has taken a less than savory path. As you will recall, we've been associates much of your adult life and I've watched you far more closely than you've likely realized. Though I disapproved of many of the clients you've chosen and the manner in which you represented them, I never felt it my responsibility to scold or offer advice.

"In recent weeks, however, my attitude has taken a rather dramatic change, and I hope you will see the value in it."

Rawlings shifted in his chair, uncertain where the conversation might be going.

"All of what I have to say is not negative. Far from it. You are a bright young man with a promising future, once you've stopped to look ahead to it. I'm not being overly optimistic when I say that a day might come in your life when you could sit on the bench as a fair-minded judge, even run for political office and do good for the people of the community.

"But none of that will be possible if you return to helping set guilty scalawags free and lining your pockets with their ill-gotten gains."

John briefly considered getting to his feet and leaving. He raised a warning hand and said, "My business is none of your—"

Before he completed his thought, Profer slammed a hand against his desk. "Sir, I have given this speech considerable thought, and I'll thank you to hear me out before storming to the door. Your arrogance and unwarranted pride are matters we can discuss at some later time."

Rawlings silently returned his hat to the corner of the desk and settled back into his chair.

"My purpose today," Profer continued, "is to make you a proposition. I am an old man, nearing my final days. From this disheveled office I have fashioned a good and honorable career, doing the best I could to see that people were treated justly and with every manner of fairness the law has to offer."

He paused and took a deep breath. "I would like for you to assume my practice."

Rawlings was speechless at first, then said, "My first thought is to say how overwhelmed I am by the offer. Second, I have to wonder what people might think about being represented by someone accused of murder."

"I have taken the liberty of sending a letter to the governor, detailing the unfortunate circumstances of you being falsely accused. Attached to it is a letter from Sheriff Langston, admitting his part in the plot to cast blame on you. The same letter, along with his willingness to resign his badge, has been sent to our mayor.

"I will personally represent you until this matter is favorably resolved and publicly announced. Thereafter, it will be up to you to make yourself and your family proud."

Extending his hand across the desk, Rawlings tried to offer his thanks, but Profer waved him away. "Go, discuss what I've suggested with your wife. And if she gives the idea her blessing—which I believe she will—ask if she might consider tidying up this office a bit before you move in."

* * *

IN THE APARTMENT, young Alton didn't understand why his mother was crying. She hugged him, explained that hers were happy tears, and sent him to play with his toys. "This is such a wonderful opportunity, a fresh start," she said. "I'm so happy for you and know you'll do well."

As she spoke, John watched his son hurry toward his room. "I will do my best to make you and Mr. Profer proud," he said. "First, though, there is something that needs to be done."

Mandy knew he was referring to the unsettled matter involving Colonel Abernathy. "There are people dealing with it," she said. "It will all be over soon."

"Not until the man who ordered my son kidnapped and mistreated is dead," John said. "And I intend to see that happen."

The warmth Mandy had been feeling just a moment earlier turned to a chill.

CHAPTER 23

To pass time, Dalton was soaping his saddle when Lanny approached and informed him he had a visitor. "She's sitting out front on the bench, waiting," he said. "A little boy is with her, wanting to see Too."

Alton's eyes lit up when he saw Ben, followed closely by the dog whose tail was already wagging. "He's glad you've come to see him," Ben said, then smiled at the boy's mother.

"I was hoping for a minute of your time," Mandy said.

Dalton called out to Lanny and asked if he would show Alton the horses, then took a seat. It was still early in the day, so the full effect of the summer sun had not yet arrived and a soft breeze teased Mandy's hair.

"I'm on my way to Mr. Profer's office to see if I can put it in some kind of order," she said, brushing away a stray curl, "though I think I may have been assigned an impossible task."

Ben laughed and nodded. "Yeah, I've been there," he said.

She told him of the generous offer that had been made to her husband, then of their later conversation.

"I'm worried he might try something foolish," she said. "He's so angry over what happened to Alton—so am I, truth be known—that I'm afraid he's not going to have any peace until Colonel Abernathy pays dearly for what he's done. I think John feels it's his responsibility to see that happen.

"I'm hoping you can talk some sense into him, convince him not to attempt anything alone. He's more likely to listen to you than anyone. I don't think you know how much he looks up to you. He has since we were kids."

Dalton could hear the concern in her voice. "I'll speak with him," he said.

"You know," she said, "I don't think I fully understood how important my family is to me until all this happened—John being put in jail, my son taken. From it all I've learned not to take anything for granted. Now that we're all safely back under one roof together, I want to do everything I can to see that it stays that way. Can you understand?"

"I do. John needs to realize just how lucky he is."

"He's a proud man, as you well know. Too proud at times. But he's no fighter, Ben, not someone who can face up to the likes of the Colonel. If he tries, I know he'll get hurt, and I can't let that happen."

"We'll see that it doesn't."

They sat in silence until Alton returned to excitedly report on the livery tour he and his new friend Lanny had taken. As she rose to leave, Mandy leaned toward

Dalton and kissed him lightly on the cheek. "Thank
you for taking care of my husband," she whispered. "I
love you both. I always have."

Ben watched as mother and son walked away, hand
in hand, his thoughts wandering back to long-ago days
when a single choice could change the course of one's
life.

R AFF BAILEY WAS becoming increasingly concerned
over the plans the Colonel was making. Several
times a day he was called to the main house to listen as
some new element was added to the plan of attack.
Day-to-day work at the Shooting Star had been reduced to a minimum as cowboys abandoned their
regular duties to attend bunkhouse meetings, review
more maps, and be reminded to make certain their
weapons were cleaned and in good working order.

At the most recent gathering, it was promised there
would be bonuses paid to all once the plan was successfully carried out.

"Just how many folks can we expect to encounter?"
one of the wranglers asked after Abernathy had dismissed them and returned to the house.

"That's what I've been told to determine," Bailey
said as he rolled his eyes.

"And let me guess: Once you've accomplished that,
we'll have us another meeting."

T HE WARNING THAT none of the Colonel's men were
allowed to visit any of the Half Acre saloons had
not barred them from coming to town. Thus, Bailey

was free to ride along the Fort Worth streets without concern he might be stopped and arrested. He was just another cowboy in town to shop for a new pair of boots, have his hat steamed, or attend the livestock sale.

With little notice, he slowly rode past the apartment hotel and the old lawyer's office where armed guards had last been seen. He counted three at one place, four at the other. Though each man held a rifle, none seemed too alert to their assignment.

Before checking out the livery, he decided to have dinner at the café down the street. Tired of a steady diet of bunkhouse food and Luisa's roadhouse tamales, he ordered the special of the day—smoked brisket, turnip greens, butter beans, and a slice of fresh-baked bread. He had almost finished and was trying to decide between the apple pie and the peach cobbler for his dessert when Anson Kelly slid into the booth across from him.

"Haven't seen you in town since you made a fool of yourself out front of the livery," Kelly said, removing his hat and placing it on the table. He smiled at the waitress and asked for a glass of sweet tea.

Though no longer interested in dessert, Bailey continued to stare across the room at the pie case, trying to ignore his visitor. Several customers left their meals half eaten, paid quickly, and left.

"You here on personal business or sent by your boss?" Kelly said.

Bailey remained silent. Beneath the table, one foot began to tap nervously on the floor. When he pushed his chair back and started to get to his feet, Kelly placed a firm hand on his arm. "No need rushing off," he said. "Let's have us a talk while I finish my tea."

Suddenly wishing the Colonel hadn't sent him to town, Bailey slumped back into his chair.

"Some of us have been talking about you boys out at the Shooting Star, wondering what you're up to these days," Kelly said. "Fact is, we've been expecting to see you. It's even been suggested that that fellow Abernathy you work for you might even show his cowardly face this time."

Finally, Bailey spoke. "I've got no idea what you're talking about."

"Oh, I think you do."

"You're crazy."

Kelly smiled and shook his head. "No, anybody who wants to do harm to friends of mine is. Word's gotten around that your boss has a powerful grudge against Ben Dalton. That right?"

Bailey didn't reply.

"See, I've come to admire Ben a great deal. He's a sworn marshal, you know. Just like myself. And we've agreed that folks who disturb the peace and try to make good folks uneasy have no business in town. Even your friend the sheriff has come around to our thinking. Whatever it is the Colonel is paying you ain't enough for the hellfire that'll rain down if you come back and try creating some kind of dustup."

"Like I said, I've got no idea what you're talking about." Bailey was no longer attempting to hide his concern. Sweat was gathering beneath his eyes and his face had turned pale.

"Well, I was just thinking out loud," Kelly said, "making conversation. If you're finished eating and have done your business in town, I suggest you ride on back to the ranch. And if you're of a mind, tell the Colonel we had this talk."

Bailey quickly got to his feet, rapidly dusting his hat against his thigh before putting it on.

Kelly, still seated, still smiling, told him not to worry about paying. "Dinner and your tip for the waitress are on me," he said.

B AILEY RODE STRAIGHT to the Shooting Star and Kelly immediately visited Dalton at the livery. "Things will soon come to a head," he said. "Abernathy sent a scout, that fella who shot up the livery a while back, to look things over."

"Any idea what they're planning?" Ben said.

"Only that they'll be coming here, not waiting for us at the ranch. Whatever they're planning, I didn't sense a great deal of enthusiasm for it. My guess is that Abernathy has scared his people into doing his bidding, whether they want to or not. We best start getting ready."

Duke Keene listened to the conversation and offered his solution: "Why don't we just saddle up, ride out there, and shoot the man dead as a doornail. That'll quickly put an end to all this foolishness."

Though neither Kelly nor Dalton replied, both felt it was a plan worthy of consideration.

W E'RE NOT GOING to surprise them," Bailey said as he stood in front of the Colonel's desk, careful to avoid mention of his encounter with Anson Kelly. "They've got lookouts all over town, including all around the livery. I haven't seen so many rifles since the war. A lot of people are going to get hurt if we—"

"There's no 'if' about it," Abernathy said.

Before he could continue his embellished report, three other ranch hands entered the office, hats removed and eyes focused on the floor.

"What's this?" the Colonel said.

"We apologize for interrupting," a young wrangler named Brett Sawyer said, "but we've come to settle up on our wages so we can be leaving. We hired on to tend your cattle, Mr. Abernathy, not be in a shooting war. We've talked about it and don't feel this is our fight or any of our business."

Abernathy's face turned red and he began cursing under his breath. "Are there others who feel the same?"

"Yes, sir, but they didn't want to come here with us."

"Cowards, are they?" Abernathy said.

Before the young cowboy could answer, the Colonel drew his pistol and fired a single shot across his desk. Sawyer's eyes widened as his hat fell to the floor. He clutched his chest as blood began to ooze through his fingers and there was a low rattle deep in his throat as his knees buckled.

The others watched in stunned silence as he lay on the floor, gasping his final breath.

"Drag him out to the bunkhouse," Abernathy said, "and make sure everyone sees how traitors are dealt with at the Shooting Star."

Even before they left his office, Abernathy was again poring over his maps, a smile on his face.

CHAPTER 24

T HE MARE WAS quickly aware that an inexperienced
rider was in the saddle. The two-year-old dapple
gray moved along in a jerky gait, occasionally pitching
her head against the reins and briefly balking when
being turned in a different direction. John Rawlings
wondered if he should have selected an older, less stubborn mount. But in the horse barn near the cattle
yards, the manager had assured him she would be ideal
for the day trip he planned, so long as he allowed her
occasional stops for rest and water. He had pocketed
the dollar rental fee and smiled when he told the young
lawyer there would be no extra charge for helping with
the bridle and saddle.

Rawlings had ridden little since his boyhood days in
Aberdene, generally walking or riding in a buggy to
his destinations in the city. Yet as they made their way
farther south, into the rolling hills and through bright
displays of summer wildflowers, man and horse made
their peace. Rawlings welcomed the unclaimed spaces

and fresh breeze. The sweet smell of leather beneath him and the sight of foxes and coyotes hurrying from his path were an enjoyable experience he'd almost forgotten.

One day, when things returned to normal and his son had grown, he wanted Alton to be introduced to this world where people didn't crowd streets and have to climb stairs to reach their home. There was a gentleness to the open range that made John homesick and envious of his friend Ben, who had made the decision to live his life in a quieter, more peaceful environment.

As he rode, Rawlings briefly dismissed his mission and found himself thinking back to their days growing up, and of the event that had begun their friendship.

It was the final day of the school year, and Ben was astride his mule, LuLu, headed home to tend his chores. John was still standing on the school steps, saying good-bye to several young girls who had crowded around him.

A boyfriend of one, the son of a local hog farmer with a reputation as one of the toughest bullies in school, approached the gathering and made it clear he didn't like the attention Rawlings was being given. "Just because he's a pretty boy and his folks got money don't make him nothing special," he said, grabbing his girl by the arm and pulling her down the steps. When she cried out, Rawlings, though skinny and no fighter, tried to shove the bully away.

As he did, two other farm boys appeared from the side of the schoolhouse and together they began to taunt young Rawlings. One slapped him hard in the face and another tripped him, sending him facedown into the schoolyard dirt. As the girls looked on, the three began kicking and punching, laughing and calling their outnumbered victim names.

Turning to see what was happening, Ben Dalton kicked his heels into LuLu's side and was not even out of his saddle before he reached the melee and put out a scuffed boot that knocked one of the attackers away. He quickly dismounted and buried a fist into another's rib cage before pulling the other off Rawlings and landing a blow that broke the youngster's nose.

It was over in minutes. The three thugs limped away, one wiping blood from his face. Something about "this ain't over" was called back in a less than enthusiastic tone.

Ben reached a hand toward Rawlings and helped him to his feet.

Dirty and embarrassed, John brushed at his pants as the young girls looked on silently. He whispered a thank-you to Dalton.

"Sorry for butting in," Ben said, "but three-on-one didn't appear to be a fair fight. I figure you could have handled them yourself one at a time."

He was walking back to LuLu when Rawlings called out. "I've seen you in school, but I don't know your name," he said.

"Ben. Ben Dalton. You're Johnny Rawlings, right?"

By the end of that summer they had become the best of friends.

When he stopped at a stream to let his horse drink, those days still replayed in his mind. And as they did so, he realized how dependent he had been on Dalton's protection. And now, years later, they were adults and nothing had changed.

It was time, he had decided, to fight his own battle, time he confronted the doubts of his own self-worth.

Since his son's return, ugly images of what the child endured had haunted him. In sleep, he heard Alton's tiny voice crying out and had visions of the fear and despair on his wife's face. That he had been hiding away to avoid a return to jail, not even aware his child had been kidnapped, and providing no help finding him, shamed him. And always running through those troubled thoughts was the image of the Colonel, the culprit of his nightmares.

His plan, which he'd shared with no one, was hardly well-conceived. He'd even had difficulty locating the pistol his father had given him as a gift on his twentieth birthday. And when he did find it, he realized he couldn't remember the last time he'd fired it. He was only vaguely aware of the location of the Shooting Star ranch until he stopped into a dingy roadhouse and was given directions by a foulmouthed Mexican woman. And once he arrived, he had no idea how he might get past the watchmen he'd heard Dalton and Anson Kelly talking about.

All he knew was that he wanted the chance to look Raymond Abernathy in the eye, then put a bullet in his head.

M ANDY RETURNED HOME, tired after hours of trying to sort out Shelby Profer's office and miffed that her husband had not come to help. At least he could have stopped in and taken Alton home for his afternoon nap. She was ready to chastise him but found the apartment empty.

Rushing downstairs, she found B. J. Wong, who was still keeping watch. He was immediately aware of the urgency in her voice when she asked that he leave his post long enough to deliver a message to Ben Dalton. "Tell him," she said, "that my husband is gone and might be in trouble. I think he'll know where to look for him."

Only minutes after Wong relayed the message, Dalton and Anson Kelly had saddled their horses and grabbed rifles and, with only a couple of hours of daylight left, were headed south.

"For a big-shot lawyer," Kelly said, "your friend don't seem all that smart."

Dalton didn't bother to disagree.

IN THE DISTANCE, Rawlings could see the guardhouse and quickly turned the mare toward a thick line of scrub oaks. After a mile, he found a secluded spot and dismounted to contemplate his next move. From his vantage point he had a good view of the seemingly endless fence line and a small herd of cattle grazing in the nearby pasture.

He held his breath as two ranch hands slowly rode past. A half hour later, they returned, headed in the opposite direction. As the sun began to set, Rawlings mentally timed the route of the guards. They rode by several times, obviously assigned a certain stretch of fence to protect, usually carrying on a conversation that John wasn't close enough to hear. Neither seemed too concerned that their area of responsibility might be breached.

The early-evening sky had turned a clabber gray by

the time Rawlings tethered his horse and made his way toward the fence. He estimated he would have at least a half-mile walk to the Shooting Star headquarters.

He made it less than three hundred yards.

A rider he'd not seen galloped toward him from the opposite side of the herd, pointing a rifle. "I've got permission to shoot you where you stand," the cowboy called out, "or you can toss away any weapon you've got and come along with me."

W ITH HIS HANDS tied behind him and a rope around his neck, Rawlings walked unsteadily toward the ranch house, the guard close behind him. His plan had failed badly.

He was breathing heavily and bathed in sweat by the time he was pushed through the door of Colonel Abernathy's office.

"I see we've got ourselves a visitor," the Colonel said, "and he looks somewhat familiar. Rawlings, isn't it? What bring you out this way?"

He got no response.

Abernathy gave a slight nod to the guard, who stepped forward and delivered a blow to John's midsection.

The Colonel watched him gasping for air and smiled. "A man trespassing this time of the evening could get himself shot. Wouldn't violate law one, which as a lawyer you already know. But before I shoot you, I'd like us to have a conversation."

Rawlings's only response was to glare at Abernathy. The guard hit him again, this time in the back of his head so hard that he stumbled forward, close enough to the Colonel to smell his foul breath. Finally, he spoke.

"All you need to know is that I came here to kill you for what you did to my little boy," he said. "Though I've obviously failed, there are others waiting to do what I couldn't. Even if you shoot me, I can rest in peace knowing your miserable life will also soon be over."

"You might get yourself a chance to live if you'll tell me what I need to know. Killing you will give me little satisfaction, only soiling the room and making it necessary to dig a hole to put you in. All you need to do is tell me what your friends in town are planning to do."

"I don't know. Wouldn't tell you if I did."

Without prompting, the guard delivered another blow to Rawlings' head, this time hitting him in the face hard enough to cause his ears to ring and blood to spew from his mouth and nose.

"Take him away," Abernathy said. "See that he gets a good beating, but don't kill him. I'll let it be a preview to his people of what's to come Saturday if what's left of him makes it back to town."

Two other guards had located John's horse and brought it to the compound. After he received the ordered beating, they lifted him into his saddle and tied him down.

Rawlings was unaware when the mare began to trot down the trail, past the guardhouse, and into the still-warm darkness.

D ALTON AND KELLY were halfway to the ranch and about to give up their search for the night when they saw a horse standing in a meadow, grazing on wildflowers. Riding closer, they realized that a motionless figure was slumped in the saddle.

"I fear that's him," Kelly said as they slowed their approach, hoping not to spook the horse.

Rawlings' face was so swollen and caked with blood that it was almost impossible to recognize him. He was unconscious and one arm dangled loosely at his side. Dalton gently placed a hand to a wrist that appeared to be broken and was surprised when he felt a pulse. Seconds later he heard a barely audible moan.

"He's alive, but just barely." Ben cut away the ropes that bound Rawlings to the saddle and laid him on the ground. "I fear moving him, so I'll stay here while you ride to town and get the doctor. Tell him we'll need a wagon."

He was pouring water from his canteen onto a bandanna and wiping Rawlings' face as Kelly rode away.

T HROUGHOUT THE NIGHT, Dalton tried to keep his wounded friend comfortable. He had removed the rent horse's saddle and blanket and fashioned a makeshift bed and pillow, and poured sips of water into John's mouth while watching out for any of the Shooting Star men. He talked quietly, urging Rawlings to be strong until Doc Thorndale arrived. "We're going to get you back to Mandy and Alton," he said.

It was almost dawn when John opened his eyes and tried to focus on his friend. "Am I dead?" he said, making a pained effort to smile.

"Not even close. You're going to be fine just as soon as you get home and in a decent bed."

In the distance he could hear the clatter of a wagon

approaching. Showing its driver the way was Anson Kelly. Duke Keene was holding the reins while the doctor sat next to him, his medical kit in his lap. Resting between them was a shotgun.

They were pleased to see Rawlings lift his head as they pulled up next to him. Duke nodded his approval and began chuckling. "Don't see any need for a burying today," he said. As the doctor examined John, the livery owner told Ben he'd put hay and blankets in back of the wagon. "I also brought you some coffee, though it might be cold by now."

"He's in pretty bad shape," Doc Thorndale said, "but he'll make it. I seriously doubt that would be the case if you boys hadn't found him. Near as I can tell, he's got only one broken bone—his wrist—but more cuts and bruises than I can count. The ride back to town won't be comfortable for him."

Dalton hitched Dolly to the back of the wagon and sat next to Rawlings. Each rough spot Duke drove over caused a muffled groan behind him.

The sun was up as they neared Fort Worth and John reached his good hand out to Dalton, signaling him to lean closer. "How many more times do you figure on having to rescue me?" he managed to whisper.

Ben laughed. "As many times as it takes, I reckon," he said.

As the wagon neared the doctor's office, he could see Mandy, with Alton in her arms, waiting on the porch.

A STEADY PARADE OF visitors came to the doctor's office to check on Rawlings. His wife had left his side only long enough to make arrangements for a friend to watch Alton. She had asked Ben if it would be all right for Too to stay with her boy, and he'd taken him by the apartment. Shelby Profer did his best to act as if he were displeased that such a fool's errand had been undertaken but ultimately placed a gentle hand on John's shoulder and wished him a speedy recovery. Lanny Butler came with Duke, who brought a bowl of chili for Mandy. "If you're determined to sit and be nursemaid, you need to keep up your strength," he said. Sheriff Langston stopped in long enough to assure John that his assailants would soon pay for their actions.

Dalton and Kelly waited until late in the day to visit. The warm towels Mandy was applying had reduced some of the swelling to her husband's face and a plaster cast was on his injured wrist. Doc Thorndale had stitched cuts to his chin and forehead.

"Ain't you a sight," Kelly said as he stood at the foot of the bed. "I bet seeing you scared little Alton plumb out of his britches." Dalton made no comment as he shook Rawlings' good hand.

Mandy didn't leave her chair at the bedside but looked up at the two men. "The doctor says you two finding my husband saved his life," she said, "and for that I will be forever grateful. Thank you both."

John slowly pushed himself into a sitting position and motioned Ben to come closer. The swelling and the pain medication the doctor had given him made speaking difficult. "Saturday," he said in a gravelly whisper. "They're coming Saturday." He then eased himself back onto the mound of pillows behind him and closed his eyes.

"You did good, John," Ben said. "You paid a high

price, but you found out what we needed to know. Get yourself some rest and let us take care of things from here on."

As he and Kelly prepared to leave, Mandy got to her feet. "Ben, can I have a word?" She kissed her husband on the forehead and followed the visitors into the hallway. Anson, sensing they needed a private moment, told Dalton he would see him back at the livery.

"John's going to be okay," Ben said. "You need to get some rest. Go home and be with your boy."

Mandy nodded, but he knew she would ignore his suggestion.

"I've asked far too much of you already and have no right to ask for more," she said, "but I have one more thing I hope you'll do for me. And God help me for even asking."

"Anything . . ."

"Kill that evil man, Ben," she said. "Kill him and put him out of our lives forever."

T HAT EVENING, THOSE who had visited Rawlings earlier assembled in Profer's office. Mandy's cleaning efforts had made it possible for everyone to find room to sit or stand without worry of being caught in an avalanche of books and papers.

Sheriff Langston was the last to arrive and the first to speak. "Until the mayor sees fit to accept my resignation," he said, "I remain the sheriff and plan to do my best to protect this town and the people living in it. I can't do anything about what's gone on before but feel bad about it and accept my punishment. But now I'm here to help. Me and my deputies.

"I know Colonel Abernathy better than anyone else in this room and can offer a guess of what he's capable of doing and how he might go about it."

Profer, seated behind a reasonably clean desk for the first time he could recall, applauded Langston. "Any insight you might provide, any thoughts you can share, are welcomed. You were not invited here so we could stand in judgment. Please continue."

"I can't speak to any real success he had during his service with the Union," the sheriff said, "but I know he enjoys thinking like a military man. Whatever he's planning will be carried out as if he was making an assault on Confederate enemy. Those under his command are ruled by their fear of him and will blindly follow his orders. No one will be safe, mainly because he has no regard for anyone standing in his way."

"What you're saying," Dalton said, "is he's flat-out crazy."

"And has been made more so by your presence," Langston replied. "I know this for a fact from previous conversations we've had. More than once, he urged me to kill you myself, even offering generous payment once it was done."

Dalton felt a rush of concern as he listened, not for his personal safety but for the possibility that by coming to Fort Worth he was responsible for all that had happened—and would happen.

Kelly read his thoughts. "The only one responsible for all this is Abernathy himself. Sooner or later, someone was bound to stand up to him. And once that happened, there was going to be a firestorm. Poke a man not thinking straight in the eye and he'll seek revenge a hundred times over."

Langston also offered reassurance. "It embarrasses me to say it, but what you've done," he said, looking across the room at Dalton, "is what I should have a long time ago."

"So," Profer said, "we know the enemy, when he plans to attack, and, most likely, where. What is our plan to defeat him?"

"I'd just as soon him and his men didn't fill my livery full of bullet holes or burn it down," Keene said. "That, and I hate to think of innocent folks, particularly young'uns, getting themselves hurt."

"He's got only one way to get here," Dalton said. "I say we should confront him before he can get this far."

CHAPTER 25

"I CAN'T TELL YOU how weary I am of riding this trail," Anson Kelly said. "Seems every time I do, something bad occurs." He, Dalton, and Sheriff Langston had decided they should scout out a place to await the arrival of Colonel Abernathy's hands. At the meeting in Profer's office it had been agreed that it needed to be a good distance from town.

Most of the landscape was flat or marked by gently rolling hills, offering no place a group of men and horses could hide. Only when they neared Luisa's roadhouse did Langston have an idea. "Out back of her place," he said, "there's a small creek bed and its banks are cut pretty deep. I think a dozen or so men and horses could wait there with little chance of being seen. As I recall, there's also some mesquite trees that would provide cover.

"My only concern is that if Miss Luisa gets word of our plan, she'll alert the Colonel. She's a powerfully mean old woman."

"Why would she tell him?" Kelly asked.

"She'd figure he might pay for her information. Money's all she ever thinks about, even in her sleep I expect."

"What if we offered to pay her to stay silent, maybe even suggest she close up and take herself a brief vacation?" Dalton said.

"I fear we'd be taking a risk."

"Well, we might have to. All we can do is go in and speak to her."

"I've got to admit, she does cook up fine tamales," the sheriff said.

H E HAD MISJUDGED Luisa's utter disdain for Raymond Abernathy. Not only was he always rude and dismissive to her when he visited the roadhouse, but he'd still not paid her for her role in the kidnapping of the Rawlings boy. She also had suspicions that he or one of his men had taken her dog.

Her curses were in Spanish, but it was clear she had strong issues with the Colonel. Only after Sheriff Langston, whom she immediately recognized from his occasional meetings with Abernathy, assured her he felt the same way, did she warm to him. And then only slightly.

But by the time she delivered a heaping plate of tamales and tortillas to the table, she had agreed to keep their plan a secret in exchange for the five-dollar gold piece the sheriff placed in her hand. The men, however, failed to convince her that for her own safety it might be a good idea to visit her sister in Fort Worth for a few days.

"Por favor," she said, "I wish to see what happens with my own eyes. The Colonel, he is a good customer, but not one I'm going to miss. I will pray he's soon dead."

After their meal, they walked down to look at the small ravine. Less than a hundred yards from the road-house, it was wide enough to provide a hiding place and the creek had dried to nothing more than a few shallow pools of water, barely enough for the horses to get drinks.

"This will work," Kelly said, "as long as the old lady keeps her mouth shut."

"She will," Langston said. "I just showed her my badge and promised she'd wind up in jail if she goes back on her word. Plus, I told her I knew for certain that it was the Colonel himself who stole her dog."

I N TOWN, PROFER drove his buggy to the stockyards and began recruiting men to forgo their usual week-end visits to the Half Acre saloons and do battle with Colonel Abernathy and his hands. He was pleasantly surprised to be able to quickly hire a half-dozen bored cowboys eager to join in a fight.

"If my counting is correct," he told Keene, "we'll have fifteen, including those I've already hired as guards. In the event Mr. Dalton agrees, we can leave the sheriff and his deputies in town to watch over things in case any of Abernathy's men were to make it this far. I want to be assured your establishment isn't harmed, nor mine for that matter."

"I'll be going with Ben and them," Duke said.

Profer smiled and rested a hand on Keene's shoulder. "I think you'll have a difficult time persuading them to allow it. My assumption is they would prefer that two old fools like ourselves stay out of their way."

"I can't just sit here," Duke said as he brushed the lawyer's hand away. "If you'll recall, I need to settle up for my barn nearly getting burned down. I'm owed."

"I suspect we can find something useful for us to do," Profer said, "though for the time being I think we would be wise to keep it to ourselves."

A puzzled look crossed Duke's face. "I'm still going to invite myself," he said.

"Then, sir, I fear you will be gravely disappointed."

As they spoke, neither had been aware of Mandy Rawlings standing in the doorway of the livery, listening. "I want to help," she said. "Just tell me what I can do."

Profer smiled at Keene. "See," he said, "our own little army is fast growing."

A S THE DAY of the planned mission neared, Raff Bailey was increasingly nervous. The Colonel, disappointed by the lack of enthusiasm in the bunkhouse and fearing a revolt, had threatened anyone who thought of breaking ranks with a bullet to his head. "I'll tolerate no disloyalty," he had said during one of the endless planning meetings he conducted.

Bailey watched his boss's grip on reality fade, then completely disappear. The Colonel had started drinking heavily again and rarely slept. If he wasn't pacing in his office, he was standing on the porch of the ranch house, muttering to himself and staring out at something no one else could see. He had worn the same clothes for days and pushed aside any food the cook offered.

When the woman from the roadhouse arrived with a pistol on her hip, demanding the return of a dog Bailey knew nothing about, he knew all vestiges of sanity had vacated the Shooting Star.

"Tell Señor Abernathy I wish to speak to him," she said. "Pronto."

To get past the guards, she had explained that she was delivering tamales to the Colonel.

Abernathy staggered onto the porch and for a moment didn't recognize the overweight woman wearing a ragged serape and a floppy black hat. When he did, he wanted to know what she was doing on his ranch.

"I've come for my dog," she said, her words slightly slurred.

Bailey couldn't decide who was more drunk, Luisa or the Colonel.

"I've got no idea what you're talking about," Abernathy said.

"You stole my dog. First, you refuse to pay me for what I did for you, which is bad enough, then you take my dog. You are a pitiful excuse for a man."

Abernathy's temper exploded. "Get out of here. Go. Vamonos."

Luisa spat curses in Spanish and drew her pistol. The Colonel was laughing until she pulled the trigger. He screamed and grabbed at his thigh as blood began to run down the leg of his pants and into his boot. For a moment he stood like a statue, stunned, then weakly braced himself against the door. By the time Luisa mounted her horse and was riding away, he was writhing in pain, unable to hear her parting threat.

"Return my dog or the next time I will kill you," she called out.

Abernathy lay on the porch, pale and delirious. "What dog?" he said. "I got no dog. Don't even like dogs." His last words before passing out were to demand someone bring him his bottle of tequila and get the doctor.

Bailey was already on his way to the barn to saddle his horse.

Dalton was just leaving the doctor's office after paying Rawlings a visit when he nearly collided with the ranch hand. "I'm in a rush to speak with Doc Thorndale," Raff said, "but when I'm done I'd like me and you to talk."

"We've got coffee over at the livery," Ben said.

It felt strange, offering such a casual invitation to one of the Colonel's men, someone who soon might attempt to kill him. Yet the two men were sitting together on Duke's bench as Bailey described the bizarre scene that had played out at the ranch.

"Abernathy going to be okay?"

"All I know is he was bleeding pretty bad when I left to fetch the doctor," Bailey said. "My guess is he's too ornery to die."

In truth, the Colonel's condition didn't concern Dalton, except to make him wonder what it might do to the Saturday plan he'd been alerted to.

"Crazy, ain't it? Poor ol' Doc Thorndale doesn't know which way to turn. In his office, he's got a fellow who was beat up out at the Shooting Star. Now, he's on his way out there to tend to the person who ordered that beating."

"Doctors don't swear allegiances," Ben said. "Their only job is to heal folks, then let God decide what side to be on."

Bailey drained the last of his coffee. "I've been look-ing for an excuse to come to town," he said. "You know something's about to happen, and I'm wondering if you've got any suggestion as to how it might be avoided."

"It's your boss who started all this."

"I know. I know. And now he's so angry and out of his mind that there's no reasoning with him. I don't mind telling you, he scares me flat to death."

"Any chance him now being laid up might give him pause?"

"As long as he's got a breath remaining, he's going to see to it you're a dead man. You and all who are on your side."

"So he's still planning to bring the fight here." Dal-ton stopped short of admitting he was aware of the date Abernathy had set.

Raff nodded. "There's not a soul out at the ranch who wants to be involved, me included, but, yes, he's made up his mind. What little is left of it." He also stopped short of mentioning the Colonel's planned schedule.

"Too bad the roadhouse lady was so drunk her aim wasn't better," Dalton said.

"Ain't that the truth."

"To answer your question," Ben said, "I see no way for this to have a peaceful ending."

"I fear you're right," Raff said as he tossed the dregs from his cup. "I want you to know I've got no personal bad feelings toward you. I've thought of just hightail-ing it out of here—so have a lot of others—but if we were to do so the Colonel would just have us hunted down and shot. He's said as much. We're left with no choice in the matter.

"I best be on my way and catch up with the doctor."

Dalton watched as he walked away, struggling with the insane thought that they might soon be shooting at one another.

Duke approached and Ben told him of the shooting that had occurred at the ranch. "I don't reckon there's any way things can get much crazier," he said, chuckling for the first time in several days. "Too bad the old lady didn't first consult Kelly and take dynamite along with her."

Dalton briefly smiled at the suggestion, then turned serious. "As long as Abernathy's still alive," he said, "nothing's changed. We've still got a fight on our hands."

Keene left him sitting on the bench. "I'll be back shortly," he said as he headed down the street. He needed to visit with Shelby Profer.

A T THE RANCH house, the maid had gotten Abernathy to his bed and was applying pressure to the wound when the doctor arrived. She had a pile of bloodstained pillows beneath the injured leg and was trying to convince her boss to forgo more tequila and sip water from the glass she held to his lips. His forehead was shiny with sweat and his breathing shallow. Delirious, he kept calling for a dog.

"Normally," the doctor said, "I'd advise against it, but in these circumstances I suggest you allow him more alcohol. The less aware he is of what's about to take place, the better."

He cut away the bloody pants leg and removed a set of instruments from his bag as the maid washed the badly swollen thigh. "The bullet needs to come out as

quickly as possible to avoid blood poisoning setting in."

The Colonel screamed as Doc Thorndale poured
alcohol into the torn flesh, then passed out.

"As much as I hate to," the doctor said once he'd
removed the bullet and stitched the wound, "I'll stay
the night to make sure he recovers."

The maid left to find the cook and ask that she prepare a meal for the doctor.

T HE FIRST HINT of daylight was showing through the
     nearby window when Abernathy woke with a loud
cough, followed by a pained grunt. He looked over at
the doctor who was dozing in a chair and called his
name. "I assume I'll live," he said.

Dr. Thorndale rubbed sleep from his eyes, stood,
and stretched without replying.

As the maid arrived and began fussing with his pillows, the Colonel eased himself into a sitting position.
"Has anybody found that crazy old woman and killed
her yet?"

The doctor made little attempt to hide his disdain
as he gathered his equipment into his bag to leave.
"You'll be fine," he said, "since no arteries were damaged. I would suggest you remain in bed and keep the
leg elevated for a week or so. Attempting to walk before that might very well tear away the stitches and
cause more bleeding. I've instructed your maid about
regularly changing the dressing. Unless you have questions, I'll be on my way." Without waiting for a reply,
he was out the door.

No sooner was he gone than Abernathy was yelling

at the maid, telling her to find Raff Bailey and bring him to his bedside.

"If I was a praying man," Bailey told one of the cow-hands as he left the bunkhouse, "I'd be asking that the Colonel's going to tell me he's decided to call things off until he's feeling better."

Such would not be the case.

CHAPTER 26

SHELBY PROFER HOOKED his thumbs into his vest pockets and leaned back in his chair as Duke surveyed the room with a look of amazement on his face. "If it wasn't you sitting behind that desk," he said, "I'd guess I came to the wrong place."

The lawyer smiled. "I have made arrangements with an excellent cleaning lady," he said. "Things are now so perfectly organized that I'm unable to find anything."

Keene removed his hat, settled in a chair, and began telling what had taken place at the ranch. "I just overheard it from one of the Colonel's own people. He's laid up, shot bad in the leg."

Profer pondered the welcome news. "This," he said, "could dramatically alter the plan I had in mind and offer us an even better one to consider."

"I don't recall you ever explaining the first one."

"No matter now. With Colonel Abernathy lame and bedridden, it is highly unlikely he will be leading any advance against our associates. Being homebound reduces him to nothing more than a vulnerable adversary in need of comforting. That's what we'll plan to do, pay him a get-well visit."

Duke wasn't following.

"You're familiar with the phrase 'While the cats are away . . .'" We, sir, shall be the mice. There will be details yet to work out, but what we'll do is go to the Shooting Star after Abernathy's men have left to do battle with Mr. Dalton and Mr. Kelly and the others we've enlisted.

"I see the possibility of our bringing a quick and justifiable close to this matter. We'll discuss this further after I've had more time to think about it. And, of course, this is just between you and me."

As Duke rose to leave, the attorney had another request. "Is it possible you own a sidearm I could borrow? Time is of the essence, and I feel the need of a bit of practice."

Keen walked back toward the livery with a bemused look on his face. He wasn't all that certain that Profer's plan, whatever it was, had a chance of working. And he certainly couldn't picture the old lawyer replacing his cane with his Peacemaker.

He might have felt a little better if he'd known Profer in his younger days.

To earn money for law school, he had worked as a buffalo hunter up on the Texas High Plains. In addition to becoming an excellent marksman with a rifle, he also gained necessary experience with his sidearm since it was regularly necessary to fight off raiding Comanches and other buffalo hunters attempting to steal the hides they had collected. The reason for his limp and the use of a cane was not his age but the fact that a horse had fallen on him during a fight with Indians, breaking his leg. Even as Profer was trapped beneath the fallen horse, he had been able to shoot and kill several members of the raiding party.

By the time his leg was injured he had earned enough to fund his education and left buffalo hunting to enroll in school. Since then he had neither ridden a horse nor held a gun.

Long after Duke was gone, he sat at his desk, tapping the head of his cane against the floor. He was not nearly as confident about his still-murky plan as he had let on. Gunfights were an exercise for the immortal young, not philosophical elders. Still, as he had watched events play out and come to know the defenders of his community, he had felt a growing need to make a contribution, to perform a final gesture that would demonstrate he still had worth.

In his mind, this had never been a standoff between two groups of men eager to return to the frightful kind of battle many had known as Confederate soldiers. They had survived one war and did not deserve to be forced to fight another. All this growing madness was the fault of one evil and greed-driven man, Colonel Raymond Abernathy.

And now, if what Duke had told him was true, he, too, was crippled. Profer liked the idea of things being even. Another old saying passed along by his father came to mind: To kill a snake, you cut off his head.

A T THE SHOOTING Star, it was as if Profer had read the minds of those who drew their pay from

Abernathy. Upon learning he had been shot, to a man they were disappointed to hear that he had survived. The only remaining question was whether their boss would go forward with his insane plan.

Raff Bailey had returned from the Colonel's bedside with the answer.

Most of the cowhands were younger and Bailey wondered if they had fully grasped the danger of the mission Abernathy planned for them.

"I'm duty bound to tell you that he will reward each man with five hundred dollars and a half-dozen head of cattle," he said. "There's also a sizable bounty for any man who kills the old lady who shot him. He again emphasized that anyone who chooses to take his leave will be hunted down and shot."

One of the wranglers asked his advice. "If he's stove up and can't leave his bed, how's he to know who chose to take off or just got himself killed in the fighting and didn't return?"

"Any chance of him coming to his senses and forgetting the whole thing?" another asked.

"I've considered the same things," Bailey said. "He's a stubborn man, and he's bound and determined to carry this out. Whether you choose to participate is a decision every man has to make on his own. You've got only two remaining days to think it over. Meanwhile, he's requested that a couple of men station themselves outside his bedroom door."

He didn't mention that less than an hour earlier, while standing at the Colonel's bedside receiving instructions, he had considered shooting him.

"What are you planning on doing?" another cowboy said.

"The Colonel tells me I'm to be the leader, but I'm not here to demand that any of you follow. Think things out and make your own decisions before Saturday morning." With that, he turned and left the bunkhouse to take a ride and clear his head. As he walked away, several cowboys were already stuffing their belongings into saddlebags.

Up at the house, Colonel Abernathy lay in bed, still in pain, his leg badly swollen, and frowning at the bowl of stew the cook had brought him. He was unaware that just a hundred yards away his plan for revenge was crumbling.

IN DUKE KEENE'S livery, a similar meeting was taking place. The men hired by Profer were sitting on hay bales or leaning against the doors of the stalls, most of them drinking the strong coffee that Lanny Butler had prepared. The last to arrive were Sheriff Langston and Profer, who had talked briefly before entering the barn.

There was a smattering of laughter when Dalton described the incident that had had played out between the Colonel and the old woman from the roadhouse.

"Unless they load him in a wagon and haul him along," Ben said, "it seems highly unlikely that he'll be accompanying his men Saturday. Fact is, I'd like to think the whole thing might get called off. But knowing how crazy he is—probably even more so after his encounter with Miss Luisa—that's not likely.

"I'll not hold anyone to their promise to be a part of this, but I still feel strongly that we need to be sure they don't get to town. We don't want innocent folks involved, so best we're prepared. Anyone who wishes to can walk out the door without apology."

No one left, so he continued. Since they had no idea when on Saturday the ranch hands would be coming, the plan was to assemble at the livery late Friday afternoon and ride to the site near the roadhouse. There, they would wait through the night. "If they arrive early Saturday morning, we'll be ready. If they choose to wait until nightfall, maybe we can get Luisa to cook up something for us since she's determined not to leave."

"I think everyone would like to shake her hand," Duke said, "even if her aim's not exactly what I would have wished it to be."

T HOUGH HE'D WANTED to attend the meeting, John Rawlings had been told by the doctor to remain in bed for a few more days. Doc Thorndale had allowed him to return home and, while much of the facial swelling had gone down, he was still experiencing headaches and dizziness. When told of the encounter between the Colonel and Luisa, his laughter quickly turned to a grimace as pain shot across his face.

Mandy entered the bedroom with a tray of biscuits and apple butter. Alton, getting used to the discoloration on his father's face, followed her and climbed onto the end of the bed.

"I'm glad he's not old enough to know what a fool his old man made of himself," John said as he reached for a biscuit.

"I'll not argue about you sometimes being foolish," his wife said, "but one day he'll be proud to know that his daddy is a man of considerable courage. I'm proud of you, too. Still a little mad that you allowed yourself to almost be killed, but proud just the same." She leaned toward him and gently kissed his forehead.

They sat quietly, sharing the breakfast and watching as Alton slipped a biscuit to Too, who had joined them. "I'm guessing Ben's going to have a hard time getting his dog back," John said.

"Knowing him, all he's concerned about is that Too has a good home and is being well cared for. Besides, he told me he's got a dog of his own waiting for him back in Aberdene."

John was silent for a moment, then said, "You've enjoyed seeing Ben again, haven't you?"

Her only reply was a slight nod. And then they sat silently, watching their son playfully wrestle with Too.

CHAPTER 27

F OR SHERIFF LANGSTON, it felt strange not being the
  person in charge, detailing plans and assigning
responsibilities. Too late, he was realizing how badly
he had tarnished his badge and lost his way. Though
there had been no formal dismissal from the mayor, he
realized he had little authority, not to mention self-
respect, remaining. Even his deputies had become
dismissive.

He had accompanied Profer to an isolated meadow
north of the stockyards, searching for a place the lawyer could try his hand at shooting Duke's pistol.

"What exactly is it you're preparing for?" the sheriff
said.

"'Preparing' is the operative word," Profer said. "In
the event I'm in a compromising position, I want to be
ready to protect myself. Nothing more, nothing less. I
have no plan to challenge anyone to a duel or compete
in a fast-draw competition. I just want to be able to

shoot straight should it become necessary." He elaborated no further.

Langston laughed and took the pistol, cocked the trigger, and demonstrated how best to aim. "Just like pointing your finger," he said. Profer didn't bother telling his instructor of his previous experience with firearms, instead allowing himself to be treated like someone who had never held a weapon before.

It all came back quickly: the feel of the gun in his hand, the heft of the steel, and the quick jolt that made his arm tingle each time he fired. For a half hour, Langston watched Profer shoot at tree limbs, fallen logs, and a fleeing rabbit, hitting his target more often than either had expected. After there was no more ammunition, the sheriff praised him in the same gentle manner he might use to applaud a schoolboy for learning his multiplication tables.

They climbed back into the buggy as the day was beginning to fade toward evening. A cool breeze blew across the flatland and the horse had calmed once the shooting ended. "Pretty country, isn't it?" the old lawyer said. "Peaceful. That's as it should be. That's how I hope it will be again, once this unfortunate matter with Colonel Abernathy is settled."

He sensed Otto Langston's uneasiness as he spoke. "We've not talked about it," he said, "but I bear you no ill will for things that have happened in the past. We all lose our way at one time or another. The important thing is to get back on the right track and seek a way to make amends. I sense that's now your intent."

Profer then began to lay out his plan. "Since I'll be needing your assistance, I hope you will convince Mr. Dalton that instead of riding with him and the others, you'll need to man your post here in town on Saturday," he said. He then put a finger to his lips. "Just between us, mind you."

They were almost to town before Profer spoke again. "Since you've known him for quite some time, I'd be interested in hearing your personal feeling about this fellow Abernathy."

The sheriff took a deep breath and gazed into the distance, as if collecting his thoughts. "He's never been a likable man, one who cares what others think of him," he said. "His goal since I've known him has been to accumulate enough money and power to make folks fear him. Not respect, fear him. Me included, I'm sorry to admit. Then, when someone finally stood up to him and some of that power and fear began to disappear, he turned meaner than ever. My guess is that getting himself shot by a woman recently might have been his last straw, knowing people are now laughing behind his back.

"Strange as it sounds, getting shot may have been the best thing that could have happened for him. See, I could never picture him being a part of a gunfight, even one he encouraged. Now, thanks to that roadhouse lady, he can lay safe in bed and not be criticized for keeping away while others do his dirty work."

"Sounds like you're describing a coward who doesn't much want to admit his shortcoming."

Langston nodded. "I'd say that's as near the truth about Raymond Abernathy as you're likely to get."

A FTER PROFER LEFT him at his office, Langston found a single deputy on duty. He said the other was on patrol and that everything was quiet, even down in

Hell's Half Acre. The sheriff told him to go on home. "If need arises," he said, "we'll send for you."

When the deputy left, he tamped tobacco into his pipe and settled behind his desk. There was a hollow feeling in the pit of his stomach as he watched smoke slowly rise toward the ceiling. From across the way, he could hear someone moaning in the drunk cage, and a slow-moving wagon passed outside. He let his eyes roam the small office that had been his second home for over a decade and suddenly felt old and tired. He tried to remember the time when he had been a good law enforcement officer, respected by the townspeople he'd sworn to serve, and it seemed long ago. A shiver ran down his back as he wondered if he would have another chance at the return to grace he so badly wanted.

Lost in thought, he didn't hear the door open and was unaware that Ben Dalton was standing in front of his desk until he spoke.

"I was on my way back from the café and saw you through the window," Ben said. "It appears you were daydreaming."

"Reckon I was," the sheriff said. "Don't seem to get much time for that these days."

M ILES AWAY, COLONEL Abernathy, the man Langston had allowed to destroy his reputation, had drunk himself into a nightmare-filled stupor and was restlessly dreaming of an even worse kind of loss.

While his boss slept, Raff Bailey wandered the compound alone, trying to grasp the situation in which he found himself. All he'd ever wanted was to cowboy, to work with horses and cattle and tend the land. Some day, he hoped to have a small spread of his own, maybe up north in Montana or the Dakotas that he'd heard good things about. He just wanted to be alone and be left alone.

Even when he'd worn the Confederate uniform he'd never considered himself much of a fighter. And that drunken afternoon in town when he shot up the livery still embarrassed him.

Yet here he was, expected to ramrod another man's foolhearted plan to prove his importance, to polish his misguided ego, regardless of the cost. The Colonel was asking him and the others to risk their lives simply so he could settle a grudge. If it weren't for the fact it was likely a suicide mission, the idea of riding into town to attack a livery, of all places, would have been laughable.

He roamed past the empty corral, then through the barn, where pigeons softly cooed in the rafters, giving the nighttime its music. He walked out toward the pasture, where he could see the distant Longhorns still grazing in the moonlight. And as he did so, he knew the peace and quiet was soon to be forever lost.

Already, a half dozen of the workers had packed their things and left. Even the Sloan brothers, who had kidnapped the little Rawlings boy, had stolen away in the dead of night. Not even enough were left to continue the patrolling of the fence line the boss had ordered. He mentally counted the number who had chosen to remain and earn Abernathy's blood money bonus. Eight, maybe ten, counting himself. Secretly, he hoped others would have the good sense to take their leave before Saturday.

Still, he'd not offered advice, feeling it wasn't his place to do so. His only warning had come after the Colonel placed the bounty on the head of the old Mexican lady at the roadhouse. "Anybody who kills a woman, no matter how fat and ugly she is, can figure on getting shot by me," he'd said.

Bailey wasn't sure why he had decided to stay. Certainly, it wasn't out of loyalty to the Colonel, nor was it even the promise of an extra five hundred dollars in his pocket. Whether reasonable or not, he held to the slim hope that he might find some way, a miracle, that would keep his young co-workers alive.

And as he wandered through the dark, avoiding the tortured dreams that he knew sleep would bring, he found himself thinking of the only sure way of resolving things. But he just couldn't bring himself to walk into Abernathy's bedroom and end the misery.

He silently prayed someone else might.

IN TOWN, SHELBY Profer was also awake, wondering if there was anything in his law books that defined a legal difference between cold-blooded murder and mercy killing. The thought was pure folly, of course, especially since he had already reached the conclusion that in some instances they could be one and the same.

Whatever the penalty might be for such a crime didn't even cross his mind.

PART FOUR

—— ◇ ——

REDEEMING GRACE

CHAPTER 28

A BOOMING CLAP OF thunder rattled the windows of Colonel Abernathy's room, causing him to wake suddenly. For a moment, he was aware of neither where he was nor what time it might be. Sitting up, he was preparing to put on his pants before he felt the still-throbbing pain in his leg. When he tried to stand, his knee buckled, sending him sprawling onto the floor. He cursed as he used the bedpost to pull himself up and hobble to the window.

Outside, the morning sky was filled with dirty gray storm clouds and a torrential rain beat against the side of the house. Lightning flashed on the horizon. God was playing another cruel trick on him and he was glad there was no one to see the tears of frustration that ran down his face. The day he had been looking forward to was close and could now be spoiled by weather, of all things.

He had struggled back to the bed by the time the maid arrived. The fall had caused his stitches to tear away from the wound and he was bleeding again. He grimaced and cursed as she changed the dressing.

When Bailey arrived, rain dripping from his hat and hoping to learn that the next day's plan had been canceled, Abernathy was composed and drinking coffee. "Fine weather for a ride into town," he said.

Raff felt a deep sigh escape and didn't reply. There was no point in arguing.

"Could be it'll break before time to leave tomorrow," the Colonel said. "If not, it'll give us an advantage we hadn't figured on. They'll not expect us coming in weather like this. Go back out and tell the men to be ready to ride out after Saturday supper."

Having not said a word since entering the room, Bailey left to pass along the message.

E XCEPT FOR A lone wagon that was stuck in the mud, the streets of Fort Worth were empty. Duke was busy setting out buckets to catch water that was coming from leaks in the livery roof. Dalton stood in the doorway, looking skyward. He was trying to do the impossible—think like Colonel Abernathy.

"No one with good sense would even consider getting himself out in this," Kelly said as he joined him and held a palm out into the stinging rain. "But we've already agreed he's not dealing from a full deck. Most likely, he'll carry out his plan even if it causes his men and their horses to drown while on their way. He's probably thinking since we're looking at things with some measure of logic, it'll give a crazy man an advantage."

Dalton agreed. "We'll head out tomorrow morning," he said as he watched two young boys race into the street and begin dancing in the ankle-deep water. "Come rain or shine."

From inside the livery, they heard Keene call their names. "Me and Lanny could use some help emptying these buckets," he said.

For many, the unexpected downpour was a godsend. With their crops just coming up, the farmers were delighted. Dried-up creeks would be running again, livestock tanks were already near full, and the parched landscapes would soon be turning from brown to emerald green. Thanks would be sung from every pew in town on Sunday morning, if people could manage to get to church.

Even Sheriff Langston and his deputies had smiles on their faces. The normal rush of weekend revelers weren't as likely to crowd the Half Acre saloons if they had to slog through heavy rain and muddy streets to get drunk and start fights.

One of those not pleased, however, was Shelby Profer. He had planned to use his buggy for the trip to the ranch but was now resigned to riding a horse for the first time in years. He needed to get word to Duke to pick him a gentle one.

The day before, he had invited Keene and the sheriff to dinner and finally disclosed some details of what he had in mind. After Langston assured him he knew an alternate route that would take them to the back side of the Shooting Star, he said they should plan to arrive in time to watch Colonel Abernathy's men leave, then make their way to the compound after it was deserted. Most likely, there would be guards left behind to watch the main house and they would determine how best to deal with them when the time came. The ultimate goal was to make their way to where Abernathy was recuperating. His earlier conversation with the sheriff had convinced him there was no chance of the Colonel joining in the attack he had planned. "The most important thing," Profer said, "is that he proves to be the coward Otto says he is. Otherwise, our trip will serve no purpose."

"I don't reckon I need to guess what your plan is once—if—we manage to make it inside the house," Duke had said.

"That," Profer replied, "will be entirely up to him." He lifted a glass of beer and said, "Before I offer a wishful toast to our success, I feel it my duty to advise you both that my strength is tending to matters inside a courthouse, not planning wild west adventures. But with your able assistance and a measure of good fortune, I think it will work."

Langston and Keene lifted their glasses. Though no one mentioned it, the three men, each from a vastly different walk of life, shared one thing in common. The best times of their lives were behind them. The lawyer and Duke were getting well up in years and the sheriff had destroyed his future. With not much left to look forward to, they had little to lose.

S UCH WAS NOT the case with some of the young cowboys who had accepted the offer to help defend the town. Lanny Butler had been pouting for several days, upset that Dalton said that under no circumstances would he be allowed to join in the ride south. Ben had attempted to soften the blow by insisting he was needed at the livery with Keene should something un-expected arise, but it failed to mend the young man's wounded pride.

"He's too young to be risking his life," Ben said to Duke after hearing Butler's final plea. "Especially on something of this nature." He thought back to the North-South war and the many boys he'd seen killed or wounded in needless battles. "Getting yourself killed after you've had a chance to live a full life and make your mark is one thing. Dying before you've even had a proper start is another."

Duke agreed and promised to talk with Lanny.

Meanwhile, he was secretly making plans to violate Dalton's instruction that he, too, stay in town Saturday. His pistol had been cleaned and loaded, a rain slicker was folded and tucked away in his saddlebag, and he'd decided which horse he would have Profer ride. The apprehension he'd once felt was turning to a warm rush of excitement he hadn't experienced in years.

R AFF BAILEY HAD been pleasantly surprised that most of those who had decided to leave their jobs and final paychecks behind were the young ranch hands. What remained were aging men in the final years of their ability to do the kind of work that had earned them a living for decades. The Shooting Star was their last stop and it was unlikely any had made plans for whatever time they had left. To them, the Colonel's bonus promise was like stumbling onto a pot of gold.

Jippy Sandoval was a good example. He had worked cattle for twenty-five years across three states, survived droughts and raging floods, suffered arthritis pains and poor eyesight, and, being a terrible poker player and lover of whiskey, was constantly broke and counting the hours until the next payday. He could neither read nor write but once could calm a wild mustang in a half day's time. With no family and few he could call friends, he had nothing to look forward to. And since he had to borrow a pistol from one of the departing wranglers, it was unlikely he was a very good shot.

Such was the caliber of men Bailey would be leading into battle.

CHAPTER 29

Saturday morning broke clear and dry, the storm clouds replaced by sun and a bright blue sky. The rain had not ended until late the previous night, causing Dalton and Kelly to wait until well after dawn to head toward the Glen Rose Valley. "It's unlikely the folks from the ranch will be traveling early," Anson said. "Even if they do, we'll meet up with them long before they can get here."

Ben detected an unusual sense of dread in his friend's voice.

"I'm just getting a little homesick," Kelly said. "I'm ready to get this over and done so I can get on back to Brush Creek." He laughed. "Never thought I'd be saying that."

Dalton had also been thinking a good deal about home. "If I'd had any notion of the trouble I was going to start," he said, "I'd have stayed in Aberdene and minded my own business."

Kelly grinned. "Oh, I doubt that. I'm thinking you

had good reason to come running like your tail was on fire. I can even call her name if you like."

Ben made no comment except to say, "Well, at least I wouldn't have imposed on you to get involved."

WHEN THE GROUP—Dalton, Kelly, and eight others—arrived at the roadhouse, they saw that their planned hideaway could no longer be used. Water was rushing over the creek banks, rising toward the back of Luisa's little adobe building. She had difficulty finding enough dry wood for her stove to heat her tamales for the arriving men.

"Not sure I can recall ever seeing a lady cook wearing a sidearm before," Kelly whispered.

"My suggestion is you only tell her she looks nice and that her tamales are the best you ever ate," Ben replied.

"Yeah, and that we're mighty proud she's on our side," Kelly said.

Aside from eating and cleaning mud from their boots and the horses' hooves, there was nothing to do but wait. As the day dragged on, the tension built and some began to wonder if Abernathy's men were even coming. Others suggested they mount up and ride out toward the Shooting Star to see if they could intercept the people they were waiting for.

When Luisa offered to pass around a couple of bottles of tequila to calm nerves, Dalton told her he didn't think it a good idea. She took a long drink from one of the bottles herself, then put them away.

It was dusk when Dalton finally saw tiny flickers of light in the distance. As they got closer, he said, "It appears they're carrying torches. Spread out and find the best cover you can."

He climbed into the saddle, placed a Winchester across his lap, and took a position in the middle of the muddy road. Since it was him they were coming for, he was going to make things easy. Behind him, rifles and handguns were pointed in the direction of the oncoming riders.

AN HOUR EARLIER, Langston, Keene, and Profer had watched from the shelter of a grove of scrub oaks as Abernathy's men mingled outside the bunkhouse, waiting to leave. They saw the torches being lit and the men carrying them lead the way toward the ranch entrance. It was difficult to tell from such a distance but there appeared to be six, maybe eight, of them. They were riding two-by-two at a good pace. "I know the Colonel's horse," Langston said, "and don't see it. He's staying behind, just as we expected."

The sheriff had led the way out of Fort Worth and onto a trail used by Shooting Star cowboys to herd cattle to auction. It reached the fence line of the ranch a hundred yards from the back porch of the main house.

Profer was the first to dismount, glad to be back on solid ground. "If it wasn't for my bad knee," he said, "I'd give strong consideration to walking back to town." He was dreading the distance to the ranch house.

Langston took the lead since he was most familiar with the layout of the ranch. "My guess," he said, "is that the Colonel will want those watching over him to stay close. So most likely, they'll be standing outside the door of his room." He added that somewhere in the house would be the cook and maid, whom they would need to silence.

A smoky ring circled a bright moon, lighting their way as they reached a corral, then walked along the edge of the garden. It didn't appear there was anyone standing guard on the porch. "We'll go in through the main door," Langston whispered. "Abernathy's room is upstairs."

They had only taken a few steps inside the house before a chorus of screams erupted. Relieved to finally have Abernathy quieted, the women were in their nightgowns, having tea before they retired for the evening. Pistol in hand, Duke rushed to the kitchen to quiet them.

Alerted by the noise, the two guards raced to the top of the stairwell and began shooting in the direction of the shadowy intruders. Profer ducked behind a china cabinet as Langston returned fire. One of the guards let out a loud grunt before lurching forward and tumbling down the polished stairs. The other watched in stunned dismay until the sheriff took aim and shot him in the chest. Seconds later he, too, was on the floor.

Keene had returned after quieting the women and helped Langston move the bodies away so they could make their way to the second floor. Profer stared briefly at the two dead men, grotesquely entwined, their lifeless eyes open. He hadn't even been aware that he'd drawn his pistol.

The three men held their breath as they made their way down the dark hallway that led to the master bedroom. The sheriff broke the silence. "He'll be armed," he whispered.

After they had positioned themselves near the closed

door, Langston called out a warning. "We're coming in," he said, "and unless you want to die in your bed, you'll put your weapon aside."

The reply was two booming shots that left gaping holes in the door.

"Your men are dead and the women are downstairs in their sleeping clothes," the sheriff yelled. "You've got nobody to do your fighting for you. You're all by your lonesome."

"Otto? That you?" Abernathy replied.

"It is, and I've got others with me. We're armed and ready to blow your head off if need be. Do yourself a favor and allow us to come in without more shooting." As he spoke he pushed the door open just enough to see the foot of the bed. Quickly, Duke shoved him aside and rushed into the room, pointing his Peacemaker at the bewildered Colonel.

His shotgun, which he'd not had time to reload, lay across his chest.

"Don't kill me . . . please." Abernathy's voice was weak and pleading as Langston approached the bed and pushed the barrel of his pistol against his forehead.

"It's something I should have done a long time ago," the sheriff said.

Shelby Profer stood at the foot of the bed, his pistol now at his side, letting his eyes roam the room. On one wall was a large oil painting of the Colonel, proudly astride his horse, his pearl-handled pistol on his hip. Atop a nearby table was a clutter of mementos: trophies and ribbons won by his prized cattle and medals he'd been awarded while a Union soldier. Next to it was a well-stocked liquor cabinet, complete with rows of crystal glasses. A half-dozen pairs of polished boots were

lined up neatly on the floor of an open closet. It was the
room, the lawyer thought, of a self-absorbed man.

"Arrest him," he said.

Keene's eyes widened. "We ain't going to kill him?
We come all this way, wading through mud up to our
shinbones, and now we're not . . ."

Profer nodded toward the sheriff. "Do your duty and
place the man under arrest." He didn't bother explaining that in correspondence with the Texas governor he
had been assured that Colonel Raymond Abernathy—
murderer, swindler, kidnapper, and thief—would, once
captured, be tried in an Austin courtroom. Shelby Profer, Esq., would come out of retirement to serve as pros-
ecutor. If the attorney general approved, John Rawlings
would be his second chair.

Keeping his pistol to Abernathy's head, Langston
told Duke where he could find rope in the barn.

"Hook up a wagon while you're there," Profer said,
"and do it quickly. We've got one more thing to do."

"Should we allow him to get dressed?" Langston
said.

The attorney looked in the direction of the closet.
"Yes, of course. I think his Union uniform would do
nicely."

WHEN BAILEY AND his men saw the lone rider waiting in the road, they came to an abrupt halt.
From the distance, it was impossible to see who it was
or determine what kind of threat he might represent.
Almost a half hour passed before Bailey instructed his
followers to remain in place and began slowly riding
toward the figure.

"This is as far as we'll allow you and your men to go," Dalton said as Bailey neared. He warned that there were others with him, armed and ready to see that they advanced no farther. "I'd like to see this matter end without bloodshed," he said, "and would appreciate hearing your thinking on the matter."

"You know I've got no personal grudge against you," Bailey said, "but if we turn back, the Colonel will—"

He was interrupted by distant yelling and the creaking sound of a wagon headed their way. Keene was standing in the driver's seat, holding the reins in one hand and waving wildly with the other. Profer was at his side, hanging on for dear life, and Langston trailed on horseback. The wagon rolled past the stunned ranch hands and on toward Dalton and Bailey.

"Y'all done any shooting yet?" Duke said as he reined the horses to a halt.

In back, the Colonel sat, bound and gagged, his leg bleeding again. "He's on his way to jail," Sheriff Langston said.

Raff Bailey was the first to laugh. "Well, I guess we can go home and tend the cattle," he said as members of Dalton's group emerged from their hiding places and gathered around the wagon, looking at the prisoner as if he were a carnival sideshow exhibit.

No one seemed disappointed that not a shot had been fired. Except, perhaps, Luisa, who came running from the roadhouse, screaming curses in Spanish as she approached the wagon. Before anyone could stop her, she slapped Abernathy hard in the face and again demanded that he return her dog.

CHAPTER 30

SHERIFF LANGSTON HAD decided he would not leave his office until Abernathy was transported to Austin. He would sleep there, have his deputies deliver his meals there, and not let his prisoner out of his sight until a telegram arrived to notify him with details of the transfer. Regardless of what arrangements were made, he planned to deliver the Colonel personally. For the first time in months, he felt good about himself.

From the dingy confines of his cell, Abernathy glared at his captor. "I should have known you would betray me," he said. "All that money I paid you, a sorry, weak little man. I hope you slowly burn in hell."

The sheriff's only reply was to assure him that Doc Thorndale would be stopping by regularly to tend to his wound, changing the bandages and making sure there was no infection. "We'll want you healthy for your trip," Langston said.

"What about my place, my cattle?"

"Raff Bailey has been instructed to look after

things until a decision is made about how your property will be dispensed with. I've also told him he should make himself welcome to your tequila."

Abernathy, his uniform still muddy from the wagon ride, slumped against the wall, a defeated man.

T HE CELEBRATION WAS not what anyone had expected. Everyone was too tired, the rush of adrenaline faded to simple relief that the matter had been settled quietly. Shelby Profer assembled those he had hired and paid them, pleased that none had been injured and knowing that he was making a generous donation to the economy of the Hell's Half Acre saloons. Lanny had made coffee and was washing down the horses, paying particular attention to Dalton's Dolly. Mandy arrived with a large basket filled with sandwiches, her husband and her son at her side. Too followed, his tail wagging, as he was greeted by everyone on hand.

John Rawlings, his bruises finally fading, thanked everyone again for bringing an end to the unhappy saga that had so disrupted his family. He was not yet aware of Profer's plan for the prosecution of Abernathy but, like most lawyers, was already anxious to see all loose ends neatly tied.

"It troubles me that we still don't know who killed Thomas Cookson," he said.

"I reckon we do," Duke said. "Before we left the ranch the other evening, I was speaking with Abernathy's maid about that very thing. She recalled that on the night the banker was shot, her boss arrived home late, his shirt spattered with blood. He insisted she wash it immediately and say nothing about it to anyone.

"I figure a good lawyer like yourself could easily convince a jury that it was Colonel Abernathy who done the killing and get him hanged for it."

Dalton found Anson Kelly in the rear of the barn, helping Lanny clean the horses. He extended a hand to shake but Kelly ignored it, instead wrapping him in a bear hug. "It's been a pleasure getting to know you," he said.

"Right back at you," Ben said. "I guess you'll be heading on to Brush Creek."

"First light tomorrow. What about you?"

"Soon. Though Mr. Profer says that the folks in Austin will likely hire a couple Pinkerton men to come along with the marshals to take custody of the Colonel, the sheriff seems bound and determined to go along for the ride. If he does, I might just tag along myself."

Kelly responded with a knowing grin. "And I 'spect you've still got matters here that need tending."

"That I do," Dalton replied. "There's a little stray dog I've seen a time or two down by the laundry. I figure if nobody there wants him, I might take him to Luisa at the roadhouse. He's not Too, but I figure he'll make her good company."

As he spoke, he heard Keene in the doorway, welcoming the mayor to the gathering. "Seeing how it's an election year," Kelly said, "he's probably trying to figure a way to take credit for all you've done."

"You know it wasn't just me," Dalton again reminded him.

In another part of the barn, Profer was nibbling on a sandwich while explaining to Rawlings why he would need to share his office a while longer before turning it over to him permanently. "Tell your missus I'll try not to clutter up the fine cleaning job she's done, though I'll make no promises."

John was overwhelmed when told that he might soon be visiting Austin.

The mayor slowly made his way through the crowd, shaking every hand he could find, until he reached Dalton and Kelly. "My city," he said, "owes you both a large debt of gratitude. My secretary is having proper citations drawn up as we speak.

"Earlier today, I paid a visit to Sheriff Langston and he informed me that as soon as this Abernathy situation is completely resolved, he plans to turn in his badge. Going to retire and raise goats, if you can imagine. I tried to convince him that bygones are bygones and that I'd like for him to stay on. But he can be a stubborn old coot once he gets his mind made up.

"So, I'll soon be in need of a new sheriff. Either one of you interested?"

Dalton and Kelly looked at each other for a moment, and then Ben replied first. "I appreciate it, but I already have a good job back home."

To his surprise, Kelly said he would go back to Brush Creek and think about it.

As the mayor turned to leave, he tipped his bowler to Mandy Rawlings as she approached. After John had shared his good news with her, she turned the duty of handing out sandwiches over to her son, who immediately slipped one to Too once her back was turned.

Dalton was smiling as she walked toward him.

"I guess you'll soon be on your way to Aberdene," she said.

He repeated the plan he'd earlier shared with Kelly.

"So you might still have time to come for supper

one evening soon. You have a standing invitation, so
you'll need only to tell us when."

He didn't tell her what he was thinking, that he
probably wouldn't be seeing her again. Nor did he
mention that every time he did so, a numbing melan-
choly stayed with him for days.

There was a long silence as they stood looking at
each other. Mandy reached out and touched his hand.
"It's been so good seeing you again," she said. "We'll
all miss you, me most of all." Somehow, she knew she
wasn't likely to see him again.

Dalton was relieved when Duke interrupted. "Soon
as those not invited take their leave," he said, "I've got
a bottle of celebrating whiskey hid away."

O NCE EVERYONE WAS gone and Keene's bottle emp-
tied, Ben walked across town to the jail. Inside,
Otto Langston sat alone at his desk, smoking his pipe.

"You really going to raise goats?"

"That I am," the sheriff said, "and be proud of doing it. Once the Colonel is put away to get his due, I'm
through."

Once enemies, now friends, the two men fell silent
as an air of discomfort suddenly swept through the
room.

"You did a fine thing, Sheriff Langston. Folks are
going to remember that for a long time to come," Dalton said as he turned to leave. "I'm proud to know you."

CHAPTER 31

DISCUSSIONS ABOUT HOW best to transport Colonel Abernathy to Austin seemed to drag on endlessly, bogged in paperwork and changing of minds. In one telegram, it was suggested that taking the train might be best. Only a few days later, they wanted to know how Sheriff Langston felt about traveling by stagecoach. If they decided to move him by wagon or on horseback, how many men should be assigned to ride along?

"Like I told Mr. Profer, it would have been a whole lot simpler if we'd just killed him," Duke said after Dalton mentioned the most recent correspondence. "However, I can't say I much mind picturing him rotting away in that jail cell day and night either."

When Langston asked Ben if he had a preference, he opted for making the trip on horseback. "It'll take us longer, but I'd prefer being in the fresh air." The sheriff agreed and sent a two-word reply to the attorney general. *WE'LL RIDE*, it said.

Meanwhile, if there was ever any doubt about Abernathy's mental state, it became clear, to some at least, during his stay in jail. One moment he would be calm, even polite, then explode into a tantrum of rage, lashing out at everyone he believed was his enemy. He would go for long stretches of refusing the food brought to him by Langston or one of the deputies, then later scream that he was being starved to death. Once, when Doc Thorndale visited to check his wound, the Colonel was certain he was Jesus, coming to forgive his sins. At other times he would cower in his bunk, pointing across the tiny cell at an invisible menace, certain the devil had come to steal his soul.

Thorndale, for one, thought it all an act designed to make him or a deputy drop his guard long enough for Abernathy to attempt an escape. Langston agreed.

"The only thing crazy about him," the sheriff said, "is him thinking he might get out of here. It won't happen until the day we put chains on him and head out for Austin. Once we get him there, I don't care if he goes crazier than an outhouse rat."

It was almost three weeks before the day finally arrived.

A state marshal and two Pinkerton agents arrived unannounced at the sheriff's office, carrying orders from the attorney general. Stern-faced and far from friendly, they left no doubt who would be in charge. Only after Langston said he would refuse to release the prisoner to their custody did they agree to allow him and Dalton to travel with them.

They told the sheriff to plan on leaving under the cover of darkness to avoid any public spectacle. He was assured they had a map of the route they planned to follow, but they wouldn't show it to him. None bothered to introduce himself by name.

"Might get myself thrown in jail before this trip's over," Langston told Dalton when he arrived at the livery to alert him to be ready to leave as soon as the moon was up.

B EN WAS PACKED and ready long before the sheriff stopped by. His duffel bag was packed with his few personal belongings and Duke had filled his saddlebags with provisions. Lanny had a small sack of oats for Dolly waiting by his saddle.

His plan was to head directly to Aberdene once they had finished their business in Austin.

"It's gonna get plumb lonesome around here," Duke said. "With Kelly done gone and you fixing to leave, it'll be just me and Lanny. Most of the time I've enjoyed having you as company."

"Most of the time?"

"On occasion, your snoring got a bit loud. Sometimes woke me and scared the horses." Keene reached into his hip pocket and withdrew an envelope. Handing it to Dalton, he said, "I saw Mrs. Rawlings in the café and she asked me to see that you got this. Her instructions were that you're not to read it until you're on your way."

A S EVENING APPROACHED, Dalton and Lanny sat on the bench outside, both having difficulty saying their goodbyes. "I'll forever be indebted to you for saving my life," Ben finally said. "You can be sure I'll never forget that. What plans do you have for yourself?"

"I'm thinking that once there's a new sheriff I might apply to be a deputy, or at least be the jailer again. I've decided I want to be a lawman." He almost added "like you," but stopped himself.

"Only a fool would hesitate to hire you."

B Y THE TIME Ben and Dolly arrived at the back of the jail, Colonel Abernathy was already in the saddle. He had a chain around his waist that connected to his handcuffs, and he was dressed in a faded gray jumpsuit. Instead of boots, he had a ragged pair of house shoes on his feet. Even in the moonlight, one could see how sunken his eyes were and how unkempt his beard had become. He no longer looked like one of the wealthiest cattle owners in North Texas.

No one spoke until the marshal said, "We best be going."

Dalton hesitated for a second. "I like to know who I'll be riding alongside," he said.

"Thaddeus Willowby. Most just call me Thad," the marshal said. He was the only one of the visiting lawmen to reply, and his were the last words spoken until they were well on their way.

T HE SUN WAS up but the morning still reasonably cool by the time they neared the tiny community of Cedar Valley. "I'm needing to relieve myself and stretch my sore leg," the Colonel said.

They found a shaded pool beneath a spring and dismounted. One of the Pinkertons told Sheriff Langston to ride into town and see if there was a café where he could buy some biscuits and bacon. "I'm not inclined to parade our prisoner through town," he said.

"That an order?" Langston replied. The sarcasm in his question was obvious.

"Nope, just a polite request."

Dalton watched Dolly drink her fill and fed her a handful of the oats Lanny had sent along. He then led her to what little shade a cluster of young cedars offered and sat. He was anxious to read the letter Duke had given him.

H ER HANDWRITING WAS the neatest he'd ever seen. *Dearest Ben*, it began.

I have tried several times to express how thankful I am for all you have done for me and my family, but felt a need to also put it in writing. Had you not answered my request for help, I hate to think how bad things might have been for us. God bless you for being such a good and loyal friend.

I think your influence on John has pointed him in a direction he was searching for but couldn't seem to find. And as you probably already know, little Alton has come to love you dearly. I'll make sure he never forgets the kind man who gave him candy and brought Too into his life.

You should know that I love my husband and my family dearly. Also that my feelings for you are something I will forever treasure. As I have done over the years, I shall keep you in my heart and in my fondest thoughts. You are the wonderful man whom I long ago let get away.

Since I may never see you again, I wish you every happiness, my dear, sweet Ben, and will close with this thought:

I'm so glad we danced.

Love, Mandy

He carefully folded the letter and placed it in his pocket, then closed his eyes and tried, perhaps for the last time, to picture her face.

"I've got biscuits and a jug of coffee," Langston said as he returned, "but there wasn't no bacon."

THE FIRST DAYS were tedious, causing Dalton to give second thoughts to his wish that they make the trip on horseback. He and the sheriff rode at Abernathy's side while the others stayed a few yards ahead, leading the way. There was still little conversation aside from the Colonel's constant complaining about his leg.

At sundown they would find a place to camp, always sure there was a sturdy tree trunk to which they could chain their prisoner. A fire would be built and coffee brewed, and strips of dried jerky and what was left of Langston's biscuits sufficed as the lone meal of the day. They would rotate shifts through the night, closely watching Abernathy and listening to his constant moaning.

"Not exactly traveling in style, are we?" Dalton said as he gnawed at the jerky. No one responded to his observation.

"There's got to be roads or maybe cattle trails out this

way," the sheriff said to the Pinkerton agent who was studying his map by the light of the fire. "Why is it we're riding cross country, through bushes and along rocky ground? It ain't good for the horses, or my rear end."

"The fewer people we encounter, the better," the agent finally replied. "We'll do the leading, you and your friend just do the following. As I recall, nobody said you had to come along."

None among them was aware they had been followed since passing by Cedar Valley.

A FTER CLAUDE AND Calvin Sloan decided they had no wish to risk their lives so Colonel Abernathy could get his revenge and left the Shooting Star, they wandered the Fort Worth stockyards in search of work. And with the Half Acre saloons once again welcoming them, they spent whatever wages they received as day workers as quickly as they were earned. Finally, after the fog of yet another drunken night lifted, they agreed it was time to get out of Cowtown and go in search of more permanent employment.

The brothers headed east after hearing that the Colonel's plot had failed miserably and that he had been arrested and would soon be taken to Austin and tried. To celebrate the news, they enjoyed one last drunken evening before leaving.

They found work building fences for a young Easterner who had recently bought a small farm near Cedar Valley and were drinking coffee in the local café when a man they recognized walked in. He was wearing a badge and ordered as many biscuits as the cook could spare.

It didn't take them long to figure out what Sheriff Langston was doing away from home. Neither did they need much time to devise a plan that might earn them far greater reward than they were earning by digging postholes and stringing barbed wire.

Once again, they fled their jobs in the middle of the night after stealing a half-full jug of whiskey from their employer's work shed.

W E'LL SOON BE nearing Lampasas," one of the Pinkerton men said as the final embers of their campfire slowly floated into the night air. "With an early start we should be there by noontime. Someone can ride into town and find us something a sight better to eat than jerky and wild berries."

From beneath the tree to which he was tethered, Abernathy said, "I'd genuinely appreciate a bottle of tequila to dull the pain in my leg." The response from those huddled around the fire was silence broken only by the hooting of a nearby owl.

The agent looked over at Dalton. "Me and you will go in and do the buying this time," he said. "Your friend couldn't even find us bacon when we sent him."

Langston huffed and walked toward his bedroll.

A change in the landscape greeted the tiring travelers the following morning. Gently rolling hillsides were lush with vegetation and the riders forded stream after stream that provided welcome drink for their horses. While Dolly had her fill, Dalton stepped down and bathed his face in the clear, cool water.

As predicted, they saw Lampasas in the distance as

they crested a hill. Off to their right was an inviting meadow that would make a good resting place.

Langston allowed the Colonel a few minutes to stretch his legs, then chained him in the shade of a nearby tree. "I don't mind telling you, I'm getting mighty weary of tending you and looking at your ugly face," the sheriff said. "I'll be glad to have this trip over."

Abernathy growled and spat in his face. It was going to be one of his "crazy" days.

A S THEY MADE the short ride toward town, the Pinkerton agent finally introduced himself. "Name's Eli Watkins."

"I was beginning to wonder if you had one," Dalton said.

They had reached a rutted wagon trail leading to the town before Watkins spoke again. "I apologize for seeming so unfriendly, but my mood hasn't been so good since I got this assignment. Worst I've been given since joining up. I feel like I've hired out to do babysitting of a grown-up." He then looked over at Dalton with a slightly puzzled expression. "Why is it you wanted to come along?"

"I just like to see that things get ended properly."

"You going to stay around to see him hanged?"

"I might. Haven't thought that far ahead."

Watkins, suddenly eager to talk, explained that he'd previously been a sheriff's deputy out in West Texas. "Ozona. Ever hear of it? Nothing out there but dust and wind and poor folks who got lost trying to get somewhere better. Thought I'd never get out of there but got lucky rounding up some cattle rustlers the Pinkertons were also pursuing. They were impressed and ended up offering me this job. I quickly took it and never looked back."

"I'm glad things worked out for you," Dalton said.

Watkins smiled. "Reckon anyone would starve if we was to find somewhere to have us a quick drink before heading back?"

"You're the man doing the leading. I recall you making that clear before we started out." It was obvious Dalton had no interest in developing a friendship.

"Seeing as how I've got state money to spend, I'll buy," the agent said.

LYING ON THEIR bellies atop a hill, the Sloan brothers watched two riders leave, apparently headed toward town. They tried to muffle their laughter as they saw Sheriff Langston chain their former boss to a tree and the others stretch out in the grass, putting their hats over their faces.

"We'll need to keep the sun to our backs as we approach," Calvin said. "That way, they're not likely to see us until we right on top of 'em."

Claude had always followed his brother's lead, even when it had gotten them into dozens of fights and tossed out of more saloons than they could recall, and once landed both in the Brownsville jail. He just nodded and patted his sidearm.

Minutes later, he was standing only a few feet behind Thad Willowby when he fired a shot into the back of the marshal's head.

The dozing Pinkerton man bolted to a sitting position and was drawing his pistol when Calvin let out a crazed yell as he pushed his Colt into the agent's chest and shot him twice. The agent fell back slowly, blood oozing from his mouth, and was dead before his head hit the grass.

Sheriff Langston raced toward his horse to get his Winchester and was pulling it from its sheath when a bullet tore through his shoulder, spinning him around to face the men attacking him. He recognized both from the days when he'd paid friendly visits to the ranch and started to call their names but was unable to get out a word. A second shot knocked him back into the spooked mare. Langston weakly lifted his hand in an attempt to reach the saddle horn and remain upright but lost his grip. He slid slowly to the ground as his body gave a final shudder and a strange, smile-like expression crossed his face.

The bloody massacre took only minutes. Then the brothers approached the Colonel.

Abernathy had watched in stunned silence, certain he would be next to die. When the gunmen approached, he closed his eyes and waited for the sound of another shot. Instead, he heard Calvin's high-pitched voice. "We've done you a big favor," he said as he knelt in front of the shackled prisoner. "Now, you can do us one. That, or you get shot dead like everybody else."

"What? Anything. Just don't . . ."

Sloan leaned forward and patted the Colonel's face. "Our offer ain't a real complicated one. If you're willing to pay—and pay good—we'll set you free and take you somewhere safe. If that don't interest you, we've got plenty more bullets."

"How much do you want?"

At that moment it occurred to the brothers that they hadn't discussed an amount they hoped to earn for their brutal efforts.

"Five thousand," Calvin whispered.

"Nope, ten thousand," his brother replied.

They turned to the Colonel. "Now that we've had a discussion between ourselves, fifteen thousand dollars seems a fair price," Claude said.

Abernathy didn't question their tortured math. "Fine. Good. I'll do it. It's a deal. Just get me out of these chains and away from here."

"When can we figure on getting the money?" Claude asked.

"It's back at the Shooting Star," the Colonel said. "Locked in a hidden safe. We'll have to go there to get it."

Claude stepped over the dead marshal and began searching the sheriff's pockets for the keys to unchain Abernathy. They decided it best to keep him handcuffed. "Hurry up," Calvin said. "We need to be gone before the others get back."

When they were ready to leave, the freed Abernathy asked them to wait another minute. Holding his hands against his throbbing thigh, he limped from one body to another before bending over the marshal. "These look to be about my size," he said as he began removing the dead man's boots.

D ALTON HAD SAT impatiently in the Lucky Lady Saloon, watching as Watkins ordered one whiskey after another. "Much more and you'll not be fit to ride," he said. "Come with me or not, but I'm going to the café next door and get some brisket and corn bread, maybe some collard greens, to take back to the others."

"Think we should bring along something to drink?" Watkins said.

Dalton rolled his eyes. "We're not having us a social." He watched as the agent downed one more quick swallow. "You sure you weren't fired from that job in Ozona? Maybe drank a little too much?"

Watkins grinned. "Well," he said, "I'd appreciate you not sharing this, but actually, it was one of those mutual decisions. My choices were to quit or get run off."

T HE SCENE THEY returned to quickly sobered Watkins and caused Dalton to be sick to his stomach. "Dear God in heaven," he said as he dismounted and rushed toward the sheriff's lifeless body. Watkins checked on the others.

"You think it was Indians?" the agent said.

Dalton's reply was filled with anger. "Wasn't Indians," he said. "It was somebody here to befriend Abernathy." He was looking toward the tree where the chain lay tangled on the ground.

"Folks in Austin are going to be mighty unhappy when we don't show up with a prisoner."

"He'll never make it that far," Dalton said as he knelt to gently cover Langston with a blanket. "I'll see him dead long before that, him and whoever did this." He stopped short of blaming the agent for the deaths but couldn't help wonder if their associates would still be alive had they not delayed so long in the saloon.

"You stay here and keep watch," he said. "I'm going

to ride back into town and get some help tending to the bodies." Watkins offered no argument when Dalton said he would take charge of whatever they did next.

The distraught agent continued to mumble his concern over what his superiors' reaction would be.

S OON, DALTON WAS back, a wagon following. On board were the local sheriff and a doctor. He had already explained as best he could what had happened. He had visited the Western Union office and sent a telegram to Duke Keene, saying that someone needed to come get Langston's body and begin arrangements for a funeral. In the message, he indicated he wouldn't likely be able to attend since he had other business to take care of.

As they placed the bodies into the bed of the wagon, Dalton pulled the cover from Langston and removed his badge, wiped specks of dried blood from it, and put it in his pocket. As he did so, the Lampasas sheriff asked what they planned to do with the others and their horses. Dalton told Watkins to give the men some money and asked that the horses be cared for at the local livery until he returned. The other bodies, he said, were the agent's concern.

T HEY COULDN'T HAVE made it too far yet," he said as he began carefully examining the ground for any signs that would indicate the direction they had headed. He found nothing as Watkins stood motionless, staring silently at the bloodstains left behind.

Finally, the agent spoke. "I'm, uh, thinking it's my

duty to go on ahead to Austin and report what's happened," he said. "I'll also take along the bodies of the others so they can be given a proper burial." He paused for a moment, then continued. "I reckon I'll most likely lose my job over this."

That was the least of Dalton's concerns as he stood in the shade of the tree where the Colonel had earlier been chained. He felt an urgency to do something but knew it was best he think things out before acting.

Who could have planned this? What cause did they have for doing it? And most important, where were they headed?

It was long after Watkins had ridden away that an answer to the last question came to mind.

T HE SLOAN BROTHERS finally agreed to remove the Colonel's handcuffs after he promised to add one of his prized Longhorns to their fee. They were also sharing the jug of whiskey they had stolen, thinking it might help end the constant complaining from the man they had rescued.

With luck, they figured, they could reach the Shooting Star in two days, three at most, and be rich.

I T WAS EARLY the following morning when Dalton found evidence that he was headed in the right direction. A cold campfire and an empty whiskey jug remained beneath a limestone outcrop that had obviously provided shelter to the cross-country travelers. There was also a discarded bandage, stained with small brown spots that were either blood or salve.

Grass was still pressed down in three spots around the dead fire where men had slept.

He now knew how many there were and was more certain than ever where they were going. He would no longer attempt to trail them but instead take a more direct route to the ranch.

With luck and cooperation from Dolly, he would be there to meet them when they arrived.

As he rode, the burning anger that had initially driven him began to subside, replaced by fond recollections of Otto Langston. Dalton had badly misjudged a man's ability to change, finally realizing how badly the sheriff had wanted to atone for his earlier greed and violation of his sworn duty. In the end, he had become a decent man, a friend, and Ben was glad their paths had crossed. He pulled the badge from his pocket and polished it against his sleeve. "You would have made a fine goat farmer," he whispered as he picked up his pace, once again headed for the Shooting Star.

W OULD HAVE BEEN mighty nice if you boys had done a bit more planning," Abernathy said as they stopped to allow the horses to rest. He was feeling better and more clear-minded than he had since Miss Luisa shot him. He was hungry for something more than the lone rabbit Claude had shot and the wild figs Calvin had picked. "No matter," he said, "we'll be arriving home soon and I'll instruct my cook to prepare us a meal you'll long remember."

And, he secretly thought, there will be someone in the bunkhouse who will gladly kill both of these idiots in exchange for keeping his job.

"Reckon those other two are following us?" Calvin said.

"I doubt they've even figured which way we headed," his brother replied. "Another day's ride and it won't matter anyway. We'll have our money and be on our way south to the border. Only person they're interested in is the Colonel, anyway."

"We're going south?"

"You got a better idea?"

"All I know is we got ourselves thrown in jail last time we were down that way."

Claude grinned and shook his head. "Don't concern yourself," he said. "This time we'll be too rich for anybody to mess with."

CHAPTER 32

D ALTON ARRIVED AT the ranch just after sundown and immediately went in search of Raff Bailey. "I think we've got trouble coming," he said after finding him in the barn, bottle-feeding a prematurely born calf. He quickly recounted the murders that had occurred. "The only reason I can figure for Abernathy not also being killed is that they have some use for him. Either that, or he was in on it from the beginning." He asked if any of the ranch hands had disappeared recently.

"Things have been pretty normal here since the Colonel was locked up. Everybody seems happy to be back cowboying like they hired on to do. Mr. Profer spoke to the bank and arranged that some of Abernathy's money be released to pay wages and take care of whatever's necessary to keep the ranch running.

"Mind you, we've had some sorry folks come

through here in my time," he continued, "but I'm hard-pressed to call the name of anybody who would help Abernathy out of the goodness of his heart. Now, if he was to offer money, that's a different matter."

"Anybody come to mind?"

"Probably about half of those who hightailed it back when the Colonel started talking about coming after you and your friends. Ones who jump to mind are the Sloan boys, brothers lacking in good sense and willing to do anything for a dollar. They're the ones he paid to kidnap that little boy."

"And cut Brent St. John's throat while doing it," Ben added.

"I 'spect they done that without a minute's regret."

"Gotta be them," Dalton said. "Somehow, they're figuring on getting a big payday from the Colonel, either for setting him free or by threatening him. Whatever the reason, they're headed here because this is where Abernathy's likely left some money."

Ben felt comfortable talking freely with Bailey. Aside from the afternoon he got stumbling drunk and decided to shoot up the livery, he had never seemed a problem maker. When they faced off near the road-house, it had been obvious he wasn't interested in a shootout. And since then he had worked hard to see that everything at the ranch went smoothly.

"When do you expect they'll be coming?" he said.

"Should be soon if this is where they're headed. I was thinking about settling into your loft and keeping an eye out."

"I'll fetch us a spyglass and keep you company," Bailey said.

* * *

T HE CLOSER THEY got to the Shooting Star, the more
   Abernathy's mood seemed to improve. When they
reached the edge of the far pasture and saw cattle grazing in the late-morning sun, he clapped his hands and
let out a yell. "Ain't that a pretty sight?" he said. "It's
mighty good to be home."

"Where's the money?" Claude said.

"Be patient. I'll show you, but first let's get us something to eat. I've also got tequila. It's hid away, same as
your money. No need for you boys to be impatient."

O N THE DISTANT horizon Dalton saw the three riders approaching. "That's got to be them," he said.
As Bailey began to raise his rifle, Ben put his hand to
the barrel, pushing it down. "I'll be doing the killing,"
he said.

He climbed from the loft and led Dolly into the
safety of an empty stall, then found her a bucket of
oats. That done, he placed Langston's Winchester on
his shoulder and walked slowly to the front porch of
the ranch house, took a seat in the Colonel's favorite
chair, and waited.

The Colonel's maid opened the front door slightly
and peeked outside. Seeing the man with a rifle, she
quickly closed it and hurried to the kitchen to warn the
cook. Bailey went to the bunkhouse to instruct his men
to remain inside.

As Dalton sat, his rage, unlike anything he'd ever
felt, returned. He pictured Sheriff Langston, lying
dead in a strange place, his final dream shattered;

thought of little Alton, scared and calling for his mother as he was taken away; of the child's father, brutally beaten and blamed for a crime he had nothing to do with; and of Brent St. John, losing his life for doing nothing more than trying to protect others.

An eerie calm fell over the compound as Ben awaited the sound of the men arriving. He watched as a mother hen and her chicks stopped chasing garden bugs and scurried under the porch. Drying bedsheets on the nearby clothesline made a soft snapping sound as they were whipped by the breeze. His finger already lightly pressed against the trigger, his thoughts went back to the conversation he'd had with Mandy, of the last request she'd made of him. "Kill him," she had said.

Bailey stepped onto the porch, carrying a rifle he'd brought from the bunkhouse.

"This isn't your fight," Dalton said.

"I figure maybe it is," he replied. "It's time this mess the Colonel started comes to an end so everybody can get on with their lives."

The three riders were in high spirits as they loped their horses toward the ranch house. Abernathy was laughing, his pain briefly forgotten. The brothers chattered away, excited in the knowledge that they were close to their money.

They all fell silent as they arrived at the hitching post.

Claude was the first to see the two men and reached for his pistol. He didn't even get it out of its holster before the crack of a rifle shot fractured the morning calm. His hat flew away and his frightened horse reared, pitching him to the ground. As blood streamed from his chest, he struggled to his knees and tried again to get a grip on his sidearm. It fell from his hand when Bailey's second shot found its mark just below his neck.

The other horses were stomping the ground and bumping into each other as Dalton called out to Abernathy. "Good seeing you again, Colonel."

As he spoke, Calvin Sloan fired a shot that zinged past his ear and buried into the front door.

Bailey aimed to return fire but was distracted for a split second by the sudden sound of a fast-approaching buggy, its driver yelling at the top of his voice. Sloan fired a second shot that ripped part of Raff's shirt sleeve away as it grazed his shoulder and knocked his rifle from his hands. Dalton stepped forward to shield him and returned Sloan's fire. His bullet hit Calvin in the face, causing a spray of teeth and blood. He was dead before he slumped forward in his saddle and slowly toppled onto the body of his dead brother.

In the brief moment of confusion caused by the buggy, the Colonel kneed his horse and was galloping toward the open door of the barn. Ben aimed his rifle again but didn't have a clear shot because of the frightened horses in his way.

As Abernathy limped into the darkness, the buggy came to a jerking halt in front of the porch. Duke Keene stepped down and looked at the Sloan brothers. "Good riddance," he said as he stepped over their bodies.

"After getting your telegram, I started trying to figure where you might be headed. Looks like I guessed right." He was carrying his shotgun. "How many's left?" he said.

"Just the Colonel," Dalton said.

Duke smiled and nodded his head. "There's three of us and just one of him. This'll be easy." He was wrapping a bandanna around Bailey's injured arm as he spoke. "Just a scratch," he said. "I've seen way worse."

"He's got weapons in there," Raff said. "Rifles, shotguns, and a barrel filled with ammunition."

"If we hadn't already done it once, I'd suggest we just set the building on fire," Duke said.

He had barely finished his sentence when a shotgun blast came from the loft, tearing a large hole in the awning of the buggy. "Mr. Profer ain't going to be happy about that," Duke said. "I borrowed it to get out here. Lanny and John Rawlings took my wagon to go get the sheriff like you asked. Mrs. Rawlings is talking with a preacher about setting up a funeral service."

Two rifle bullets buried into the porch railing.

"We need cover," Dalton said, motioning toward the front door. Moving inside and peering from a window, they could see the advantage Abernathy had. From his perch, there was a panoramic view of the compound.

"Reckon he's crazy enough to think he can shoot his way out of this?" Bailey said.

From across the way, Abernathy answered his question. "I know I'm going to die before the day's done," he shouted from the loft, "but it'll not be at your hand, Ben Dalton. I'll not give you that satisfaction."

As he spoke, ranch hands began cautiously making their way out of the bunkhouse, weapons in hand, preparing to surround the barn. "Odds just got even better," Keene said. "Doesn't appear the Colonel has many friends, does it?"

Bailey looked over at Dalton. "What's your thinking?"

"Let's just wait for a spell. If he doesn't come to his

senses and decide to walk himself out, I'll go in and get
him. No way he's getting away again."

T HERE WAS AN occasional shot from the loft, but
both the Colonel and the men waiting in his house
seemed satisfied to just let time pass. The day dragged
and by midafternoon Dalton suggested they alternate
watching the barn and napping. He took the first watch
and never surrendered it. "The only kind of tired I
have," he said, "is the one you get from sitting, doing
nothing."

The cook shyly peeked out from the kitchen, holding a tray of sandwiches, cups, and a coffeepot. Duke
got to his feet and went to take it from her.

Dalton aimed at a small iron bell hanging over the
opening to the loft and fired off a series of quick shots.
"Don't want him dozing off," he said as it sounded for
a moment like church services were about to begin.
Keene nodded his approval and handed him a sandwich.

By dusk, frustration had set in. "The old fool's just
sitting up there, waiting to get himself killed," Bailey
said. "I think it's about time we accommodate him. I
don't want this going on into the night."

Dalton got to his feet. "Keep his attention for a few
minutes," he said as he handed his rifle to Duke. "Use
this instead of your shotgun," he said. He explained that
while they peppered the loft with shots, he would make
his way out the back door and try to get to the side of the
bunkhouse without being noticed. "Once I get that far
I can ask for cover from some of your cowboys."

"Think you'll get a better shot from over there?" Duke asked.

"Nope, but it's the best way I can think of to get in the barn. Then it'll be just him and me."

I NSIDE, DALTON KNELT behind a feed barrel to let his eyes adjust to the darkness. The only sound came from Abernathy's abandoned horse, chomping at a bale of hay. In the stall across the way, Ben saw Dolly nuzzling the oats he'd left her. The rafters were empty and silent since the pigeons had swiftly deserted their roosts when the gunfire began.

Only when a volley of shots came from the house, answered by a shotgun blast from above, was Dalton certain of the Colonel's location.

Seated to the side of the loft door, behind a barricade of hay bales he'd hastily fashioned, Abernathy alternately rubbed his swollen leg and took quick looks toward the house. Beside him were several long guns and a bucket filled with bullets and shotgun shells. The effort of arranging the bales and the rising heat inside had bathed him in sweat, and pains were shooting through his wounded leg. Parched from a lack of water, he still managed a hoarse curse when he saw the cowhands leaving the bunkhouse to circle the barn.

He was resigned to his fate but determined to have one last taste of revenge before dying, unaware that the focus of his anger was waiting below.

Dalton was struggling to decide his next move. He counted the rungs on the ladder leading to the loft, aware that he would be vulnerable should the Colonel hear him approaching. He holstered his Peacemaker after again making sure it was fully loaded and began taking off his boots. He also removed his hat.

Certain Abernathy would not come to him, he would have to confront him in the loft.

When several more shots came from the house, he left his hiding place and hurried to the bottom of the ladder. Above, he could hear the Colonel mumbling to himself as he reloaded one of his rifles.

In his sock feet, Dalton climbed a few careful steps at a time, only when there was gunfire from Bailey and Keene. After several minutes he reached a position where the floor was at eye level and he could see Abernathy's back, his attention focused on the house. The loft was filled with stored hay that would offer Ben some measure of protection—if he could reach one of the stacks.

He ducked back below the loft's floor level and waited for another exchange of fire. Instead, the next sound he heard was the Colonel's voice.

Rising to his feet, Abernathy cupped his hands to his mouth and shouted, "Dalton, show yourself. I'll make you a proposition. What say we both walk out into the open where we can face one another? Best shooter wins. Simple as that." Then there was a spate of maniacal laughter.

As he was calling out his challenge, Dalton quickly climbed to the floor of the loft and dove behind a stack of hay bales. Their sweet scent mixed with the smell of smoke and gunpowder.

"I'm here waiting," the Colonel said as he aimed his rifle at the doorway of the house, hoping a target would emerge. "Come on out and we'll get this done with." He had no intention of it being a fair fight.

Dalton got to his feet, now no more than ten feet from Abernathy. "Let's just do it right here," he said.

The startled Colonel turned and fired toward the sound of the familiar voice, his shot nowhere close to doing harm. He ducked behind his barricade before Dalton could shoot back.

As soon as they heard Abernathy shoot, Bailey and Keene stepped out onto the porch and began firing repeatedly. Raff yelled at the ranch hands who were huddled behind water troughs and a nearby cistern. "Go, go, go," he yelled, then returned to shooting in the direction of the loft.

The cowboys rushed into the barn, pointing their guns in all directions before realizing that Dalton and the Colonel were above them. "Colonel," one of the hands called out, "you've got no chance. There's guns pointed at you from everywhere you're inclined to look." For emphasis, he fired a shot into the floor of the loft.

Abernathy replied by putting the barrel of his shotgun against the floor and blowing a sizable hole through which he could see some of the men whose salaries he'd once paid. "You're traitors, every one," he yelled as he fired a second shot.

Then he was suddenly on his feet, standing with his back to the door, his feet spread wide, looking toward where Dalton was hidden. There was a calm, almost angelic expression on his sweat-drenched face. "I'm feeling mighty tired," he said, "and am ready for this to end. I figure you are as well.

"But know this, Ben Dalton: I've got no apologies for

things I've done. Look at this ranch, all the fine cattle, my house. I made more money than you'll ever see. I did myself proud putting all this together. My life was good and getting better. Then you came and ruined it, came from God knows where just to give me all this misery.

"Now you're here, wanting to kill me. I'll not allow that to happen."

Dalton had moved from behind the hay bales, his eyes fixed on the Colonel's shotgun, which was pointed in his direction. He didn't see the handgun until Abernathy lifted it from his side, placed it against his temple, and pulled the trigger.

For a moment everything moved in slow motion. The Colonel briefly remained upright as his pistol fell from his hand. Then he began to gently sway. Finally, he slowly fell into open space.

Duke Keene was among the first to reach the body. "He died just like the sorry coward he was," he said, then looked up to the doorway of the loft where Dalton was standing. "Come on down and let's go home," the livery owner said. "I've got some explaining to do to Mr. Profer about the roof of his buggy."

For some time, Dalton didn't move, unsure how he felt about what had just happened. There was a calming evening breeze on his face as he slowly holstered his pistol. He watched as Bailey and the cowhands gathered around the Colonel's twisted body, talking in low whispers. The cook and the maid left the porch to join them.

It would be a while before he would know if he'd accomplished what he'd set out to do when he answered Mandy's call for help. All he knew at the moment was that it was finally over.

For the time being, that would have to be enough.

EPILOGUE

DESPITE DUKE'S URGING, Ben decided not to accompany him back to Fort Worth. He had already said his goodbyes before leaving on the ill-fated trip to Austin, and he was now more anxious than ever to get home to Aberdene. If he had learned anything for certain, it was that he had no business being in a big city.

His thoughts had begun to turn to the farm and his dog, Poncho, and how his deputy, Rolly Blair, had fared in his absence. He was strongly considering offering him the job permanently. Maybe he would raise a few goats himself in honor of Sheriff Langston.

He felt a twinge of guilt at not staying to attend the funeral but decided he'd rather remember his friend as he was in life. When Duke was climbing into the buggy to leave the Shooting Star, Ben pulled the sheriff's badge from his pocket and requested that it be placed in Langston's casket.

The following morning, as he and Dolly made their

way into the open range, he reflected on the people who had recently come into his life, not Colonel Abernathy and his kind, but those for whom he had developed strong feelings. Duke, with his cranky wit and kindheartedness, would be impossible to forget. Same with the fancy-talking Shelby Profer; innocent young Lanny, who had once saved his life; and Anson Kelly, whom he judged to be a better lawman than he could ever be.

He was pleased that he had rekindled his friendship with John Rawlings and gotten to know little Alton, who he was sure would grow up to be a good master for Too.

And, of course, there was Mandy. He needed only to close his eyes to see her face, to again feel her close to him on that summer evening when they had danced. He reached to touch the pocket where he carried her letter.

That, too, would have to be enough.

ACKNOWLEDGMENTS

Editor Tom Colgan's reaching out to ask if I'd be interested in writing a Western was a moment for which I'll forever be indebted. That was five novels and many enjoyable days at the keyboard ago. Award-winning writer friends James Ward Lee and Jeff Guinn again provided thoughtful advice, criticism, and encouragement, as did agent and talented historian Jim Donovan. And, of course, a tip of the Stetson is due to Ralph Compton, whose boots are far too big to fill.

Ready to find
your next great read?

Let us help.

Visit prh.com/nextread

Penguin
Random
House